STEN AND THE PIRATE QUEEN

STEN AND THE PIRATE QUEEN

ALLAN COLE

From the Novel Series by Allan Cole And Chris Bunch

WILDSIDE PRESS

*For Kathryn, my forever love as we enter our fourth
decade of marriage and sixth decade of friendship.*

And
The late Frank Gessel: Keep the stregg cold for us, brother.

And
Our new granddaughter, Ariana
Making her book dedication debut.

And
Scott Braun
My stalwart friend and physician

AUTHOR'S NOTE

This tale is set between Sten #2, *The Wolf Worlds*, and Sten #3, *The Court of a Thousand Suns*.

CHAPTER ONE

GREGOR

"Sten's coming to kill me," Gregor said, wall-eyeing the panic room door as if expecting his enemy to kick it down and come charging in, AM2 battlerifle blazing. "He's out there right now."

"Oh, sweetie, I wish you'd quit saying things like that," the joygirl said. "And here I told your father's people we were making such great progress with your therapy."

"But it's true, it's true," Gregor wailed. "I feel it in my bones. It's like he's in this room, waiting until I have one happy moment, then he'll cut my throat ear to ear, while that pal of his—Alex Kilgour—laughs his head off."

"Honey love," the joygirl said with an artful pout, "besides you, the only living being in this room is me. And I'm sure I'm nothing like that Sten of yours."

She took his hands and forcefully pulled them to her, then moved them over her body while squirming lasciviously.

"See what I mean, cutie pie?" she whispered lustfully. "It's all girl all... the... way... down."

Gregor's eyes started to close and a dreamy smile stole across his face. Then the monitor gave a "beep" and he snatched his hands back with a shriek.

"It's Sten, I tell you," he cried. "Right out there." He pointed a shaky finger at the far wall—a floor to ceiling monitor displaying the luxurious seaside grounds of Wichlandia—his father's first of a planned chain of frontier world resorts.

Twin moons bathed the dozen or so cliff-side villas in soothing golden light. The terraced cliffs and the surrounding grounds were true works of landscape art, with exotic trees and plants clinging bonsai-like to the rocks and cascading down to the sea, where steamy hot springs were nestled in moss-covered boulders. Booming surf broke over the sides to the delight of partiers frolicking in the grotto.

A black-hulled fishing boat made its way offshore, phosphorescent seas parting before its carved raptor bow, twin eyes glowing on either side of the beak. The crewmembers—all humanoid—were rowing toward shore, scarlet oars flashing in unison like wings. It had been a good catch, witness the multitude of silvery bodies spilling out of the holds and flopping onto the deck. And with the twin moons and seas ablaze with color the view alone should have been worth the outrageous prices Lord Wichman—Gregor's resort king dad—charged. Artists would someday capture the scene and sell their works for small fortunes.

But all that was lost on Gregor, whose feverish, bloodshot eyes searched the scene for signs of his enemy:

Sten.

The man who had fooled everyone into believing that he hailed from common origins and had risen in the esteem of the brass through sheer ability and merit to become an admiral's flag lieutenant.

Lies. All lies.

It was Sten who had undermined Gregor's career from the very beginning—all the way back to basic training, eventually orchestrating his ouster from the Guard.

And it was Sten—using lofty connections he claimed no knowledge of—who had brought Gregor to ruin and near death in the Merchant Marines.

Gregor shuddered to think what would have happened if his father hadn't pressured the Eternal Emperor into rescuing him from a kangaroo court of mutineers who would have found him guilty and sentenced him to death.

And it wouldn't be a death anywhere near so kind as being hauled before an Imperial firing squad, where you would at least die with the dignity due an officer in service to the Eternal Emperor.

No, it would be that monster Rual who did the murderous deed.

Rual—second in command of the thugs and traitors who had seized Gregor's ship, the *Flame,* along with an entire 125 kilometer-long space train filled to the overflowing with Imperium X. After AM2, the mineral was the second most valuable substance in the Empire.

Rual, with her mad eyes, skeletal frame and clawlike fingers.

Rual, with her long shark's-tooth-like knife, working gleefully under the direction of the psychotic Zheng, a serial killer and leader of the mutineers.

Adding lying insult to injury, the mutineers falsely claimed they had evidence that Gregor had cheated them out of their wages. Fed them substandard food unless they paid a surcharge. Clipped them in illegal gambling games they were strong-armed into playing. The traitors even claimed they had evidence that Gregor regularly pocketed the money for badly needed repairs that were never done, leading to many injuries and at least one death.

More lies.

There was absolutely no evidence of wrongdoing. Gregor had made double-damned sure of that by feeding the evidence into a plasma furnace that atomized every claim.

All had seemed lost, but at the very last minute, Gregor's father had circumvented Sten in a wheels-within-wheels leak-proof conspiracy, fooling the Emperor, his dreaded spymaster Ian Mahoney, and Venatora, the beauteous pirate queen who ruled over an army of fanatical women pirates.

And Sten.

Yes, Sten, who conspired to take Gregor aboard his own ship—the *Jo'l Cash*—and slap him in chains before hauling him before a court martial board.

Gregor didn't believe for a nanosecond that Sten would allow him to live long enough to reach Prime World, much less stand trial. Really. If anyone believed that, Gregor's father had some nice swampland on Clematis III he'd love to sell them.

Obviously, that had all been a cunning Sten ploy to fool the brass. Gregor knew full well that Sten had been planning to kill him all along. Of this, Gregor was certain. Just as he suspected that Sten had somehow kept Rual alive and the moment Gregor stepped aboard the *Jo'l Cash,* Rual would leap out, screaming bloody murder, slashing Gregor until his flesh hung in ribbons.

He shivered. Stomach roiling. Throat constricting. Gag reflexes cutting in.

"Are you cold, Sweetie?" the joygirl purred. "Let Mitzi get you a nice little cup of hot narcochai."

Numb, Gregor could do little more than nod. Not sure she caught it, he croaked, "Please."

"No trouble at all, cutie pie," Mitzi said. While she spoke, she moved to the bureau where she had a variety of sex toys spread out on black velvet. When she'd first arrived, slipping into the room on a perfumed cloud, Gregor had been intrigued and no little aroused.

The joygirls and joyboys who plied their art in Lord Wichman's resorts were renowned for their skills in the erotic arts. So to say that Mitzi was merely beautiful would be an understatement.

Her body had been sculpted to perfection. Joints enhanced so she could offer her clients impossibly pleasurable positions.

And her toys were unlike anything Gregor had ever seen before. With all kinds of interesting protrusions, textures and electronic delights.

For a few minutes he had been fooled into complacency. Here was

Mitzi—so lovely, so willing, so… so… so *everything*!

And he was perfectly safe. The panic room had been built to his most exacting standards, with beyond state of the art security.

And hadn't his father assured him that no one knew that Gregor was in residence at Wichlandia?

And hadn't Gregor personally tasked his own private security force with checking Mitzi out before sending her to his room?

And she had come up aces, hadn't she?

Safe as safe could be.

With soft music, sweet words and a few glasses of a heady narcochai drink he was soon relaxed enough not to panic when she slipped into his bed.

But as he embraced her luscious form the bloody face of Rual came charging out of his backbrain!

And with her came the ghostly figure of Sten!

Hissing, "Slice him, Raul! Slice him good."

But it was here that Mitzi showed off her real skills. "There, there, little darlin'," she soothed as his heart picked up speed and sweat broke out on his brow. "Just come into Mitzi's arms and she'll make you feel all better."

Slowly, surely, she brought him under control. The weeping subsided to occasional sobs. Then she wiped his face, undressed him, helped him swallow a pill with the last of his chai, and then led him to a tub that had been filling up with hot, soothing water.

But just as he lifted his foot to step into the perfumed soap suds, he thought he caught a flash of red out of the corner of his eye.

Startled, he drew back.

"What's that?" he cried.

"What's bothering you now, sweetie pie?" Mitzi asked.

Gregor caught the impatience in her voice, but waved it away.

"There!" Gregor shouted, pointing at the monitor. "On that boat."

Mitzi made an exasperated noise. But Gregor was certain. He'd by clot, seen what he had seen.

"Looks the same to me," she said.

"There it is again," Gregor cried. "That flash of red. It's a gunsight! I just know it!"

"Really, honey pie," Mitzi said. "There's nothing there. Just lights for the fishermen to find their way home."

Gregor's panic turned to a sudden cold fury. "You're one of them," he shouted, pointing an accusing finger at Mitzi. "You're with Sten!"

"Please, sweetie pie," the joygirl begged. "You know that poor little old Mitzi would never harm a fly, much less a handsome man like you. All the other girls are jealous of me."

Gregor wasn't listening.

He hit the panic button. The door to the room irised open and two burly bodyguards burst into the room.

Gregor pointed at Mitzi. "Get her out of here!" he shouted. "She's one of them. She's with Sten."

"Sure boss, sure," the larger of two soothed. She gave Mitzi a conspiratorial wink. "We'll take care of everything."

At the door, Mitzi turned to say, "I'll be back when you feel better, honey pot. Then we can have a lovely time making up."

As they left one the guards snagged a wheeled cart with all of Mitzi's paraphernalia and drew it with them. A moment later they were gone.

Gregor listened intently as—one by one—the series of pick-proof locks clicked into place.

He threw himself onto the bed, laughing maniacally. "You can't fool me, Sten," he babbled. "I can see right through your nasty little game."

It didn't occur to him that the locks were more to keep him in, than trouble out.

* * * *

In the hallway, the guards and Mitzi laughed about Gregor's latest antics.

"Can't believe the guy," the woman guard said. "He just turned his back on the best joygirl ride this side of Prime World."

"It wasn't his back that he was turning," Mitzi giggled.

The male guard lifted a bottle of champagne out of the old-fashioned ice cooler and popped the cork, while the others held out glasses to catch the overflow.

"Best gig I've had in years," Mitzi said. "A thousand credits an e-hour and I don't even have to put out. He couldn't if he tried. Not with that wet noodle hanging between his legs."

Everyone had a big laugh at that. There are few things funnier than a rich man's son brought low.

Mitzi downed her wine, exchanged a few more jokes at Gregor's expense, then leisurely made her way back to her quarters.

Once in the privacy of her room she went to the hiding place beneath her bed and fished out the tiny comm.

She pressed it into her ear. Static. Then a voice. She could hear waves crashing in the background.

"He's onto us," she said into the unit.

"Clottin' hell," came the voice. "That tears it!"

It was Sten.

CHAPTER TWO

STEN

"Hit it!" Sten said. "We've been blown."

"Efter all tha' bleedin' work," Kilgour grumbled, as he signaled the grizzled captain to turn about. "Freezin' me knackers off all night, n' boilin' in me britches all day."

"Mitzi says he's convinced we're lurking out here waiting for him to drop his guard," Sten said.

"Weel, he's got us deid tae rights oan 'at one, young Sten, doesnae he?" the heavy worlder said as he helped the crew stash the sail. "Jist like we're lurkin' oan his auld man."

"True enough," Sten said. "But Gregor acts like we're trying to kill him, instead of just spying on him."

"Ah've ne'er binsae insulted in me life," Kilgour harrumphed. "If Ah wanted tae kill th' wee scrote, he'd a been boobies up in th' noonday sun long ago."

Sten's comm buzzed. It was Mitzi again.

"Gregor's shouting for Security to turn out the guard," she said. "But everybody is making nice, agreeable 'yessir,' 'right away, sir' noises and ignoring him."

"Did you get a chance to plant that bug on him?" Sten asked.

"That's a no go," Mitzi said. "He's ordered bodily scans twice a day. I'll just have to stay close to him like silk on skin."

"What about his old man?"

"I'm writing up a report now," Mitzi replied, "and I'm laying it on thick, although I'm not sure he really cares. Sometimes it feels like he's just keeping his kid on ice for something down the road."

"I expect it won't be something nice," Sten said.

"Wouldn't bet against that," Mitzi said, then signed off.

Kilgour groaned in frustration. "Ah love ye loch a brither, wee Sten," he said. "But Ah'm sick't ay yer face an' sick't ay th' soon ah yer voice, an' Ah'm sick tae death of watchin' Wichman an his bampot bairn circle aroond th' jakes bowl before we flush it.

"Fur th' life ay me Ah dinnae ken why Mahoney an' th' wee Emp don't jist lit us tweep th' bloody pair of 'em an' lit us gang home."

Sten sighed. "I'm just as sick of all this as you are," he said. "And Ida. And Doc. But you know as well as I do that we have a clot more on our plate than the Wichmans."

Alex snorted. "Hoo coodst Ah forgit? There's also yer wee burd. The lady pirate. We've been trackin' 'er aw over th' Possnet Sector as well."

Sten flushed. "Venatora is not—I repeat—not! my girlfriend. She's a mission target. Nothing more. Nothing less."

"Aye, laddie," he scoffed. "Jist keep tellin' yerself 'at an' mebbe yoo'll believe it in a century ur three."

Sten started to argue, but gave it up. His friend knew him too well.

"This is the nastiest, most boring bit of business we've been stuck with since Mantis school," Sten said. "In one big tub of glop we've got the Wichmans, Queen Venatora, and her fellow pirate captains, and then the trickiest of all—the Tahn. It's like playing three-dimensional billiards. With the table changing form and purpose no matter how much we finesse the cue ball."

Kilgour grimaced. He said, "Ah, dinnae ken, laddie, when it aw went tae th' home ay th' devil himself. What th' clot happened tae th' guid auld days when all an honest Mantis fellaw hud tae dae was kill everybody, clean up th' bluid an' gang home for a wee bevy."

Silence settled in. Other than blowing steam, griping about things they couldn't change was pointless.

A chill wind picked up and Sten huddled deeper into his slicker. Miserable as this duty was, it was better than his previous life as a delinq on the run in a factory world where Migs like himself were the lowest of the low. They had so little value to the Company that they had ordered the death of hundreds of Migs—including Sten's entire family—rather than chance a leak of their secrets.

He smiled a bitter smile remembering how, back in basic training for the Guards, Gregor had insisted Sten was actually a member of the Imperial ruling class with friends in high places. How else could Gregor explain Sten's superior ratings?

Hard work? Study? Practice?

Never!

Such words had never been a part of Gregor's lexicon.

Kilgour nudged him, and Sten caught sight of a stealthy little all-terrain craft slipping away from a dark cove. In a few minutes it was bumping against the fishing boat.

Lieutenant Mk'wolf popped up from the hold, mustache twitching and teeth gleaming through the dark camo makeup. "Got her done, boss," he said. "Vid and sound in every room and all through the grounds."

"Explosives?" Sten asked.

Mk'wolf pointed toward Wichlandia's sparkling lights. "Got 'em all along the perimeter," he said. "Then the admin wing. Plus an extra big load for the armory."

He handed Sten a small black box. "Just say the magic word and the whole place will go up like a volcano."

"And that word would be?"

"Whatever you choose, boss," Mk'wolf said.

The face of the man Sten hated more than any other flashed into his mind. The one responsible for murdering his entire family back on Vulcan. Never mind Sten had already killed the man. Literally ripped his heart from his chest. A single death was far too small for the likes of the Baron.

"Program it for 'Thoresen'," Sten said.

Kilgour nodded, understanding. "Good choice, laddie," he said.

Mk'wolf hesitated, then said, "Yessir, Thoresen it is."

Sten smiled to himself. He knew Mk'wolf didn't have the faintest idea what they were talking about. But he was smart enough not to press the issue.

"Any thoughts on what Gregor's old man is up to?" Sten asked.

Mk'wolf said, "He spends most of his time getting ready for the official grand opening of Wichlandia. It's quite the event. Big shots and glitterati from all over the region are gagging for invitations."

"What about the Tahn?" Sten asked. "Have they been around."

"In droves," Mk'wolf said. "He's become quite the Tahn darling. Every day they're out cruising the grounds on those little grav sleds playing some sort of silly little game that none of us can make heads or tails of. Except every time we think we're onto something, Wichman changes the subject and the rules of whatever deal he's trying to cook up."

"What silly game would that be?" Sten asked, burying a smile. He knew very well what it was, but he wanted to see Kilgour's reaction.

Mk'wolf shrugged. "Not sure, boss. They drive little gravcarts around this big field for hours at a time hitting a little white ball with clubs. Never did find out what the game is called."

Sten watched Kilgour's face in fascination as Mk'wolf went on to over explain the mysteries of Wichman's sport. Kilgour's big round mug seemed to swell larger and larger as the lieutenant spoke, the color deepening until it was practically scarlet.

When Mk'wolf stopped to draw breath, Kilgour exploded.

"Ah'll hae ye ken 'at silly little game ye waur blasphemin' is known fur 'n' wide as th' king ay sports. Nay, the king AN' th' queen of sports."

He jabbed Mk'wolf's chest with a thick finger. The lieutenant was knocked a step back with each jab.

"The game's called golf, cheil. It's golf yoo're malignin'. Golf! Created by bonny Scotsmen loch meself thoosands ay years ago tae benefit aw beingkind."

Then the fury went out of him. His color returned to normal. He sighed, shaking his head.

"Ah d'nae ken Ah'd taken oan a barbarian fur a shipmate. Ah'm sore disappointed in yer, laddie."

Mk'wolf gave Sten a what-the-clot-happened look. A slender, well-built human with a hawk face, Mk'wolf was a born cynic, and had a what-the-clot attitude about most things. But Kilgour's tirade was a little overboard.

Sten took pity. "One question, Lieutenant."

Mk'wolf snapped a salute. "Sir?

"Did you plant a few extra bombs in the bar?"

"I took the liberty of doubling the charge," Mk'wolf said.

Sten slapped him on the back. "Good lad," he said.

Mk'wolf handed Sten a fiche. "It's stuffed full of evidence. Deals and more deals. Almost all involving sanctioned goods."

Sten's eyebrows rose. He lifted the fiche. "You mean we have Wichman on here selling illegal weapons and machines."

Mk'wolf shook his head. "Nothing so damning as that, sir," he said. "The old man is too sneaky. He hints about this, that, and the other. Then backs away, saying he'll have his people study the matter and report back." He pointed at the fiche. "What we have there are Tahn bigwigs bragging about making those deals after the fact. Meeting Wichman's people in secret. Setting up corporate cutouts. That sort of thing."

"So, there's no smoking fiche?" Sten said, his face falling.

"Nothing solid enough to call in the Guard," Mk'wolf said. "But there's one thing on there that might interest you. It seems there's a some kind of a Tahn big shot on his way to Wichlandia. He'll be here in a few days, and Wichman has his spies and dirty tricksters working overtime putting together possible deals."

"Did you catch a name?" Sten asked.

"Lord Fehrle," Mk'wolf said. "But we didn't get much more than that."

In his ear, Ida spoke up. She was monitoring the situation from their ship—the *Jo'l Cash*—which was parked behind the shield of Wichlandia's smallest moon.

"Fehrle's the senior member of the Tahn High Council," she said. "Only reason a muckety like Fehrle would be there is for something really big."

"Any idea what it might be?" he asked.

"Nossir," Mk'wolf said. "Except that Wichman's people have been talking to the pirates a lot. All back channel stuff."

"That's not much help," Sten said. Soon as the words came out of his mouth, he was sorry he'd spoken.

"Best I could do, boss," Mk'wolf said, face darkening with disappointment.

The last thing Sten wanted to do was add to a growing morale problem. For what seemed like an eternity they had been cruising the Possnet Sector, following villains and spending days on pointless stakeouts.

Sten clapped Mk'wolf on the back. "Come to think of it, this could be the breakthrough we've been looking for. We even have a name we can report. Lord Fehrle. Great work, lieutenant. I'll be sure to sing your praises to Mahoney."

He was rewarded by the looks of pleasure on the faces of Mk'wolf and his crew. A reminder, Young Sten, he chided himself, that there is a lot more to leadership than gathering your forces and charging the barricades.

Ida broke in. "Speaking of our Satanic Majesty," she said, "I just got an 'eyes only' from Mahoney."

"What about?"

"Want the bad news, or the bad news?" she said.

Sten sighed. "Bad news first," he said.

"Mahoney wants to talk."

Another sigh. "Okay, what could be worse than that?"

Ida snorted. "Easy, sweet cheeks. What he called about."

"Which was?"

"Venatora is on the move."

For the second time that night, Sten cursed.

* * * *

He stood under the fresher while hot, soapy cleansing agents rat-a-tat-tatted against his body, penetrating every fold of skin, pore, and hair follicle.

Even so, he could not seem to relax. Sten palmed the controls, making the stream hotter, stronger, but no matter how hard it hammered against him, he could not remove Venatora's image from his mind.

Venatora.

The first time they met, she'd vowed to kill him.

Quite different from the last time, when promises of a different sort burned in her eyes.

Between those two events Sten and Venatora had played a high-stakes game of wits, wagering their lives and self esteem on each move.

They'd first met over a Xypaca fighting pit, totally absorbed with one another. Shocked by the intensity of their emotions. Crossing mental swords in their own very private battle of wits and nerve, while all around them adrenalin-charged gamblers shouted or groaned, depending on the fortunes of the small beasts fighting to the death for the gamblers' enjoyment.

Sten had won the first encounter—but barely. Venatora accused him of cheating. He had, but only a little. He accused her of being a poor sport who was trying to renege on the wager—one hundred thousand credits.

In the end, she'd paid up, teasing him with the prospect of a rematch in some other, equally adrenalin-charged event.

With Sten and Venatora facing one another in a fighting pit of their own devise.

Sten: Mantis assassin.

Venatora: Pirate Queen.

She ruled the Himmenops, a fierce race of warrior women biologically chained to their queen. The Himmenops' sleek little pirate ships roamed the Possnet Sector, looking for opportunity. And with the discovery of the rich Imperium X deposits, there was a mouth-watering plentitude of that.

And they weren't the only trouble in the region. Unruly pirates like the Himmenops constantly trolled the sector looking to steal everything from space trains bearing raw ore, to an ever-increasing demand for goods and services for the thousands of beings flocking to the region.

Imperial forces were overwhelmed by the sheer number of attacks. Culminating in the theft of an entire Imperium X space train by mutineers rebelling against the Eternal Emperor.

That convoy had been commanded by Gregor, taken hostage by the mutineers led by two psychotics who used Gregor's inhumane treatment of the crewmen to foster the rebellion. Then the mutineers parked themselves and the spacetrain just off Venatora's stronghold for weeks, negotiating between Venatora and the Emperor via his most skilled Mantis assassin—Sten.

In a complicated cat-and-mouse game—one that saw Gregor and his fabulously wealthy father attempt a double-cross—Sten had won in the end, penetrating the Himmenops defenses to steal back all but a handful of the ore-bearing cars.

To Sten's disgust, Gregor and his old man had been declared heroes by the Emperor—who was playing his own very far behind the scenes cat and mouse game with the Wichmans and the Tahn.

Which then led to what seemed to be an endless mission in the desolate Fringe Worlds.

A mission with two objectives:

(1)Gather evidence against Lord Wichman and Gregor, then kill them, while blaming the Tahn.

(2)Wipe out the pirates who plagued the area. Starting with Venatora.

Sten was inching his way toward achieving the first objective. When he did, he'd have no problem at carrying out the kill orders.

As for the second…

Venatora.

Venatora.

Venatora.

The name pulsing in his chest.

Her image was seared in his memory after their first meeting in a mining company gambling hell known as Rec Area 477.

She was tall, slender, her skin a gleaming ebony, her hair, long sable tresses that spilled over one bare shoulder, her breasts round and firm and high, her hips and thighs a beckoning paradise.

That one glimpse, accompanied by a strange, almost giddy feeling of yearning.

But yearning for what?

And the answer came back: Venatora.

Mahoney said she was a splicer. A biological creation of a mysterious cabal known only as "The Fathers."

Pheromones enabled her to command absolute obedience from the Himmenops, an apian-like all female society ruled by a queen. And then there were the Zabanyas. An elite corps of women who were specially bred to guard the queen. Large, heavily muscled humanoids. Albino white. Silver hair. Glowing pink eyes.

A startling contrast to the dark-eyed ebony beauty who ruled them.

Sten vividly recalled their first and only kiss.

When their lips touched he felt like he was submerged in a warm river of sensations.

He reached out—meaning to embrace her. A gentle hand on his chest firmly pushed him away.

Sten tried to speak. But all he could manage was a strangled croak.

Then, somehow he managed: "Venatora. We must—"

Two fingers touched his lips, silencing him.

And she said, "We shall, Sten. We shall."

Then she was gone.

Vanishing into the dense spaceport bar crowd. Her last words echoing in his mind: "We shall, Sten. We shall."

Now here he was. Months later. Once again on endless patrol. Wondering what she meant by those parting words.

Wondering if she ever thought of him.

CHAPTER THREE

VENATORA

Just before the jump, she thought: "Sten!"

She jolted up in her command chair. Hackles prickling.

"Check again, Marta," she said.

"But, Highness, we already—"

Venatora snapped: "Check again!"

"Yes, Majesty," Marta said, voice tight with frustration.

And so she'd repeated the order—a rare occurrence for the Pirate Queen—mistress of all the Himmenops. But Marta was not only her Segunda, her second, she was also a trusted friend who had every reason to question her.

Venatora had to admit she'd been behaving obsessively of late. Seeing Sten's hand in every setback. Every delay.

But she had grounds for worry. Since their last encounter at that spaceport bar Venatora's spies had filled in and corrected many assumptions about Sten.

He was not the flag lieutenant of an Imperial Admiral but, in fact, the emissary of the Eternal Emperor. It was whispered that he was a skilled assassin. A member of the highly secretive Mantis Section. The catspaw of the Emperor's rule. When the Emperor wanted something done quietly, with no public blowback, he turned to Mantis operatives like Sten for everything ranging from simple wetwork to the toppling of governments.

In Venatora's case, she was certain Sten had been ordered to perform both deeds: kill her and then destroy the Himmenops pirate culture.

Father Raggio assured her that Sten had met his match in her. That her warrior skills, coupled with her heightened pheromonic powers, would foil any attempt Sten made to carry out his orders.

Not only that, Father Raggio said, but she might be able to bring Sten into their fold. To bond with him. To manipulate a gene or two from his DNA chain and add it to Venatora's.

"What an amazing achievement that would be," Father Raggio said.

Venatora wanted nothing to do with Father Raggio's scheme. Wasn't it enough for her to manipulate her own people to create what Raggio said would soon become a "super race?" A race of people directly under control of the Holy Fathers. Made stronger still through Venatora—adding to the cut-and-paste DNA progeny that would be the result of the Fathers' experiments.

His scheme was not without controversy. Father Huber, Raggio's main rival for leadership of the Council of Fathers—led a group that was vehemently opposed to the scheme. It was even whispered in the halls of power that Huber had formed an alliance with Venatora's own chief rival, the rebel Princess Anthofelia.

Venatora's well-honed survival skills told her that her best course was to kill Sten the moment she laid eyes on him.

If she didn't, he would surely kill her.

Never mind the white hot passions that came to a boil when they'd last met.

In Sten, she sensed, she had found a man whose duty would outweigh any of his internal passions.

Worse still—Sten seemed to have a similar pheromonic effects on Venatora. In short, she was as attracted to Sten as he was to her. And the more she ramped up her powers, the more she seemed to be drawn to him.

Venatora was certain that in the end she had the will to overcome Father Raggio's demands.

But—and this was a big BUT. When it really came down to it, could she kill Sten?

Sharp pain brought her out of her reverie. She looked down and for the first time noticed that her right fist was clenched so tight her nails dug into her flesh.

Then, all around her, she felt the prickling sensation of snooper sensors scanning her ship. Moments later, Marta once again issued the all clear.

Venatora ordered the jump.

As a myriad of colors swirled about and through her as she and her ship passed from one sector to another, she had the crazy thought that Sten might be waiting on the other side.

Despite all her navigational cutouts and switchbacks, could he have tracked her?

If so, what would be his intent?

An embrace?

Or a blade?

* * * *

On the overhead monitor, Tortooga looked like a vast junk yard. Ancient wrecks, played out freighters, chopped up passenger liners, and yachts stripped of everything of value, mingled with cast off engines and machines so old no one remembered their purpose.

When Venatora had first seen it years before she'd laughed when Father Raggio said it was the most notorious pirate stronghold in the Fringe Regions. Supported by all the pirate captains in the region, Tortooga was the place where territorial concessions were auctioned off and leadership disputes settled.

And it was here—at the annual Gathering of the Captains—that her reign officially began as the queen of the Himmenops.

And it was here that her rule was being challenged by an upstart, self-styled princess who was determined to win the favor of the other captains.

Venatora paced the deck as the Tortooga pilot guided her ship through the detritus of several centuries worth of raids. The attendance of a local pilot was a requirement for all visitors. Without their presence and constant reassurance that everyone's intentions were peaceful, several gigantic laser cannons would turn interlopers into molten plas and steel.

Behind her, Marta was at the comm board, monitoring those very same giant laser cannons. Meanwhile, two of her most trusted Zabanya guardswomen had taken station at the entrance of the bridge. A third, Palsonia, lingered near the pilot, dagger at the ready in case she tried to betray them.

On the central overhead monitor, Venatora watched as Captain Skink's warship—a creaky battlewagon that dated back to the Mueller Wars—maneuver while a swarm of drone minifighters clung to her, like remora servicing a megashark.

Skink's ship, the *Swagman*, might have been old, but like the ships of most pirate captains it was armed with a dazzling array of weapons. Even so, they were no match for Venatora's pride and joy—the *Takeko*, a sleek little *Stiletto* class ship named for an ancient warrior woman. The fact that Venatora had a reputation for shooting first and asking questions later, also tended to give her rivals pause.

And so when Venatora fingered her comm and barked, "That's close enough, Captain," the monitor showed Skink responding instantly, retro thrusters lighting up to slow the ship.

The monitor blurred, then the left side was swallowed by the image of a short-snouted crocodilian Parlitas, with the mottled green features and turret-like eyes common to his desert-world species. It was Skink, fellow pirate and self-proclaimed Governor General of Tortooga.

Founded by his great grandmother and her siblings, the fortress was that rarest of things: a neutral zone in the always restive Possnet Sector where pirates could rest up between raids, repair their ships, take on supplies, sell their loot and deal with quarrels between the captains.

"Please, Your Highness," Skink said. "We always guarantee everyone a safe berth for the Gathering. So I have to check you out along with all the others."

"You're close enough for a proper scan," Venatora snarled. "Do your business and get on with it."

Venatora trusted no one—especially a fellow pirate. Skink would sell his own scrotum if he thought he could make a profit.

In an oddly delicate motion, Skink covered his mouth with a claw as he cleared his throat. "There's a small matter of payment," he said, clearly uncomfortable. "Everyone has to kick in. That's the deal. Tortooga hospitality doesn't come cheap, you know."

"And a rich arrangement it is for you, Skink," Venatora said. "I should know. I pay more than any other captain."

"Pardon, Highness, but that's also part of the agreement," Skink said. "It's all based on scale. The most successful privateer captains pay the most. It's only fair. Can't expect a poor Cybom who goes pirating with her mate and a couple of pups to pay the same as the Queen Of Thieves."

Venatora couldn't help but smile at that. She quite liked the sobriquet conferred on her by rivals and admirers alike.

She said, "You'll get your money when I've been cleared and you have satisfied me that Princess Anthofelia and her supporters pose no threat."

Skink sighed. "Suspicions, suspicions. So little trust these days," he said. "Makes me sad for my nestlings' future."

"Get on with it, Skink," Venatora said. "Everyone knows that Parlitas males eat their young if they are left unguarded by their mates. So I won't join you shedding tears for your nestlings."

She almost said crocodile tears, but cut it when she caught the warning look from Marta, who could usually guess when she was about to stray over the diplomatic line.

"Such a cynic," Skink harrumphed.

But a moment later the *Takeko*'s sensors gave a series of blips as Skink's techs scanned her bow to stern. Soon, they were cleared and Venatora authorized a sizeable credit transfer from her treasury.

Moments later, they were approaching the eerie citadel that was Tartooga.

Four hollowed out meteors—played out nickel mines, actually—had been put in motion around each other. Bristling with arms, the meteors formed a virtual fortress encircling the cosmic junkyard. Closer in were the command ships of the attending captains. They ranged from large clumsy craft, to sleek raiders like the *Takeko*.

One ship—the *Gunakada*—even sported an elongated bridge and a double hump, not unlike the ancient sea creature it was named for. The *Gunakada* was Princess Anthofelia's command ship.

When her palace coup had failed, Anthofelia had seized the ship, along with several unguarded *Stiletto* class fighters and managed to carry away hundreds of her supporters. Most of whom, Venatora assumed, were living in cramped misery in those ships.

The pilot, a Wallob named Roo, was gathering up the tools of her trade, preparing to disembark. Built with thick haunches and small forelimbs, Roo had confided to Palsonia that she'd only recently returned to duty after giving birth to a single female pup. At the moment the big eyed little critter was peeping out of Roo's pouch to see if it was safe to creep out for a feeding.

Venatora strode over to Roo, holding out a handsome bonus for her work. During the approach, Venatora had noted that the pilot steered well clear of a small white yacht that had seemed overly curious.

Roo tried to refuse the bonus. "Only doin' me duty, Yer Highness," she said.

"Nonsense," Venatora replied. "I saw you out maneuver that yacht. Up to no good, was she?"

Roo ducked her head. "Fore I set out the skipper offered me money to steer close in," she said. "Don't like it for beings to think Old Roo was on the take. Bad for a pilot's reputation. We're supposed to be neutral."

"Then you deserve this even more," Venatora said, again offering the money. "It's not a bribe, but a bonus for a job well done. Take your mate out for a nice dinner tonight courtesy of your shipmates on the *Takeko*."

"Thankee, thankee, Yer Highness," Roo said, taking the money and discretely tucking it and her pup back into her pouch. "Not so many have been generous this year." She sniffed. "They groan about the takings when it comes time to pay for me services. But boast of fat purses when impressin' the joyboys and joygirls in the pleasure houses."

Venatora indicated Anthofelia's ship. "We've heard gossip that the Princess is notoriously tight-fisted. I don't know if it's true." She lifted her smooth shoulders and lowered them again. "For your sake I hope she is being falsely maligned."

Bitter laughter from Roo. "No chance of that," she said. "Word is she's payin' her people with nothin' but promises." Roo glanced around, as if people were listening in. Which, of course, they were. Marta and the others were only a few feet away, big-earing every word.

Ignoring them, Roo said, "And wasn't it the Princess herself who tried to bribe me? And when I refused, she tried to stiff me altogether. Had to get Skink to put the arm on her."

"That's interesting to know," Venatora said, nodding at Palsonia to escort the pilot off the ship.

When they were gone, she turned to Marta. "Take her the rest of the way in," she said, then resumed pacing as Marta maneuvered the *Takeko* into her berth.

There was a dry buzzing in her ear. It was Father Raggio.

She answered. "You were absolutely correct on how to play it, Father," she said. "We go in and make a big splash."

"The bigger the better," Father Raggio said.

CHAPTER FOUR

QUEEN OF THIEVES

When Venatora and her entourage entered Tortooga's infamous Gibbet Hall, she thought she'd never witnessed such a level of bloody chaos.

Things were always unruly in the Hall. After all, this is where felons from all over the region gathered to party, nurse wounds, and do business.

But this gathering made all her other visits seems funereal in comparison.

Hundreds of pirates and their sycophants were on hand to witness the confrontation between the Pirate Queen and the rebel princess. Criminals of all species and sexes shouted and fought for room enough to raise drinking appendages to the level of intake organs.

The hall was set in what had once been the rec area of an old starliner that in a hundred plus years had gone from luxury cruises to cut rate travel for pensioners. The Parlitas—Skink's forbearers—ended up taking the ship in trade for overdue berthing bills.

While the crowd bickered and complained, booze drones whizzed overhead, delivering overpriced and watered down intoxicants. Loot hung from the walls in a gaudy display of how rampant piracy had become in the region, where the price of security had outpaced the willingness of mining companies to pay up.

They'd adopted the penguin method of survival, sending out huge convoys that bent Imperial security laws to the limit—and beyond. Ships on the edges of the convoy were fed to the pirates, while the others hurried away, leaving their convoy mates at the mercy of the pirates.

The convoy routes were the main piece of business at the annual Gathering of the Captains. Over the next few days the assembled pirates would bid for the routes, which would then become the exclusive hunting territory for auction winners. Skink took a percentage of each sale for the upkeep and maintenance of Tortooga.

Taking Father Raggio at his word, Venatora made her entrance the grandest of her career. At her command, the double doors slammed open.

Marta shouted orders and twelve Zabanya guardswomen formed a phalanx—six on a side with Palsonia making a formidable tip of the spear. In the center of this wedge of warrior women, Venatora barked commands, and they all marched down the center aisle. Beings cringed out of their way, fearing what would happen if they were too slow.

As well they should. The Zabanyas were an elite group among the Himmenops. They were specially bred, raised and trained to fight to the death for their queen and colony. They were all tall, muscular and for psychological shock wore skin-tight body armor. Their white skin and long snowy white braids glistened under the lights.

They carried the latest AM2 battlerifles at port arms. Black metal girdles encircled slender waists, bearing pistols and long curved knives.

In the center, Venatora was the most splendid of all. Her tall ebony figure was draped in swirling robes of many colors and her golden crown of office completed the dazzling display. She carried no weapons in the open, but secreted a few fighting necessities beneath her flowing robes.

At the far end of the hall, five beings sat on a raised dais trying, but failing to look unimpressed.

Skink, decked out in outrageous finery, from tooled leather boots to a broad feathered hat, was in the center. To his left were Captains Manzil and Barnid. Humanoids, scarred from countless boardings. To his right, Captain Clew. Female, reptilian, with cunning yellow eyes. Venatora had once participated in a boarding with Clew, who seemed competent enough, but she had no experience with Manzil and Barnid, other than the annual conclave of captains.

There was an empty chair at the head of the table. Princess Anthofelia stood behind it. The portrait of regal beauty, with flowing silvery hair, dazzling emerald eyes, a muscular, but curvaceous body, draped in rather plain, but elegant robes that bared her arms. A red and gold Sharkwire tattoo encircled one rippling bicep.

The chair was normally reserved for Venatora. Six fierce Himmenops rebels guarded the deposed princess, battlerifles at ready.

In awful fascination, everyone watched for the inevitable confrontation. But to the surprise of the crowd and Venatora, Anthofelia snatched a battlerifle from the hands of one of her guards and leveled it at Venatora.

"One more step, you dirty boslachee," she hissed, "and you'll soon be sleeping under the feet of our Fathers."

It was the worst sort of insult for one woman to call another. Instinctively, Marta and Palsonia raised their weapons. A great silence descended on the hall. Nerves were on hair trigger.

Venatora held up a hand. "Wait," she commanded.

Marta and Palsonia were jolted as if hit by electric shocks. They looked at her, confused.

Ignoring Anthofelia, Venatora turned to Skink. "What is this, Skink?" she demanded. "Violence has always been forbidden at the Gathering of the

Captains. Open bidding has always been the rule."

Skink harrumphed. "There's those of us who think it's time for a change," he said. "At every gathering you come forward with your women and sweep up the most lucrative territories in the Possnet Sector. Why, with all your riches, you are always able to outbid every hard working pirate in the region."

Someone at the far end of the table slammed down a fist. It was Captain Manzil, scarred face flushed with fury.

"Me and my crew are sick of gettin' the dregs, Venatora," he thundered, "while you get richer every season. Makin' it impossible for anybody to catch up and match you."

There were murmurs of agreement in the crowd.

Barataria bellowed support. "You tell her, Cap'n," he said. "Whole clottin' system's been rigged for years. Rigged to keep the rest of us out, while Venatora gets richer. Guaranteein' that she's gonna win every bid at the next gathering. And we just get her leavin's."

Out in the hall, the murmurs were turning to shouts.

"Fair bidding," somebody cried. Others took it up. "Fair bidding! Fair bidding!"

The building uproar was so organized that Venatora knew that Skink had planted shills in the crowd.

Skink grinned at her, exposing rows of long yellow teeth. "Hear them, Venatora?" he said. "Sounds like a lot of the captains here are looking for change, don't it? Well, me and my kin have been talking to the captains the past few months and there were so many grievances we decided to bring the issue forward at the next gathering. It'd be more democratic, like."

Keeping her calm, Venatora shook her head in amusement. "Skink," she said, "No one has ever accused you of being the brightest pixel on the screen. Nor has anyone ever heard you calling for instituting a *'one being, one vote'* democracy.

"We're pirates, for clot's sake. We don't vote, we steal. And if the hostages' friends and family can't pony up the ransom, we space them to set an example and move on."

To Venatora's amazement, Anthofelia suddenly came unstuck. "Lies!" she shouted, pushing past Venatora to address the crowd. "Nothing but lies! She's proclaimed herself the Queen Of The Himmenops. But she's nothing of the sort. She's just a sport. A mutant. A great whore. The mother of all boslachees."

She turned to Venatora, shaking an angry fist. "I don't know what it is that gives you power over your fellow beings. But I for one am no longer affected. I'm immune to your powers, Venatora. Immune."

To Venatora's frustration, Anthofelia's declaration appeared to be true.

Try as she might to flood the short distance between them with pheromones, her efforts seemed to have no affect on Anthofelia, or her bodyguards.

She felt suddenly out of sorts. The room seemed hazy. She became momentarily fixed on the sight of Anthofelia's Sharkwire tattoo. Gold with blood red tips, that seemed to throb with an energy of its own.

Marta glanced back at her, puzzled. Even Palsonia, the always faithful Palsonia, was frowning down at her weapon, as if wondering how it got there.

A buzz in her ear. "Beware, daughter," came Father Raggio's voice. "Skink has flooded the hall with some sort of chemical. Can you smell it?"

Soon as he said it, Venatora caught the odor of dying flowers. The crowd was becoming more restive. She heard her name being cursed. And more shouts of "Fair Bidding!"

As she struggled to take all this in, Anthofelia gripped the battlerifle at both ends and raised it over her head, striking a classic rebels' pose.

What appeared to be nothing but a plain set of robes, suddenly took on a golden flow with sparkles of light running up and down the seams. And for the first time Venatora saw just how beautiful her rival was.

She was tall—nearly as tall as Venatora. Her figure nearly as lush. Her skin was ivory white and her hair a silver cloud, framing a heart-shaped face, glowing emerald eyes and lips as red and full as ripe fruit.

"I say no bidding," she shouted, her voice suddenly amplified by Skink, who also threw her image up on the big central monitor, blocking out Venatora entirely.

"I say the Possnet Sector should be open to all who are willing to fight for it."

And then she seemed to really hit her stride when she thundered, "Let pirates be pirates!"

Her cry was taken up by the crowd. "Let pirates be pirates! Let pirates be pirates!" Louder and louder. "Let pirates be pirates."

The crowd was barely in control. Faces were flushed. Beings were waving fists and claws and tentacles at Venatora.

In her ear, Father Raggio urged, "Get out! Get out now!"

There was a deafening explosion, and Venatora turned to see Clew on her feet. She had old antique hand cannon. Once again, she aimed at the ceiling and fired. Smoke and flame erupted from the barrel.

She grabbed Venatora's elbow. "Come on," she said. "Before they kill us all!"

And Clew led the way as Marta and Palsonia reformed the deadly phalanx of women warrior and they rushed off the dais and slammed into the crowd.

There were shouts and screams and no little blood as Venatora found herself trampling over pirates trying to block her exit.

And the last thing she saw as she burst though the big double doors was the victorious figure of Anthofelia filling the overhead monitor.

Standing tall in her rebel pose and shouting, "Let pirates be pirates. Let pirates be pirates."

The doors slammed shut and Marta lasered the locking mechanism into a molten mess, sealing the crowd in.

Then they were running for the *Takeko,* desperate to escape before the jaws of Skink's trap snapped shut.

CHAPTER FIVE

DEATHRUN

Racing around a corner at top speed, they were greeted by a hail of gunfire. Rock splinters flew everywhere and one of her women went down.

While the others dived for cover, Palsonia ran to the woman, heaved her over a shoulder and staggered back, firing blindly behind her with one hand, while balancing her wounded charge with the other.

Shedding her robes to reveal skin-tight body armor and belted weapons, Venatora shouted orders. Meanwhile, Marta and the others laid down covering fire, driving back a squad of armored bots Skink had sent to block their escape.

Clew grabbed her arm. "There's a back way," she shouted. Venatora and the others followed, staying low to avoid the withering fire laid down by the bots.

The corridor broke out into a wide chamber, where the mouths of a dozen or more tunnels offered more possibilities of escape than they had time to explore.

"To the right," Clew cried, indicating a narrow passageway.

Venatora hesitated. "Why are you doing this, Clew?" she demanded. "You don't have a reputation for sticking your neck out for anyone."

"There's a whole new game in play," Clew said. "Something that Lord Wichman has spent a good deal of money to cook up for the Tahn. It's called Project Demeter."

"What's that all about?"

A hail of gunfire shattered the momentary calm. Molten metal spraying everywhere.

"Come on," Clew urged. "We don't have time for this."

Venatora came unstuck. If Clew was part of the trap, so be it. They could all stay here and fight until they were overwhelmed, or they could take their chances.

An inveterate gambler, Venatora rolled the dice and they came up Run Like Hell.

So that's what she did. Shoving Clew forward. And taking off in a dead run, Marta and the others close on their heels.

They leapfrogged down the tunnel. One group hanging back to confront their pursuers, while the others moved ahead, found cover, then returned the compliment as their sisters raced to rejoin them.

Zig-zagging as they ran, bullets pinging the surrounding rock.

Clew led them to the door of a chamber, fiddled with the lock and the door irised open, revealing a changing area, with lockers and freshers and row after row of white spacesuits and bubble helmets.

They threw themselves to the floor to escape the withering gunfire that followed them in. It was so intense that it was almost impossible to raise their heads.

Their attackers were spraying indiscriminately, rounds peppering the walls and lockers, and ripping spacesuits into useless shreds.

Venatora flopped over on her back, fumbled out an incendiary pellet she'd stashed in her belt, then hurled it into the hallway.

A deafening explosion rocked the chamber. Flames scorched the hallway leading into it and she heard the satisfying screams of her attackers. Bots didn't scream when they were hit. Which meant that Skink's gunnies had joined the fight.

There was a pause in the gunfire long enough for Venatora to shout, "Block the door."

The number of pursuers must have doubled, or even tripled since their first encounter.

Palsonia jumped forward with several other women and muscled the door shut. Stray rounds found their way through, but finally the door was closed. Meanwhile, Marta and a few other women warriors ripped the lockers from the walls and piled them against the door.

Clew pointed to an exit at the far end. "We go that way," she said. "Half a klick or so and we can get to the tarmac and your ship."

Venatora didn't hesitate. She'd made up her mind to trust Clew and there was no going back now. She'd learn Clew's motives soon enough— and what this Project Demeter business was about.

If they lived long enough to find out.

An explosion rocked the door, hurling several lockers aside. Palsonia and several other women piled up more, while Marta fired blindly through the gap the explosion had forced open.

"Suit up, everybody," Venatora shouted, grabbing two suits off a rack and handing one to Clew.

More blasts hammered the door as they all pulled on their suits. Moments later, Clew was forcing the door on the other side, using her claws to rip wiring from a panel next to the door.

A few sparks shot out as she manipulated the wires, then the door gave a groan like a tired old woman, then slowly, but surely, opened.

"Don't forget your helmets," Venatora cried, as she grabbed one for herself and hooked it to a belt loop.

Palsonia and Marta cautiously checked the corridor on the other side. Nothing.

The way looked clear.

Another explosion sent lockers flying and then they charged out of the chamber to face the unknown.

Venatora was last. She paused, slipped another grenade from her belt. Ignoring Marta's pleas to run.

She counted. One… Two… And then another explosion blew the far door wide open. A torrent of gunfire poured in. But still Venatora didn't move.

"Come Highness," Marta urged. "Come now!"

Then Venatora underhanded the incendiary grenade and she turned and ran, nearly bowling Marta over.

As they raced down the corridor, she heard the grenade go off and there were more screams as the attackers were hit with the full force of the blast.

The smell of death followed Venatora as she and her women raced along the corridor, with Clew leading the way.

It wasn't easy an easy escape route. A work in constant progress, Tortooga was a warren of tunnels and chambers bored through solid nickel alloy.

Twice Clew took wrong turns and they had to backtrack.

Then she came to a place where a pair of tunnels beckoned in opposite directions.

She started down the one on the left, but was met with a barrage of gunfire. She staggered back, one limb bleeding.

Marta ran to help, but Clew waved her away. "It's nothing," she said. "All I need is a suit patch."

Clew fished one out of a utility pocket. Pressed it against the suit. There was a hiss and a few tendrils of smoke. She winced from obvious pain. Then it was over, the smell of burning plas and flesh fouled the air.

"That should do it," Clew said.

But she stumbled when she started toward the exit and Marta caught her by an elbow.

"Maybe you'd better hang back a bit," she advised. "Until you recover."

More gunfire erupted. Blasting through the tunnel with greater intensity than before. Everyone flattened against the nearest wall. The direction of the fire changed as the enemy tried to get into better positions.

But Marta and Palsonia—taking shelter on opposite walls—took turns leaping out, triggering bursts from their battlerifles, then jumping back to safety.

It was a momentary stalemate, with neither side gaining an advantage. But slowly the enemy forces grew, giving Marta and Palsonia fewer chances to return fire.

Then Marta shouted "Majesty!" and Venatora turned to see a grenade come bouncing into the room. Coming at an angle and heading straight for her.

She watched in awful fascination as it bounced toward her. Once... Twice... And Venatora hurled herself to the side, desperately trying to get out of its path.

Luck seemed to have deserted her because the grenade caromed off a wall and bounced in her new direction.

"Not a chance," Palsonia said, stepping into its path and kicking it back toward the entrance.

It hit the edge of the doorway, bounced up, and then exploded in midair, blinding and deafening everyone on both sides of the door.

Venatora was the first to recover. "Let's go!" she shouted, shoving a still-dazed Clew toward the exit. "Get us out of here."

She didn't have to repeat herself. Clew came out of her shock and stumbled for the exit. She paused, looked left, then right, then said, "This way!" and disappeared.

Palsonia and Marta took up covering position, firing through the ruins of the doorway, holding the enemy back long enough for the others to escape.

Venatora was the last to go. As soon as she vanished, the two women hurled incendiaries through the doorway, turned and sprinted after their queen.

The last airlock closed behind them. Palsonia disabled the locking mechanism and then they all raced out onto the tarmac.

Dark, airless space all around them. Grav boots keeping them from floating away as they ran for their ship. It was like running through mud, the grav boots sticking as she pulled each one free for the next step.

Then there it was.

The *Takeo*!

Venatora thought she'd never seen her ship look more beautiful. Sitting there gleaming in the starlight.

Their last hope.

The first of her women reached the ship and had the doors open, while the others fanned out on either side. Battlerifles at ready. Muzzles looking for the enemy.

For a moment, it looked like the enemy hadn't found them. Then in the darkness a humped back turret stirred.

Long barrels smoothed out on oiled bearings.

Red laser beams speared out and the turret swiveled slowly... slowly...

And then it found Venatora and opened fire.

Spent uranium rounds chewed up the tarmac, stitching their way toward Venatora.

Two of her women charged the big gun in a futile effort to shield their queen with their own bodies. And they went down in a welter of blood.

Venatora didn't have time to move. Only the blink of eye stood between her and certain death.

And then a sleek missile flashed out of nowhere, hitting the big gun square on.

A massive explosion rocked Tortooga. Venatora and the others clung to anything close at hand to keep from being swept off the surface into uttermost space.

And then Venatora came out of the shock of suddenly being alive, when she should have been dead.

She gathered up Marta, and then Palsonia and Clew. Together, they rounded up the other warrior women. Bruised and aching from head to toe.

They stumbled onto the *Takeko*. Pulled up the ramp and then closed and locked the door.

By the time Skink and a horde of other pirates came tumbling out onto the tarmac Venatora was long gone.

* * * *

Sitting off in his little *Viper* a short distance away, Sten watched with amusement as Skink argued with two other pirate captains.

They were waving their arms. Punctuating remarks with chest-stabbing fingers.

Meanwhile, their various crews gathered around—taking sides. With Venatora gone, they no longer had the unity of a common enemy. Any minute now and the first blow would be struck and the pirates would be fighting each other.

He recorded all their images for Mahoney to identify later. Then slipped away unnoticed in his little ghost ship.

Sten shook his head in amazement. A minute ago he could have carried out Mahoney's kill order by just letting nature take its course.

If he hadn't fired that missile Venatora would be dead. And it wouldn't have been his fault.

Not really.

He wouldn't have had to actually pull the trigger and kill her.

But when it came down to it, he wasn't sure if he could have carried out that order.

Mantis training or no Mantis training.

On the other hand, would he have really been able to just sit there while Venatora was gunned down? Could he allow that amazing woman be turned into a smear of gore on the tarmac.

Sten sighed. He wasn't sure he could have done that, anymore than he could have rationalized his responsibility away.

But Mahoney had changed the order. The Eternal Emperor was reviewing the situation and didn't want her dead.

Not just yet.

CHAPTER SIX

OF HEROES AND GOATS

When Mahoney stepped into his boss's kitchen, the Eternal Emperor was singing at the top of his voice, keeping time with an enormous cleaver as he whacked away at a dead animal.

At least he hoped it was dead.

"*I think I'm going to Kathmandu,*" the Emperor warbled as he slammed the cleaver down—whack!

"*That's really, really where I'm going to...*"

Whack!

"*If I ever get out of here...*"

Whack!

"*That's what I'm going to do...*"

Whack!

"*K-k-k-k-k...*"

Whack! Whack! Whack!

And with the last whack what appeared to be a bloody leg came loose from the skinned carcass and the Emperor brandished it aloft—voice so out of tune it was like being stabbed in the ear—as he shouted:

"*Kathmandu! K-k-k-k-k-k Kathmandu!*"

He spotted Mahoney. Waving the bloody leg at a stool drawn up to the butcher block counter, he said, "Pull up a pew, Ian and grab yourself a drink. Party's just getting started."

Ian helped himself to a slug of scotch, saw that the Emperor's glass was empty and filled it.

With a gory hand, the Emperor raised his glass, "Confusion to our enemies," he said.

Mahoney raised his glass: "Here's to those who wish us well," he said, "And those that don't can go to hell."

Laughing, the Emperor drowned his drink in one go. "My daddy always told me to never try to match toasts with an Irishman."

"Wise man, your father, so he was," Ian said as he refilled their classes.

Perching his hind end on the stool, he said, "Always happy to see you in a good mood, boss, that I am. But what's brought on all this cheer? Did your Prime Minister keel over on the floor of Parliament, or something?"

"Oh, if only it were so," the Emperor said.

He indicated the carcass on the table. It still wore its head and its pleading eyes seemed to follow Mahoney everywhere.

"Does look a bit like him, though, doesn't he? With those pleading eyes you can almost hear him bleat."

Mahoney laughed. "What happened, boss? Somebody trying to make a goat out of you, are they?"

"And then, some," the Emperor said. "So much so that it inspired me to make Timbuktu goat curry out of them."

He slapped the carcass. "Do us a favor, Ian, and toss the leftovers into the ice box. Thapa will be along later to collect them."

Thapa was Havildar-Major Lalbahadur Thapa, head of the contingent of Gurkhas who were the Emperor's personal bodyguards. Hailing from the kingdom of Nepal in Kathmandu, they had taken an oath to die, rather than to see the Emperor come to harm. The Emperor said they'd performed the same service for the British royal family for centuries.

Ian had only a vague idea who the British were. His boss was a fan of Elizabeth The First, who, in his view was the canniest monarch in human history.

Mahoney tossed a towel over the goat's carcass to protect his clothes, hoisted it over his shoulder, and strode over to the gleaming temperature controlled fresher that the Emperor insisted on calling an ice box. Ian hadn't the faintest idea why since there was never any ice inside.

The Emperor switched knives and started to expertly dissect the leg, then turn the choicest pieces into nearly identical cubes.

"Old Tanz stopped by a little while ago to tell tales on one of his zillionare buddies," the Emperor said.

Old Tanz was Tanz Sullamora, the richest industrialist in the Empire who had his greedy fingers in every enterprise. He hated anyone nearly as rich as himself and loved to undermine them in the Emperor's eyes by gossiping shamelessly about their private peccadilloes and disloyal actions.

In short, in Ian's humble Irish opinion, he was the biggest ass kisser in the Empire, but he was a loyal ass kisser who would go to any extreme to please the Emperor.

"You know, with Tanz I have to keep a smile fixed on my face the whole time he's talking," the Emperor said.

He grimaced. "Sometimes it feels like my face is going to fall off. I can't stand the son of a scrote, but like LBJ said, I'd rather he was inside my tent pissing out, than outside, pissing in."

Ian hadn't the foggiest who the Emperor was referring to, but this LBJ boyo sounded like a pretty savvy fellow.

He was always amazed how graceful the Emperor was in the kitchen. He seemed to be doing several things at once. Rolling the goat in spices and minced garlic; sprinkling the cubed meat with three fingers of sea salt; hooking a foot back to catch the lip of a broiler and checking the vegetables charring inside; turning back to add a few glugs of mustard oil to a heavy iron pot he called a Dutch oven; stirring in too many spices for Ian to identify, but as they cooked he definitely smelled fenugreek, chilies, and curry powder among other savory delights.

Oh, yeah, and more garlic. The Emperor loved his garlic. And Ian thought he saw his boss sprinkle in a sparing pinch or so of cumin. Then in went the goat, which he lovingly browned in the pot.

And all while he plotted the demise of his enemies with Ian.

"If you recall," the Emperor said, "in our latest negotiations with the Tahn I eased a few of the sanctions I'd slapped on them with for being sneaky drakh heads."

Mahoney shook his head. "And sorry I am that so much effort led to naught," he said.

Ian had been part of those negotiations. The Tahn pulled every crooked trick in the book to get the upper hand in business negotiations. From price wars, to product dumping, to computer sabotage, and outright theft.

Only the Emperor's iron grip on AM2 kept them at bay.

The sanctions came when Mahoney started getting reports of raids on AM2 depots on smaller worlds. Ian's spies couldn't get definite proof that the Tahn were behind the raids. Although the Tahn vehemently denied responsibility and blamed pirates, all signs pointed in their direction. Of course, pirates probably were involved. But Ian and the Emperor had no doubt they were pirates working for the Tahn.

Fed up, but cautious of appearing to be a bully by threatening military action, the Emperor imposed sanctions. Denying permits to trade with the Tahn, except for medical and other humanitarian goods and supplies.

Agricultural products and equipment were also sanctioned. The Tahn had the misfortune of settling worlds with sparse farming opportunities.

Plus, as the Emperor liked to tell Mahoney, "They're just clotting lousy farmers. All warrior culture are like that. They look down on beings who till the soil and grow their own food. Manly men—and womanly women—like the Tahn took what they wanted and pressed the farmers into unproductive slave labor gangs."

The sanctions were hard to police, but the Emperor kept squeezing until finally the Tahn were forced back to the negotiating tables. Although they still denied responsibility and blamed pirates, they made several crucial concessions in the areas of goods dumping, price fixing and industrial espionage.

The Emperor shrugged. "Of course, the reality is that sanctions cut two ways," he said. "Your competitor is cut off from badly need goods, but at the same time, your companies at home are denied lucrative markets. So they all came crying and whining to me. Old Tanz being one the loudest and whiniest. Finally, I play Mr. Nice Guy. A role I'm not well suited for. I tell the Tahn I'll give them another chance. And I ease up a bit."

Snorting disgust, the Emperor turned back to his oven. "Better keep going, or I'll burn the drakh out of the veggies."

Grabbing a towel, he rescued the tray of nicely charred veggies from the oven. Mahoney noted that they mostly consisted of skinned tomatoes, peppers, red onions, ginger, garlic and green chilies. The Emperor popped them in a blender, flipped it on, whirred them to a smooth sauce, then dumped the whole thing into the Dutch oven with the goat.

Stirring the contents of the pot with a wooden spoon, he said, "Agriculture is one area I'm not going to budge on. Keep them hungry. And then turn up the heat."

He popped on the lid. Adjusted the heat. Wiped his hands on a towel and perched on a stool.

"Hit me with another, Ian," he said. "Goat currying and Tahn plotting is thirsty work."

"Glad I am to oblige, boss," Mahoney said.

While he fixed their drinks, the Emperor gestured to the side where pots and pans bubbled and squeaked, giving off delicious smells. "Got some jasmine rice and other good stuff going on over there," he added. "And some nice Nepalese flat bread for dipping and scooping and other fun messy things."

Ian's belly rumbled. The smells had awakened the hunger beast in him.

"Douse it with Scotch," the Emperor advised. "Makes it easier to hold out for dinner."

Mahoney tossed off his scotch. Shuddered. Even so, he felt a little better.

He grimaced, "I'm better, that I am. But the cure like to have killed me."

"So, back to where you came in," the Emperor said. "Back to old Tanz Sullamora. Who was jumping up and down with joy about the sanctions being lifted. Well, imagine his surprise when his guys went to the Tahn with their order books out, and there were no takers."

"That doesn't make sense, boss," Ian said. "Tanz mainly specializes in big ticket items. Like Kurosawa engines, prefab factories, parts for expensive machines. Those were among the first things we clamped down on."

"Well, obviously the Tahn are getting those big tickets items elsewhere," the Emperor said. "Some very foolish beings dared my wrath and went behind my back to supply the Tahn."

A lot of questions that had been swirling around Mahoney's brain suddenly found a few answers.

"Wichman!" he said. "So that's what that piece of pig drakh has been up to."

"What we've suspected all along," the Emperor said, with a shrug. "Selling sanctioned goods to the enemy."

"Forgive me for pointing out the obvious, Your Highness, but that's a firing squad offense. Conspiring with the enemy. Why don't we just pick the Wichmans up and put them on trial?"

The Emperor sighed. "Things have been ticking along pretty well, lately, Ian," he said. "Longest period of peace since the damned Mueller Wars. The economy is humming along to the point where poor folks are moving up to the middle class, and the middle class is knocking on the doors of the new rich.

"By and large the public views my government as a big happy family, with yours truly as the benign patriarch. Dispensing favors to the deserving. Punishing the few malcontents—but only to bring them back into line, like prodigal sons.

"A sunny, Norman Rockwell portrait of love and loyalty."

"Gotcha, boss," Ian said.

Although he had no idea who that Rockwell boyo was, the Emperor's meaning was clear. When the time came to shed the blood of the Emperor's enemies, he didn't want any spatter to foul that carefully created image.

"Bottom line," the Emperor said, "I do not want a war with the Tahn at this time."

Mahoney sighed. "It's gonna come, boss," he said. "Mark my words. Just a matter of time, so it is."

"You are right in so many ways, Ian," he said. "But right now let's kick the can a little further down the road. Besides, as grim as things look now, I have certain irons in the fire that I'm betting will pay off in the near future. And we may be able to avoid war altogether."

"Yessir," Ian said.

He had his doubts, but in the Eternal Emperor's long time at the diplomatic gaming table, he'd rolled sevens more often than was probable.

Meaning, when he placed his last bets the dice were likely to be loaded.

The Emperor started dishing out dinner, and the meal proved to be as heavenly as it smelled. The rich, meaty flavor of the curry mixing magically with the fragrant jasmine rice. And the best bite yet, Ian soon discovered, was when he scooped curry and rice up in the delicious hunks of Nepalese flat bread.

"Now tell me about Sten and this so-called pirate queen," the Emperor said. He chuckled. "She must have a beaut of a PR department," he said. "Strikes fear in her hearts over her victims before she even hoists the Jolly Roger."

Jolly Roger? An ancient comedian? Once again, Mahoney was left puzzling over archaic terms, but he got the general gist of the Emperor's meaning.

"I don't mean to question your judgment, Your Highness," Mahoney said. "But I don't understand why we couldn't just let nature take its course. Venatora was all but dead, she was. Which is what we wanted to begin with. Plus, it seems that the whole brotherhood of pirates business that has bedeviled us for all these years is about to implode."

"Listen up, Ian, old friend, old pal," the Emperor said. "The day you stop questioning my judgment is the day you'll no longer be of any use to me. If you feel such a yes-man notion coming on fire yourself and save me the trouble. I already have more 'yes your highness' swinging Richards than Argos had fleas."

That name Ian knew. Argos was Ulysses' faithful hound during his years away from home. The Emperor's obscure speech had sent him back to the history fiches and he'd immediately been stricken with admiration for the very ancient Greeks. Whether they predated the Emperor, he wasn't sure. Lately, he'd been guessing that Emperor's origins fell somewhere between the Greeks and the Romans. Both of whom he quoted frequently.

Scholars who dug too deeply into the Emperor's background were usually discouraged. Politely, or otherwise. One historian surmised that the Emperor dated to the 21st century in the old school calendars. This didn't make sense to Mahoney, so after reading the scholar's notes, he'd burned them and dismissed them from his mind. The scholar later died in an unfortunate accident and the generous insurance payout kept the family sweet.

"Now, back to this beautiful splicer—Venatora," the Emperor said. "I'd like to know more about the beings who made her. So let's keep her alive a bit longer. Also, I have a few ideas on how we might be able to use this current thieves-falling-out debacle to our advantage. Maybe do away with the whole shebang, the Wichmans, Venatora, and the pirates with one simple truel."

Mahoney frowned. "*Truel*, sir?"

"That'd be a three way duel," the Emperor said.

Mahoney chuckled. "This I have to see, sir," he said.

"Oh, you will, Ian," the Eternal Emperor said. "You surely will. Now, pour us a couple of snifters of cognac and I'll explain."

Mahoney fetched the bottle, but he nearly dropped it when the Emperor said, "Did I ever tell you about Project Demeter?"

"Uh, boss," Mahoney said. "Sten overheard one of Venatora's allies mention a Project Demeter just before they escaped."

"Did he now?" the Emperor said, a grin as wide as Earth's moon splitting his chiseled features.

"Well, what is it, sir?" Mahoney asked.

"Food, Ian," the Emperor said. "Magical, wonderful, glorious food."

CHAPTER SEVEN

THE DEAL MAKER

Lord Wichman was a contented man. As he sat on his golden throne, leisurely performing his morning necessaries, he considered the day ahead.

First was the meeting with Lord Fehrle, the Tahn High Council bigshot who had been one of the most difficult beings Wichman had ever done business with.

For every offer, Fehrle had a counter.

For every price, a challenge.

For every proposed solution, a difficulty raised.

But as Lord Wichman blinked in the rising Wichlandian sun, he was confident that he finally had Fehrle backed into a corner he could not escape.

The notion had come to him a month or so before on a morning just like this. As he sat on his outdoor toilet, a gentle sea breeze fanning his cheeks, going over his morning intelligence reports, he'd spotted a item titled, *The Demeter Project: A Logistical Solution To Overstressed Supply Lines.*

It had been flagged for his attention by his chief of staff, Gen. Khelee, who stood before him now anxiously awaiting his comments.

The old war horse was a former Imperial Guardsman whose career had stalled out at the brigadier level and he'd been forced into retirement. Before his ouster, Khelee had enjoyed top secret clearances at the highest levels. Cast adrift, he'd become embittered and let it be known he was willing to sell his contacts in the world of military and industrial secrets.

Wichman, a man who had never served in the military, was a self-styled tough guy who'd go to any lengths to close a deal—up to and including industrial espionage and assassination. In Khelee he'd found the real deal when it came to tough guys and he'd quickly snapped him up and put him in charge of his Black Ops Division.

He'd proven himself many times over working with the pirates. Wichman believed he'd been instrumental into turning the Mutineers' Imperium X fiasco into a moderate success. It was then that Wichman made him chief of staff. Now he oversaw Wichman's chaotic business empire, including the resorts—which were a profitable cover for a host of criminal enterprises.

And it was Khelee that Wichman had to thank for keeping Gregor on ice for the day when Wichman might need him to play the fall guy.

Wichman tapped the fiche that contained the report.

"What's this all about, General?" he asked. "The title alone almost put me to sleep."

Khelee had the remarkable ability to ignore his boss's flatulent noises, fixing his eyes on a spot just to the left of Wichman's head.

"I got it off a Tahn operative, sir," Khelee said. "He was picked up in an Imperial sweep. Caught red handed stealing state secrets. I pulled strings and got him released to us."

Wichman shrugged. "What's that got to do with us? I don't care what the Tahn are up to on Prime World. That's the Emperor's problem."

"In this case, sir," Khelee said, "the operative stumbled on something his bosses would pay dearly to possess. It could be a partial answer to their logistics problems."

Wichman didn't bother stifling a yawn. Khelee caught the danger signal. Wichman Enterprises went through chiefs of staff like porcine fat through a gray Anser. One yawn was okay. Two yawns, perilous. Three yawns and you were out.

"Well sir," Khelee hastened to say, "You know and I know that the Tahn can fight well enough. They can punch way above their weight class."

Wichman blinked. A sign of interest. He liked action words like "punch" and "weight class."

Wichman said, "Even so, as we also both know, in the long run they can't beat the emperor. For three reasons." He ticked them off on his fingers: "AM2 AM2 and AM2."

"Sure, sure, boss," Khelee said. "But like you have so wisely pointed out, we can make money on a run up to war by supplying the Tahn. And after they lose the war we can sell the ruins of their worlds for a handsome profit."

Wichman raised a hand. "And don't forget the mortuary business," he reminded Khelee. "All those dead Tahn and Imperials will need to be disposed of. And their families will want to see it done properly."

Khelee nodded, "Yessir, and as you've reminded us time and time again there isn't that much difference between the hospitality business and the mortician business."

Wichman shrugged. "Bottom line is that in both cases we're selling false happiness at inflated prices."

Khelee nodded. "How droll, sir," he said. "I'll have to pass that on to the boys."

"The beauty of the burying business," Wichman continued, "is the dead can't complain if the champagne is flat, or the caviar gamey."

Khelee barked laughter "No sir, they sure as clot can't."

"Still," Wichman said, "I don't see how the Tahn stand a chance in the long run."

"To be sure," Khelee said, "But with our help we can help stave off the inevitable by preparing them for their own doom. To start with, to fight a modern war they need a plentitude of ships and guns, which we have been supplying, although not in the quantities they desire. They also needed AM2 to power their military buildup."

Wichman grunted assent. He'd made deals with Venatora, Skink and the other pirates to buy all the weapons they could steal. His minions had also supplied Fehrle with AM2 from raids on out-of-the-way storage depots.

"Not as much as they want," Khelee said, "but things are looking up now that Venatora is all but out of the picture. She fancies herself as a gambler, but from where I stand she's way too cautious."

Wichman snorted. "She's always carping that her fellow captains are too greedy for their own good," he said. "Thinks the Emperor will get fed up if there are too many raids and send in a big Imperial Force. And what with the troubles caused by Princess Anthofelia, she can't afford to lose too many people."

Khelee nodded. "All progs show that a big bodybag count would trigger a Himmenops revolt. And then she'd have a helluva lot more on her hands than a ditzy rebel princess."

The general was well satisfied with their work undermining Venatora's influence with the other captains. Skink and his cohorts had taken the bait and ousted Venatora from her seat at the Captain's High Council and moved the ineffectual Princess Anthofelia into her place.

It helped that there was some kind of a power struggle going on behind the scenes—the Fathers, Anthofelia called them. Whoever they were. Khelee's spies would find out more soon enough.

As Khelee reflected, Wichman ostentatiously yawned. Clot, he'd almost missed the danger signal. His boss was getting bored.

"But about this Demeter Project, sir," Khelee hastened to say. "It could very well throw all the Emperor's plans into a cocked helm. When I was still on his payroll, the Emperor used to quote some fellow—Napoleon, I think it was—who said that an army marches on its stomach."

Wichman frowned. "Napoleon? Is this somebody we should hire?"

"Oh, no sir," Khelee said. "I got the idea that he died a long time ago. One of the ancients."

Wichman's hand went to his mouth. A second yawn threatened. "A dead guy? Why are we talking about dead guys?"

"Yessir, sorry sir," Khelee said. "The point the Emperor was making is that if you can't supply your troops with adequate rations, a well fed enemy will soon prevail. The same goes for civilians. Left to starve, they are sure to revolt."

Khelee indicated the report. "And that project, sir, will guarantee that the Tahn will never have to fight on short rations again."

"Get to the point, General," Wichman said. He was just about through with his toilet and was ready for a shower and breakfast. "Lord Fehrle will be here soon and I need something to wow him. To get him to dip into the Tahn treasury and fill our pockets."

"It's a farm, sir," Khelee said.

"A farm?"

"Yessir, a farm."

Wichman almost yawned a second time, but then the look on Khelee's face gave him pause. He looked nervous—perhaps even frightened. But he also had the look of a man who was certain that he held a winning hand.

"Hand me my robe," Wichman said. "Then tell me more about this farm."

Khelee handed over his boss's golden robe. Grateful that it would soon cover those disgustingly skinny flanks.

And he told him about the farm.

* * * *

Lord Fehrle was a man who was not easily impressed. Tall, austere, clothed head to toe in a form-fitting black uniform with silver rank badges, he was the epitome of the Spartan warrior culture the Tahn admired above all else.

Wichman normally wined and dined his guests—plying them with drink and willing sexual companionship.

He did not make that mistake with Fehrle. Instead he had him escorted into a large chamber almost devoid of furniture, with a small refreshment table containing only pitchers of lukewarm water and small plates of dry crackers sprinkled with crystals of Wichlandian sea salt. Three large Tahn officers attended him.

Perched uncomfortably on a straight-backed chair, with only Gen. Khelee at his side, Wichman held forth.

"It's a well known fact, My Lord," Wichman said, "that the kingdoms of the Tahn have not been blessed with bounty. Of all the worlds in the Empire, the Tahn have the fewest planets capable of producing more food than their own inhabitants can consume."

Fehrle shrugged. "No matter," he said. "We Tahn are an abstemious race. We can make do on very little. We train from childhood to eat and drink as little as possible and to bear up under the most severe conditions."

"And very wise you are to take this course," Wichman said. "While the

Emperor plays in his kitchens and his subjects grow fat, the Tahn slowly, but surely, make headway. Unfortunately, however, your agricultural planets of late are producing less and less as time goes by. Making matters worse, your production costs are climbing."

Wichman wet his throat with a little water. "Despite this handicap, the Tahn have managed to prosper to the point where they are first true rivals of the Eternal Emperor in hundreds of years."

Fehrle waved an impatient hand. He was not impressed by flattery. "Go on," he said. "You didn't bring me all this way in utmost secrecy to relate facts I am fully aware of."

"Patience, My Lord, if you please," Wichman said. "And all will be soon revealed. It's true the Tahn have accomplished much—however these accomplishments have made in a time of relative peace."

He gestured. "But what if you were at war. And not just any old war—skirmishes on the borders. But a full out war with the Emperor himself. Could you accomplish so much then? Hmm?"

The room fell silent. Unconsciously, Fehrle glanced over at his men. War was not a topic thrown around lightly among the Tahn. Especially war with the Emperor.

Wichman motioned for Khelee to step forward. "My Lord," he said, "our top people have run all the progs and in their estimation a war with Emperor would fail almost before it began without a sufficient stockpile of food to feed your troops."

Fehrle nodded. "We have run the same progs," he said. "Purely as an intellectual exercise."

Khelee waved that away. "Yes, yes, it was the same with us. A simple intellectual exercise."

"We have no quarrel with the Emperor," Fehrle said, "that can't be solve through simple diplomacy."

Wichman had to bury a smile. From what his spies had told him, war with the Empire was a constant topic of conversation in the Tahn barracks.

Now he played his trump card: "Just as I'm sure that the Emperor has launched a crash program that would give him the logistical edge over the Tahn if a war should erupt."

Fehrle straightened in his chair. "Crash program? What crash program."

Wichman waved at the huge overhead monitor. "Gentle beings," he said, "I give you *Demeter!*"

The monitor flickered into life.

A beautiful little world appeared on the monitor. It was shimmering blue with streaks of emerald green. Lovely white clouds drifted through skies teaming with avian life.

Actually, it was more of a half world. It was like a ball had been cut in two. The top half was the artificial planet. The agworld. It was built on a flat plate and a closer look revealed several large drive units, and scores of docking ports of various sizes on the reverse side.

Then the view became that of a vid camera, mounted on a ship and it dipped down into the agworld's atmosphere, revealing booming seas filled with aquatic creatures, then it was moving over land, showing kilometer after kilometer of trees, many of them fruit bearing, then vast plains filled with golden grain. Which soon gave way to immense grazing herds of four-legged animals.

And there were streams filled with leaping fish flowing down from snow-capped mountains to form mighty rivers and tributaries that fed those forests and fields.

All the while the camera dipped and soared, pausing here and there and then moving on to one wonder after the next. While it moved Gen. Khelee told the tale in a deep, mellifluous voice.

"This is the first of many agricultural planets being developed in the secret labs of Tanz Sullamora," he said. "Each world can supply the needs of tens of thousands of troops. And they are all scalable. Those tens of thousands could quickly become hundreds of thousands—even millions—if more worlds are moved into place."

"But light," Fehrle interrupted. "I'm no agricultural expert, but you need not just light, but the right kind of light."

"Let there be… and all that…" Khelee said and with a wave of his hand, the camera pulled back and Fehrle saw himself looking at enormous arcs stretching from one side of the agworld to the other. All pouring rich, yellow nourishing light onto the world.

"The true beauty of all this," Wichman broke in, "is all these self-contained worlds can be operated remotely. Not one single being is required to tend the forests or the fields. It is all done with robotic workers, who do not require the resources of the agworld to feed and clothe them.

"Those arc lights are the brainchild of a team of scientists and engineers from the New Norway Sector. They not only supply nurturing light for the plants and animals, but energy to operate the robotic tenders."

He paused, looking at the struggle on Fehrle's face. A man who prided himself in never showing emotion, he could barely keep the deep feelings he was experiencing from showing on his dark features. His men were not so successful. With satisfaction, Wichman noted the looks of wonder at play on their normally blank faces.

Fehrle finally managed to control himself enough to speak without a quaver in his voice.

"But surely this isn't real," he said. "Beautiful as all this may be, it is all an artist's depiction, is it not?"

"Indeed it is," Wichman said. "One of my operatives lifted this from Tanz Sullamora's offices."

Fehrle snorted. "Well, if it isn't real," he said, "why are you wasting my time?"

"No waste, I assure you, My Lord," Wichman said. "At this very moment a prototype of that agricultural world is being moved from Tanz Sullamora's secret workshops to serve a half-a-dozen mining worlds in the Possnet sector."

"Mining worlds?" Fehrle asked. "But I thought this project was for military purposes."

"Begging your pardon, My Lord," Khelee said, "but that's just the cover. The mining worlds are in constant need of supplies, the logistics of which are not only elaborate and labor intensive, but quite expensive."

Wichman said, "The mining companies jumped at the chance to get the use of these agricultural worlds at minimal cost to them. Behind the scenes, of course, the Emperor is footing the bill for the entire project, using his oh so loyal lap dog Tanz Sullamora as his cover."

Khelee said, "As we speak, one of those worlds is being moved to within easy reach of several mining planets so desolate that not even a bean could grow on in their rocky soil."

Wichman said, "If you could get your hands on one of those, My Lord, I wouldn't be surprised if your scientists could reverse engineer the whole thing and start building agricultural worlds of your own."

Fehrle nodded. "I want one," he said. "Price is no object."

"I didn't think it would be," Wichman murmured, stifling a smile.

"With that in mind, my people have already been in touch with the pirates in Tortooga. All we need is your go ahead, and we'll steal an agworld for you."

Fehrle thought a minute then said, "What are your requirements?"

"I've taken the precaution of greasing the pirates' palms," Wichman said, "so I'm already out quite a bit of front money."

Fehrle's eyes glittered. "And you were, perhaps, thinking that I would underwrite those initial costs?"

"Plus a little more," Wichman said. "The expenses are more than I can afford if I don't have certain guarantees from you. Like half down and half on delivery."

"And what do you foresee that total cost will be?" Fehrle asked.

Wichman told him. Fehrle didn't react one way or the other. He merely nodded.

"That's quite a large sum," he said.

"Planet stealing doesn't come cheap," Wichman said.

Again, Fehrle just nodded. Then he said, "I'll need some guarantees."

Wichman sighed. "How can I guarantee something like that? It's never been done before. You'll just have to trust me."

"The last time I trusted you," Fehrle said, "I didn't get anywhere near as much AM2 as had been promised."

Wichman waved that away. "There was no way we could have anticipated the intervention of Sten, and Venatora's reaction to it. Besides, it wasn't a total loss. We managed to get our hands on some of the AM2."

"Still," Fehrle said. "Still. My fellow council members were disappointed. And so was I."

Wichman held up both hands. "What can I do to satisfy you, Lord Fehrle? What can I offer to set your mind at ease."

"There is one thing," Fehrle said.

"Name it," Wichman said.

Fehrle told him.

CHAPTER EIGHT

ON THE STALK

Through narrowed eyes, Ida watched Lord Fehrle's black-on-black stealth ship—the *Rapier*—slip into orbit. It waited there, while supply ships made last minute trips.

She said, "It occurs to me that we could save our bosses a clottin' load of grief if we inserted a goblin round up his shorts."

Doc, who was nibbling on a bowl of frozen hemoglobin berries, snorted contempt. "Violence. That's your Rom genes speaking. Your answer to everything is violence, followed by more violence."

Ida sniffed. "Nothing could be further from the truth," she said. "It's a well-known fact that we Rom prefer light fingers over hard fists."

She waved a bejeweled hand at the glittering red pustules in Doc's breakfast bowl. "You should talk. You can't wait to cuddle up to a mark and drain him of every drop of blood. That's your answer to universal peace. Blood sucking."

"Ah'm loathe t' admit it, my furry mukker" Alex broke in, "but ah think uir tubby little sister hae a wee point. Ah've got aches an' pains in every puir bone in mah body. An' that can only mean one thing: A big fat bludy war."

He shrugged. "Ur a big clottin' solar st'rm."

Sten grimaced. Watching Lord Fehrle dash across the tarmac from his grav car to his ship left a bad taste in his mouth. Even though they'd been unable to big ear his meeting with Wichman, he had no doubt that the Tahn overlord had more nasty tricks up his sleeve than a Prime World pol.

"Every time I lay eyes on that sorry excuse for a being I get the shivers," he said. "Unfortunately, we don't have kill orders. In fact, we are to keep him alive at all costs."

Ida brightened. "Well, the good news is that if Alex's bones are right we'll all get stinking rich. Because I'm going to put every penny we can beg borrow or steal into war mongering industries."

She called up a document in one corner of the monitor. It was an undecipherable mess of legalese.

"Just give me your okay, including power of attorney, and I'll put your money to work starting the next pay period."

Doc sneered. "Money, in case that part of your moral education was neglected, isn't everything."

"Oh, yeah," Ida challenged. "Name one other thing."

"It's a weel-known fact a life that aw Scotsman ur romantics," Alex said, placing a hand across his brawny chest. "So ah'd say love... pure sweet love... is more important than money."

"Do you want to be rich, or spout Bobby Burns love poems to mice and lice all day?" Ida said.

Alex eyed the document. Wary. But tempted.

"Will ye really make us rich, lass?" he asked.

"Have I ever lied to you, Alex?" Ida pressed.

"Frequently," Alex said.

"Oh sure, I've lied about little stuff, but nothing major," Ida said.

"I recollect thae ye almost killed me a coople a times," Alex said.

"But not on purpose," Ida said.

"Nae. Ah don't think it was oann purpose," Alex said.

Doc snorted. "I can't believe this woman," he said. "Be warned. She's lying through her teeth right now, Alex."

"Admit it, Doc," Ida said. "I may have bent the truth a bit, but I've never lied to you about money."

A long silence.

"Have I?"

"Oh, sign the bludy thing," Alex said. "Ur we'll never hear th' end of her infernal gypsy yappin'."

He made an impression on the monitor with his thumb. Sten shrugged, then made his own print. On matters of money, he always bowed to Ida.

After a long time—with Doc's luminous eyes fixed on her—she sighed. "Okay, Doc, I'm not going to force you to do anything against your will."

She started to close off the monitor.

That's when Doc broke. "Wait a minute," Doc said. "Don't be too hasty."

He slid off his stool and waddled over to the monitor. Jabbed his furry thumb into the indicated space on the monitor.

"Reverse psychology doesn't work with me," he said. "You didn't' really want me onboard did you? Well, I'm onto your game. Remember—the next time you try to pull a fast one, that I'm the Shrink around here."

"Sure, Doc, sure," Ida said. And with a small smile on her face, she closed down the screen.

But her hands had barely left the keys, when the monitor began blinking.

Ida frowned. "It's Mitzi," she said.

Everyone crowded around the console. Sten nodded at Ida, who made the connection.

They heard loud voices and sounds of a struggle.

Someone shouted, "No! I'm not going! I refuse!"

Sten frowned. It sounded like Gregor.

Then Mitzi's voice came in, faint and full of static. Ida fooled with the connection and the static lessened.

"Can you hear me, Sten?" she asked, voice just above a whisper.

"I can hear you. Go ahead."

"Some kind of a big deal is going down," she said. "And the Tahn want Gregor as their guarantee. As their hostage."

"Drakh!" Sten said, thinking fast. "Okay, look, hang tight and I'll send Mk'wolf's team to extract you."

"No, no, no," Mitzi said. "I've got it covered. Lord Wichman personally asked me to go along with Gregor to keep him company."

"I don't know about that, Mitzi," Sten said. "Sounds like more than I originally asked you sign on for."

"Oh, pshaw!" Mitzi said. "I'm having more fun than I ever had in my life. You're not gonna cut me out now, just when things are getting exciting."

Sten shook his head. No clottin way. Mitzi was a civilian. Recruited for one mission and Sten had gone to a lot of trouble to make sure nothing bad happened to her.

"Knock it off with negative vibes," Mitzi said. "I can feel them over the airwaves. I'm going along whether you like it or not."

Sten sighed. "Okay, okay," he said. "I just wish we had time to prepare. Set up better a better comm system, at least, so we can extract you on a moment's notice."

"Well, if wishes were wings, and all that," Mitzi said. "Just trust me, Sten. At least this way you'll have a pair of eyes and ears on the inside."

Ida broke in. "Mitzi," she said. "I'm sending you a quick software update that'll boost the strength of your comm."

"Fantastic, Ida," Mitzi said. "I knew you'd be on my side. Grrl power all the way!"

Ida grinned at this. "One thing," she said. "I can keep on updating you no matter where you go. Find a quiet place every day at say, Five Bells, and I'll push through the booster and get your report."

"Done and done," Mitzi said.

There were more shouts. "Get him! Hold him! Don't let him get away."

"Gotta go," Mitzi said. "I'm needed."

The last thing they heard before she keyed off was Mitzi saying, "Come on, honey bunch. This will be fun. An adventure. And little Mitzi will be with you all the way."

Then the connection was cut. On the monitor they saw Fehrle's ship break away from the last tender. Caught in the grip of the first stages of hyperjump it hesitated a moment. Shimmered. Then disappeared.

Ida and the others looked at Sten.

He shrugged. "Guess we'd better talk to Mahoney," he said.

CHAPTER NINE

THE DECISION

Venatora watched as Palsonia—flanked by two powerful Zabanya guardswomen—cautiously approached the airlock that led to the rebel armory.

On the floor were the corpses of two sentries. They had once been beautiful women, with narrow waists and rippling biceps—the Himmenops were known for their muscular beauty—but now the face of one had been blown away, while a large bloody chest wound marred the body of the other.

Both women sported the Sharkwire red and gold bicep tattoos that marked them as followers of Princess Anthofelia.

Venatora felt a catch in her throat. Those women were her subjects, damn it. Their deaths were needless. Pointless.

When they'd first crept into the chamber that led to the armory Venatora's spies had ferreted out, she'd tried to confront them directly.

Over the objections of Mara and Palsonia, she'd stepped into the chamber, calling: "Sisters. Sisters."

With cries of alarm the women had spun around, battlerifles coming up.

Venatora raised a calming hand, palm turned out in peace.

"No cause for alarm, my sisters," she said. "It is I, Venatora. Your Queen."

At the same time, she practically glowed with pheromonal power. Her own guardswomen sighed in ecstasy.

But the two sentries seemed unmoved. Through disbelieving eyes, Venatora saw them press their battlerifles against their shoulders. Fingers curling around triggers.

"Please, sisters," Venatora said. "Listen to your Queen, who loves you."

It was no use. The women were unmoved. And if Marta hadn't broken free of Venatora's spell the women would have opened fire and Venatora would now be a corpse like the two she was staring at now.

What was wrong? What had Anthofelia done to them? Or, more likely, her mentor Father Huber had concocted some kind of antidote to Venatora's pheromonal powers. Father Raggio had warned her of that possibility.

There was a faint hiss and a small, batlike drone sailed by, drawing her attention back to the present.

She glanced over at Marta, who was in the center of the room skillfully operating the controls of her mini-fleet of drones, which swooped around the vaulted chamber, hunting down the pinprick-size monitors that guarded the entrance of the armory.

Some were imbedded in the ceiling, others pebbled the twin columns that supported the vaulted roof.

When they found them, little spears of hot red laser beams shot out from the drones, frying the monitors.

At the armory door, Palsonia pressed a blastpak against the locking mechanism. She signaled the guardswomen and the three backpedaled until they were twenty meters away. Then took refuge behind two enormous pillars.

Palsonia glanced over at Venatora, who waited with a dozen of her best guardswomen, all of them bristling with AM2 battlerifles.

Venatora gave a thumbs up, then she and her team ducked behind an armored rhino-sized gravsled that sported a heavy ram that had been welded to its nose.

Palsonia pressed a button and at the airlock there was a blinding flash of white heat and the door sagged in on itself, molten metal running across the deck, steaming and crackling.

Venatora heard cries of alarm, then the gravsled lumbered into life, charging across the deck, with Venatora and her assault team sprinting along behind it.

The gravsled bumped over the corpses, then rammed through the remains of the airlock and then they were all through, shouting and shooting, while angry spears of rebel laser fire seared the air.

Caught up in the first adrenaline rush of battle, Venatora was at first blinded by chaos. AM2 rounds mingled with laser fire. Women were shouting furiously, although some screamed in pain or gasped in surprise as their lives were torn from them.

Then the firing stopped and Venatora found herself looking at a half-a-dozen corpses on the floor. Anthofelia rebels all—witness the gold and blood red Sharkwire tattoos encircling their right biceps.

Next to her, she heard Marta say, "Your Highness? Are you okay?"

And she came back to life, jolting up straight and tall.

"Of course I'm okay," she snapped.

She scanned her surroundings. Saw the scores of weapons—ranging from sidearms and AM2 battlerifles, to Bester grenades and other explosives—arrayed along the walls and stacked in the corners.

To Marta: "Casualties?"

"We were lucky," Marta said "We caught them by surprise. None dead on our side and only a small laser burn on Corporal Jenna's thigh."

"The rebels?" Venatora's voice was taut.

Marta sighed. "Six dead. One badly wounded."

Venatora steeled herself. "Prognosis?"

"No hope, Your Highness. She'll be dead in an hour."

"Very well," Venatora said. "Call in the others to gather up the arms and transport them back to base."

"Yes ma'am." A pause, then: "And the dead rebels?"

An almost unreasoning anger overtook Venatora. How dare they? How dare they?

"Burn them," Venatora said. "But kill the wounded one first and burn her as well."

* * * *

Late that night, in the domed fortress that was Venatora's command center, she sat with Clew, staring out at the scattered stars. Wondering if perhaps her time really was over.

It would almost be a great relief to turn her back on it all and relinquish the whole kingdom of the Himmenops over to Anthofelia. Let her have it. Let her deal with all those ungrateful subjects that Venatora had sacrificed so much for.

She could say hang it all. Shed all her troubles and go off alone on some grand adventure. She could take Marta with her for company. But not Palsonia. She was too—well, too much. Bulled through everything. Marta was all calmness and love.

Sten's face floated up. Well, why not? She could stop by on her way out the Possnet Sector and see if Sten wanted to come along.

If not—Venatora shrugged. She didn't need Sten. Or Marta. Hells, she didn't need anyone. They didn't call her queen for nothing. When she spoke, beings jumped to do her bidding.

A sudden stubborn feeling overtook her. She grabbed the dusty spirits bottle and filled her glass to the brim.

Turned to Clew, who was looking at her quizzically.

"I'm guessing that sort of a decision has been reached," she said.

"Indeed it has," Venatora said, as all the old confidence came flooding back.

Clot Skink! Clot all her brother and sister pirates! And clot the damned Tahn as well. Fehrle had been ignoring all her attempts at communication, so she had no doubt which side he was backing.

The more she thought on it, the more Clew's plan made sense. With her own farm planet that produced enough to feed all her people, Venatora would be invulnerable to all outside threats and influences.

She raised her glass to Clew and downed the fiery contents in one long, searing swallow. Venatora slammed the glass down and came to her feet.

"Let's steal a planet," she said.

CHAPTER TEN

CROSS AND DOUBLE CROSS

Sten and Alex muscled their way through the chaos that was Port Chinen, the fierce Ryuku sun boiling them alive in their uniforms.

The Imperium X boom had overwhelmed what had once been a sleepy Guards' base, suitable for a dozen or so Imperial ships, a dilapidated repair bay and rusted out barracks for the crews.

Now the base was expanding at near light speed, with ships and tenders continually landing or taking off. Overwhelming the Nav Center and causing huge traffic jams that left some ships stranded in near orbit, waiting for the nod to land.

Construction crews worked day and night building new landing sites, warehouses, repair bays and quarters for Imperial crews.

Meanwhile, the town of Chinen was in the throes of its own boom, with workshops and stores, and ramshackle housing units filling up before they were completed. Inspectors gave up trying to stay apace of the boom and started simply taking bribes at the door without even stepping inside for a cursory check.

Vehicle traffic was a nightmare of civilian grav sleds and trucks competing with armored military vehicles and mechanical monsters. To be a pedestrian was to be a person with a suicide complex. Making matters worse, there were no sidewalks and the few slideways serving the public were usually out of order, forcing those on foot into the street.

A confusion of metal blocked their way. A gravtruck carrying a load of rebar had tangled with another that had been loaded with worn out 'bots. The scene was a mess of iron bars and waldo arms and legs. An ambulance was lifting off in a hurry, so injuries had obviously been involved.

As they passed an enormous crane dipped its steel jaws into the mess and picked up the gravtruck. The diver was a crablike being who worked the controls with his claws. Sten didn't know if he was a rookie driver, or just plain incompetent, because he kept slamming the gravtruck around, sending debris from the wreckage everywhere.

Sten spotted a gap and grabbed Alex's arm. "Let's get while the getting's good," he said and they sprinted across the thoroughfare to the other side.

The two paused at the mouth of an alley to catch their breath and get their bearings.

"Clot an' double clot," Alex said. "Ah think me knackers have crawled up into me belly t' get oot of harm's way."

"Good thing we have no time for I&I then," Sten said, meaning Intercourse and Intoxication—grunt slang for R&R, rest and recreation.

Sten's left eye went to the live map on the tiny monocle on his solar specs. There was the thoroughfare they'd just bet their lives on. And here was the alleyway where they were standing.

"Where is Battaria's?" he whispered and a red dot bloomed on the optimap and started blinking like crazy. A sultry woman's voice in his ear said, "You're almost there, Lieutenant Sten. Fifty meters north. Look to the green door on your right."

"It's supposed to be just up ahead," he told Alex. "Look for a green door."

Then he yelped in surprise as his heavy worlder friend lifted him off the ground and jumped deeper into the alley.

At the same time he spotted the big crane they'd just escaped out of the corner of his eye. The gravtruck, bristling with scraps of torn metal, scraped against the storefront where they had been standing a spit-second before.

"What the clot?" Sten shouted.

"That crab critter amos got ye, laddie," Alex said. "A minute more an ye woods hae sprouted a steel bar fer a tail."

"Next time we come to town," Sten said, "remind me to requisition a nice tank."

Down the alley, they heard someone bellowing curses and looked in time to see a burly merchantman come sailing through an open door.

The merchantman landed on his overlarge bum, then rolled over with some difficulty until he was on his knees.

He shouted at the door, "Yer a weaklin', Kruger. A candy-arse joyboy with pillows fer fists."

At that moment a huge figure stepped through the door, which Sten noted was colored a sun-faded green. The figure was a horned Javan, well over two meters high, with two hundred kilos of solid muscle balanced on enormous twin pillars for legs.

"Ah'll make a wee guess 'at th' horned beastie is Kruger," Alex said.

Sten grimaced. "Clot," he said. "That's our contact," he said.

The creature known as Kruger sneered down at the drunken merchantman. "Jonsey," he said in a surprisingly high voice, "when will youse ever get it through yer thick noggin that when yer've been 86'd at Battaria's, yer stays 86'd until further notice."

Jonsey was suddenly contrite. "Aw, but Kruger, all me shipmates come here. Everybody knows Kruger's got the best chow and drink in Chinen. All I wants is a little gnosh and some narcobeer with me pals."

"Yer should have thought of that before yer busted up the place last time yer was in port. At Battaria's the rule is—No Violence."

Jonsey started weeping. Big tears spilling down his leathery cheeks, "Come on, Kruger," he blubbered. "Have a heart."

"I'll find me heart when youse find the credits for damages," Kruger said.

Jonsey climbed to his feet. "Okay, okay," he said. "I gots the picture. All yer cares about is money."

The burly merchantman turned away, but as he came to Sten and Alex he stopped. Looked them up and down, eyeing their uniforms. Sten noted that for a supposed drunk, Jonsey was suddenly extremely alert.

He sneered: "Clottin' Imperials," he said. "Big surprise." He looked back at Kruger. "Heard you was a rat, Kruger," he shouted. "Now, here's the bleedin' proof."

Kruger took a step toward him and Jonsey lost his nerve, scrambled to his feet and raced away, all vestiges of drunkenness gone.

Before Kruger could disappear through the green doorway, Alex hailed him. "Ahoy, me fine mucker," he said. "Ye woodnae happen tae be Sr. Kruger, would ye?"

The big Javan turned to them, beady red eyes glaring over the polished ivory horn, which Sten noted had been sharpened to a needle point.

"Who wants to know?" he demanded in his high, squeaky voice. Sten saw a meaty hand go to the hilt of a large knife scabbarded at his thick waist.

"Captain Sten and Specialist First Class," Sten said. "If you're Kruger, we were supposed to meet right about now."

Kruger stared at them suspiciously, carefully examining their uniforms and rank tabs. "You the Imperials Stover told me about?"

"Guilty as charged," Sten said, carefully removing his ID from his tunic breast pocket with two fingers. Kilgour did the same.

Kruger advanced. Peered down at their IDs. Checking to make sure the holopix matched their faces.

"These can be faked," he said.

"That they can," Sten said.

Kruger studied them both. Weighing. Finally, he snorted and turned back to the door.

"This way," he said," and lumbered through the opening.

The delicious odors that greeted them made Sten's mouth water. The food must be fantastic here. He didn't blame Jonsey for his tears.

Battaria's was more of a bar and grill than a drinking being's saloon. Actual living beings delivered the food and drink, rather than the usual serving 'bots. Most of the room was taken up by a variety of battered tables and chairs, serviceable to both humans and ET's alike.

From some of the rough-looking types that lined the long, polished steel bar Sten could see that it wasn't fussy about its clientele. Beings with eye patches and missing limbs mixed with burly merchantmen and uniformed port workers.

A chipped and faded mural covered the walls, depicting an ancient seaport with several sailing ships in the harbor. Sten thought he could make out a black flag on one of the topmasts, that displayed a human skull and crossbones. Their contact had said it was an old pirate's symbol known as a Jolly Roger.

Sten stepped out of the way as a young human woman hustled past, bearing a tray of the most marvelous-looking dishes. Enormous soy steaks filled the platters, surrounded by roasted vegetables and potatoes.

His stomach rumbled. He very much wanted to stay and eat. He heard Kilgour's big belly rumble in sympathy and knew he was thinking the same thing.

His hopes were dashed when Kruger led them toward a small door next to the room-length bar. Kruger palmed a switch and a door slid open. He squeezed his bulk though. Sten and Alex followed.

The room was almost entirely taken up by an enormous desk and an equally enormous stuffed chair. Built-in cupboards served as storage and filing space.

Kruger squeezed behind the desk and with a great sigh collapsed into the chair, which groaned under his weight.

"Sit," he commanded and so they sat in two faded green plas chairs with curved arms.

He eyed them, still weighing whether they deserved his trust.

Finally he said, "Drinks?"

"Please," Sten said. "Narcobeer for us both, if you don't mind."

Kruger nodded, then opened a small carved wooden box on his desk. He withdrew an overly long 'bac stick, which barely fit under his horn. He drew on it, then exhaled a thick cloud of smoke. Pause. Another intake. Then he blew three perfect smoke rings.

He nodded in satisfaction. "Youse guys are in luck," he said. "It's gonna be a good day. Smoke rings never lie."

At that moment the door swung open and the pretty young woman they'd seen before ankled in, bearing a tray with three glasses of narcobeer, capped by just the perfect amount of white foam. After distributing them, she made herself scare. Sten was sorry to see her go.

"Drink," Kruger said and Sten and Alex dutifully drank.

The narcobeer was ice cold and went down smoothly.

Alex's eyes widened with delight. "She goes doon loch velvet," he said.

Kruger bobbed his horn up and down. "It's me own brew," he said.

He took another sip, then said, "Youse gots somethin' for me?"

Sten nodded at Alex, who withdrew a small black velveteen pouch from his tunic and upended it into his open palm. A single crystal about the size of a blueberry spilled out. It glittered in his palm, shooting spears of multi-colored light.

"A Wilczek," murmured the big Javan in awestricken tones. "Ain't seen one of these babies since I shed me first horn."

"Guaranteed untraceable," Sten said.

Wilczeks were rare space-grown crystals that produced dazzling holo colors when properly handled by a master jeweler. They were also illegal as clot, since they hailed from a planet in the Catoca system that was on the outs with the Emperor for reasons that didn't concern Sten.

Besides, Kruger was Mahoney's contact. The general said he was tight with the pirates and had a passion for Wilczeks so great that he'd sell his own mother. He was also a Venatora loyalist and was angry at her betrayal by the turret-eyed Skink.

Kruger took a small box from the top drawer. It was black with a clear glass top. There were indentations on the side. He plucked the crystal from Alex's hand then gently placed it on the glass. He pressed into the indentations, and the box gave a joyful beep and colorful lights flashed on and off.

"Lovely," Kruger sighed. "Not a blemish to be found."

He picked up the stone and started to put it in his breast pocket.

Alex caught his thick wrist. "Don't be tae hasty, me braw mucker," he said. "Where's yer end?"

Kruger struggled to break free, but big as he was, he was no match for Kilgour, who just grinned as Kruger sweated and strained.

Finally, he relaxed and dropped the crystal. Alex released his hand and caught the stone midair, then dropped it back into the velveteen bag.

The big Javan grimaced and rubbed his wrist. "Whatever happened to trust?" he said mournfully.

Sten laughed. "Trust?" he said. "You're finking on your pirate mates and we're supposed to trust you?"

"Nothin' to do with trust," Kruger said. "It's just business. 'Sides, I'm Venatora's man. Next time I see Skink I'm gonna ram my tusk up his filthy bum."

"Venatora is also an enemy of the Emperor," Sten said.

Kruger shrugged, unimpressed. Sten hadn't expected him to be. The

Possnet frontier attracted all sorts of malcontents, most of whom had no love of authority of any kind—especially the Eternal Emperor.

Sten said, "You've seen the goods, now let's get down to business."

Kruger's chair groaned in relief as he rose. "This way," he said, leading them to an alcove on the other side of the room.

He swept a curtain aside, revealing a steep flight of stairs. Sten didn't count the number of levels they climbed, but the back of his legs were screaming by the time they reached a small door. Kruger pushed it open and sunlight came flooding in. Sten was momentarily blinded. Instinctively his gun hand went to the butt of his sidearm and he paused until his vision cleared. Ahead of him he heard Alex murmur an "all clear."

They emerged on the roof of Battaria's and to Sten's surprise he found himself standing in a lush rooftop garden, with row after row of vegetables and spices. Colorful flowers were planted between the rows, filling Chinen's dry, dusty air with their perfume. It was a bizarre sight on a barren planet, where all life struggled for moisture of any kind.

He looked over at Kruger, who was leaning over to sniff at the blossoms of what appeared to be a dwarf lemon tree. A smile of almost childlike contentment creased the area beneath his needle-sharp horn.

He straightened, and with great pride said, "Yer can see why Battaria's is known as the best clottin' dive in the clottin' Possnets."

Indeed. Sten swore that the moment they finished their business, he was going to dig into some of delicacies himself. From the look on Alex's face, he could tell that he was thinking the same thing.

In the distance Sten saw the imposing black bulwark of Port Chinen. A heavy, bulbous-nosed gunship lifted off and slowly rose toward the sky.

The incongruity of the lovely garden and the bristling martial scene just beyond made Sten feel out of place. There was a tug at his heart and for a moment he wished he could be whisked away to some idyllic isle where roses and citrus trees basked beneath a bright sun. And with that vision, Venatora's beautiful face swam up into mental view.

"You alright, matey?" he heard Alex say.

He shook his head to clear it, pulling himself together.

"Yeah, yeah," he said. "Sorry. Just tired."

"No need fur sorries, lad," Kilgour said. "Yer prob'ly a bit peckish. Feelin' a wee bit like tha' meself."

Sten looked over at Kruger. "This all very impressive," he said. "But we were looking for something a little more than a rooftop garden tour."

"Patience, me young friend," Kruger said. "Patience."

Then he guided them to a corner of the roof where three meter high legume vines shielded them from view. A meter-and-a-half ferro-cement post was set into the rooftop. Kruger touched a metal plate, which swung open. He palmed a switch and the post began to whirr. A moment later an old-fashioned opticom rose out of the guts of the post.

"Here's where I keep track of Skink and his boyos," Kruger said.

"Is Skink here now?" Sten asked.

Kruger shook his head. "Naw, he keeps his head low and lets his boys do the dirty work."

He looked up at the sky, judging the position of the sun, then nodded. "Speakin' of dirty work," he said, "it's just about time."

The Javan squeezed the barrel of the opticom and a long eyepiece slid out. He planted one of his rheumy eyes against the viewer—twisting his neck to get the horn out the way, and began manipulating a small wheel that controlled focus.

"Just a minute," he said. "Won't be long."

He found his target, adjusted the focus a bit more, then straightened.

"There they be," he said, motioning Sten forward.

Sten looked through the eyepiece. At first everything was blurry, but his fingers went to the controls and soon the view became crystal clear.

He was looking just to the north of the Imperial fortress, where a long, low ramshackle building leaned wearily against the constant wind. A sagging sign overhead gave it a name.

"Ryuku Mines," he said aloud. "I thought they'd gone bankrupt."

"New owner," Kruger said. "And guess who it is?"

Alex snorted. "We're nae payin' ye tae play guessin' games," he growled. "Spit it out me horned mucker, if ye want tae lay your peepers oan at pretty Wilczek again."

"Skink," Kruger said hastily. "Skink bought it. And he's been movin' blackmarket stuff in and out of it for weeks now. Mostly at night. But I had word that he's expectin' another important delivery today."

Sten almost asked when that would be when he saw an enormous vehicle lumber onto the street and head for the entrance of Ryuku Mines. A moment later red and white striped warning barriers rose from the pavement and then the roadway in front of Ryuku yawned opened. The vehicle was as clumsy as it was large, and it took the driver several attempts before it was lined up properly. Then it slowly descended into the cavern, rocking back and forth as if it were carrying a heavy, badly secured load.

After the door closed, Sten turned away from the opticom, rubbing eyes to clear them.

"What was that carrying?" he asked.

"Skink's keepin' drakh close to his chest," Kruger said. "But one of the loaders said he thought it was some big clottin' weapon system. But it won't be there long. After Skink's techs fuss with it and give it the okay, they'll be movin' it on."

How a civilian got a weapon system of that apparent sophistication through Chinen security was troubling. He'd have to alert Mahoney that someone needed to take a close look at the personnel on Chinen.

"Hey, whit th' clot is that clot up to?" Kilgour asked.

Sten looked up to see the crane they'd encountered earlier, heading in their direction. It still had that battered grav-truck in its jaws, which it swung back and forth on heavy chains.

"Hey!" Kruger bellowed. "Get yer arse away from here!"

The driver was enclosed in a cab above the crane. Was the drakh head drunk, or just incompetent?

Sten turned the opticom around and looked through the barrel. He could see the driver and to his surprise, he wasn't looking at the same crab-like ET he'd seen before.

Instead, bent over the controls was none other than the weeping drunk they'd met when they'd first arrived. Except now he was a perfectly sober villain who was staring directly at them, a huge grin on his face as he expertly manipulated the controls, swinging the gravtruck back and forth in its chains.

"It's Jonsey," Sten shouted. "And he's comin' right for us."

"Ah shoods hae known," Kilgour growled. "It was tay clottin' easy frae the start."

Sten had no idea how Kilgour figured that he should have twigged to the setup, but this was no time for an after action discussion.

He turned, looking for a way to escape. Just then the gravtruck rammed the rooftop, tearing away a huge piece of the building and hurling Sten, Alex and Kruger to the ground.

The big Javan immediately leaped to his feet and charged the roof's edge.

"Jonsey, ya filthy scrote," he shouted, holding up his hands as if to block the next swing of the gravtruck. "What the clot are youse doin'?"

But on and on the gravtruck came, arcing its burden out, then swinging in with even greater force than before.

Kilgour grabbed Sten. "This way," he shouted, pulling Sten toward the opposite side of the building.

Once again the gravtruck struck. There was a great ripping sound and then a shriek of fury and pain. Sten looked back and saw Kruger clinging to the gravtruck with one hand, and pounding the body of the crane with the other.

"Stop! Stop!" he shouted. "This is Battaria's, you clot! Battaria's."

Sten had no idea what that had to do with anything. It was obvious that Jonsey was intent on hammering the building—and them—into oblivion.

Then, Sten witnessed one of the most amazing things he'd seen in his career as a Mantis operative. As Jonsey swung the gravtruck back for another go, Kruger twisted and then jumped. He grabbed one of the steel girders and started swarming up the side of the crane toward the cab. But there was no time to see how things played out. The weight of the gravtruck was slamming back Sten and Alex's way.

"Come on," Alex shouted.

They sprinted for the roof's edge. It was a long jump to the rooftop of the neighboring building, but they didn't hesitate a second. It was jump and maybe die or stay put and die for certain.

Sten jumped.

He cleared the edge. Tuck and roll and he was back on his feet. Alex hadn't quite made it and was clinging to the edge of the building with one hand. Sten ran to help him over the side as the crane—with Kruger dangling from crossbeam—slammed into Battaria's one more time.

The whole building caved in, sending up a dense cloud of dust and dirt.

They found a gutter leading down and they clambered to the alley below. Sten heard screams and shouts coming from beings trapped inside the ruins. He smelled gas and then there was an explosion and Battaria's was consumed in flames.

Sten and Alex raced down the alley, anxious to get free before the remainder of the building collapsed into a fiery ball. But as they neared the mouth they saw Kruger drop down from above, Jonsey clutched in one meaty paw.

It was a three-point landing, the driver in one hand, the other knuckling into the pavement and his elephantine legs taking up the rest of the shock.

He looked up, blood-shot eyes wild, face and horn spattered with blood. When he saw Sten and Alex he grinned, displaying bloody teeth.

"Got the drakh head," he shouted.

He lifted the man off the ground until he was at eye level and he shook him until Sten swore he could hear the man's teeth rattle.

"I'm gonna rip his head off an drakh in his neck," the big Javan said, reaching for Jonsey's head with a meaty paw.

"Stop him, Alex," Sten said.

Kilgour reached and with little effort, plucked Jonsey from Kruger's grasp. The Javan reacted, furious. He raised a heavy fist to strike, but Sten intervened, batting the blow aside. The force was so great that it whipped Kruger around.

"I'll kill the pig humpin' smeg face," Kruger said. "Get out of me way."

But Alex shook Jonsey loose, dropped him to the ground, then gripped Kruger by the back of the neck and squeezed until his eyes bulged.

"Easy, me wee mucker," he said. "We'll be wantin' tae gab with th' clot first, than ye can have her way wi' heem."

Chastened, the Javan bowed his head. "But he destroyed Battaria's," he moaned. "It was me mum's pride and joy."

Sirens wailed in the distance and there a roar of rescue vehicles as the first responders headed to the scene.

"It was Skink who hired him," Sten said. "Wouldn't you rather make him pay for it first?"

Kruger sighed. "Okay," he said. "Skink first, then I swear on me mum's grave that I'm gonna stomp this scrote face into jelly."

CHAPTER ELEVEN

DESCENDING, DEEPLY, INTO THE HOLE

The interrogation room was deep within the bowels of Port Chinen's HQ building. Jonsey cowered in a corner, bloody and bruised but still among the living.

"Don't let him at me," he begged Sten. "I'll talk. Skink didn't pay me near enough for a Javan stompin'."

"Oh, I see," Sten said. "It was just enough to destroy Kruger's restaurant and kill everybody in it just to get me and Kilgour," Sten said.

"Times've been tough," Jonsey whined. "Only jobs're down in them clottin' mines. Some of 'em are so deep it takes a whole day just to get down to the diggin' level and start yer shift."

"Pur bairn," Alex said in mocking tones. "Better tae burn yer mates tae death, than to do an honest day's wark."

"Yer don't know what it's like," Jonsey said. "Don't see sunlight fer days, and then all's yer gets is this clottin' garbage heap topside. Then Skink's man comes along and says Kruger's rattin' to the Imperials and needed to be taken down. Big time. Set an example for other finks."

He paused, looked up at Sten, then away. "Guess he wasn't lyin' about Kruger bein' a rat," he said, a little bolder than before.

Sten made a prearranged signal and suddenly there was a loud banging on the interrogation room door.

"Let me at th' drakh head," Kruger bellowed from the other side. "He'll talk a blue streak when I'm done with him."

Then they heard Alex say, in pleading tones. "Calm down, Kruger. We ken hoo ye feel. He's a right bassard, he is. But he'll spill. Tryst me, my wee mucker. Tryst me."

There was more banging. So hard that the door seemed to bend inward. Jonsey moaned.

"Don't let him get me," he wept. "Please. I'll talk. I already said I would."

"You'll be doing more than just talk," Sten said.

"Anything," Jonsey said. "Anything."

But when Sten told him what he had to do he soiled himself.

* * * *

The everyday chaos that was Port Chinen had devolved into the sheer pandemonium of too many casualties and not enough first responders.

The two-block area that had once housed Battaria's was a boiling sea of rescuers. Yellow-suited firefighters mingled with red-vested diggers and several motorpools worth of vehicles, ranging from mini ambulances to massive removal equipment that pried up piles of debris with surprising gentleness, as 'bot searchers, mingled with real canine sniffers, ferreted out victims trapped under the still-smoking rubble.

Sten led his little party in a mad, broken field dash for the entrance of Ryuku Mines. Kilgour and Kruger—with Jonsey stuffed between them— dogged his heels as he raced from one scrap of cover to the next.

Mk'wolf and a squad of troopies waited on the other side, hidden behind one of the armored vehicles guarding the entrance of the Imperial base. It was Mk'wolf's job to take out the sentrycams that kept watch over the mining company's main doors.

Anyone monitoring the scene would see nothing more than the ruins of what had once been the best eating establishment in the Sector.

Once on the other side, Sten and his people secured the position, then covered Mk'wolf and his troopies as they repeated Sten's moves.

Mk'wolf was halfway across when a rooftop gunner opened up, stitching the road with AM2 rounds. They all dived for cover, barely escaping the barrage.

Sten and Alex leaned out, trying to get a fix on the gunner. But the smoke was so heavy it was hard to see.

Suddenly, one of Mk'wolf's people rolled out and leaped to her feet. With her helmet hanging from its chin strap Sten made out fiery red hair and it was Corporal Pegatha, Mk'wolf's number two.

She dashed to the middle of the street, aimed her battlerifle at a nearby rooftop and let loose as another barrage came pouring in. Pegatha rolled under a smashed up gravcar, just as her grenade went off.

Fire and smoke and a shrill scream left no doubt that she had hit her target. A moment later a body tumbled off the roof, carrying a chaingun with it.

Mk'wolf and his people emerged from cover and ran like hell before someone else spotted them, picking up Pegatha on their way.

They joined Sten under the sagging roof of the building. He made a mental note to mention Corporal Pegatha in glowing terms in his report.

For the time being, he just nodded at her and murmured "well done." She gave a just-doing-my-job shrug, but blushed furiously, showing how pleased she was at the compliment.

The front doors of the Ryuku building were wide open and the windows were blown out from the initial explosion. There was no one inside. The employees had either fled, or had been carried away. There were spatters of blood here and there that Sten guessed were from people hit by exploding glass.

The reception area of the bankrupt company was shabby, with sagging chairs and beat up desks. However, a second set of security doors blocked them from proceeding to the executive offices. They were brand new and made of expensive steel.

It was no surprise to Sten. He'd had Ida troll the company's records and the newly purchased Ryuku Mines had a busy transaction life. Money poured in from sources that even Ida had difficulty tracking, and went out to a string of shell companies that Ida had traced to blackmarket suppliers.

At the moment the account was near zero, but a bridge loan to carry out operations had been approved, presumably with the expectation of another large payment.

"Fargo Ltd. wouldn't risk a thin credit unless it was absolutely clottin' certain that paybacks were guaranteed," she said.

"If you have a moment to spare," Doc said, "I'd advise performing some action that would rattle the gilded cages of Fargo's Board Of Directors."

Sten sighed. "Finding what they are up to will be tough enough, Doc," he said. "Putting a bomb in their fiscal shorts is a whole other matter."

Doc's furry little shoulders rose and fell. "Just saying," he said.

And now Alex was through the doors and they all piled in, their weapons at the ready. Sten and his people went left, while Mk'wolf's party bore right.

In the center of the room there was a wide, half-moon security desk encircling a bank of monitors. The facility was unmanned, as were the half-a-dozen offices on this floor. Papers and blinking monitors filled with data supported Sten's theory that the building had been evacuated.

Kilgour did something to the main security center, then motioned for the others to follow him to the far side of the room. Kruger was right behind him, gripping Jonsey by the scruff of the neck. His heels dragged like a marionette with loose strings.

"It's right over there," Jonsey said indicating a pair of elevator doors at the far end. "They're fer the brass. Miners don't get somethin' so posh."

Alex got the doors open, scanned the operating system, then took control with the device Ida had jury rigged for them. They all pushed inside. Even with Mk'wolf's squad there was plenty of room.

This was an elevator definitely built for execs. Gleaming plas floor, tastefully decorated walls, with padded drop down seats. There was even a refreshment stand in one corner with cold drinks and snacks.

Kilgour took position next to the control panel, which had a series of numbers, indicating the different levels.

"Which one?" he asked Jonsey.

"The last one," their battered prisoner said.

Alex looked over at Sten. "Ready, laddie?" he asked.

Sten nodded. "GA," he said.

Alex pressed the bottom button and the elevator whirred, then gave a jolt. After a slight pause, it began the long journey down.

Jonsey struggled with Kruger. "Let me sit down," he said. "This is gonna take a long clottin' time. It's four klicks to the bottom."

Kruger sighed and let loose of his charge. Jonsey turned and pulled down a recessed bench. It was padded. He sank into it with a sigh.

Sten and the others followed his example, pulling down benches and getting as comfortable as they could.

The elevator moved at a steady pace, the level numbers lighting up as they reached each one, then continued downward without pause.

Everyone had been charged with adrenaline, expecting trouble from the moment they set out on their mad dash across the thoroughfare. But now they were all winding down and Sten could feel the lethargy settling in that follows hard action. And the steady drone of the gravdrives soon had him feeling sleepy eyed. He heard yawns all around him.

"Ah woonae mind a wee bite to eat," Kilgour said, rising from his bench, which immediately snapped back into place.

"Good idea," Mk'wolf said, joining him at the refreshment center.

The two of them figured out how to operate it, then started taking orders. Handing out snacks and drinks all around.

Kilgour settled back on his bench, munching a sandwich and sipping a cold drink. For desert, he bought himself a nice, ripe banana. He started peeling it, then paused. Sten had the sudden horrible feeling that a Kilgour joke was coming on. He tried to think of some way to stop it, but before he could act Alex spoke up.

"Me maw aye gart us to eat a banana fur breakfast every day," he said. He patted his rounded belly. "That's hoo ah keeps me girlish figure."

Mk'wolf frowned. "Ever since I've known you, I've never seen you eat a banana," he said.

Kilgour shrugged. "Bananas hae saved th' life ay many a Kilgour. Take me Uncle Alban fur example."

"Let's not," Sten said. "We should be planning what we're going to do when reach the bottom level."

Alex waved his objection away, "Dinae fash, lad," he said. "There's plenty ay time fur at."

And with no further ado, he launched into the story.

"Me bonny Uncle Alban had a job as a gravtrain conductor," Kilgour said. "Fur years he'd bin stoatin at his job. Every day, when th' gravtrain arrived at the station, he'd sound the whistle tae annoonce th' arrivel an th' openin' ay th' doors. Efter all a' fowks gits off an oan, he sounds th' whistle' fur th' closin' ay th' doors an th' gravtrain's departure.

"Truth be tauld, it was a bloody mindless job an' every shift he was workin' away', blowin' his whistle. Th' gravtrains came an' went, an came an' went. Over and over. Then one day he gart a big mistake. Me Uncle Alban thought a th' folk had boarded an he bleew th' whistle just as an woman wi 'er dog was still getting' oan th' grav train.

"An th' doors closed an' chopped th' old lady clean in half. Killin' her."

The troopies gasped, the loudest coming from Corporal Pegatha.

"Poor woman," she said. "But what about the dog?"

"Ah don't know about the wee puppy," Alex said, but I 'spec she was killed as well."

Kilgour took a bite of his banana, then continued the story. Sten stifled a groan. When Alex was mid-shaggy dog story there was nothing to do but let it run its course and pray that it ended soon. Sometimes days and even weeks passed before he reached the punchline.

Alex said: "Me poor Uncle Alban was clearly responsible fur the woman's death. He was foond guilty ay manslaughter. In those days, th' penalty was death by th' electric chair.

"He was put in a cell until his execution. A couple hours affair he was tae be killed th' warden came tae his cell. 'Yoo gie anythin' you want fur yer last meal,' he said.

"Uncle Alban thought, then said, 'Weel, if Ah waur tae hae a last wish it wood be for fifty kilos of banana.'

"Th' warden was stunned. 'Really?' he said. He wasn't sure if he heard Alban reit. Me uncle' cheil only nodded and said, 'Please, sir. Fifty kilos of bananas is me final wish. So th' warden fetched th' bananas and me Uncle Alban devoors all th' banana, skin an' aw. After stuffin' himself an' makin' quite a mess th' jailers took him to th' electric chair. He was strapped in an' th' electrodes attached.

"Th' executioner placed his hand on th' lever an' grimaces. He counts, 'Three... two.. one... an' pulls the lever. Only tae fin that me Uncle Alban is perfectly braw.

"Th' executioner pulled the lever again... and again... and still again... but nothin' happened. They checked the wires but everythin' was okay. Uncle Alban jes won't die.

"Th' warden was stunned. He said, "weel, only an act of God coods hae saved ye. Clearly ye jist aren't meant to die. Yer free to go."

Murmurs around the room. "And that was it?" Corporal Pegatha said.

"He went free, even after killing the old woman the dog?"

"Aye," Alex said. "Nae only 'at, but th' union got heem his auld job back as a gravtrain conductor."

Corporal Pegatha looked shocked. "So that was really—*really*—it? He goes free and lives happily ever after?"

"No, lass, no," Kilgour said. "There's maire to come. Only a few years went by—th' gravtrains comin' an' goin'. Th' whistle blowin.' Th' doors comin' open and then closin'.

"An' then one body braw day—"

There was a jolt as the elevator reached the bottom and stopped.

Sten got to his feet. "Okay, people," he said. "Charge your battlerifles. We don't know what's on the other side of those doors."

"But wait a minute," Corporal Pegatha said, clearly frustrated. "What about Uncle Alban."

"Don' worry, lass," Alex said. "You'll hear it soon enough."

Sten stifled a groan. Unfortunately, he knew his friend was a man of his word.

Then the doors came open and he heard shouts of alarm.

CHAPTER TWELVE

DEADLY CONTRABAND

Instead of charging out of the elevator, Sten held everyone back. He fished a Bester grenade from his harness and tossed it toward the sound of the voices. Kilgour followed up with one of his own.

There was a flashbang! and a puff of smoke and then Sten led the assault team from the elevator. Mk'wolf and Pegatha going left, and Sten, Alex, and Kruger—who had a tight hold of Jonsey—cutting right.

Dead silence greeted them. A quick glance caught the pile of unconscious bodies sprawled around the giant gravtruck they'd seen from the rooftop of Battaria's. The canvas covering the contents of the vehicle hid whatever it was carrying. The flexible metal straps that had held the canvas in place, however, had been loosened.

There were five human men and four women in the group. The women were mostly techs and engineers. The men were all heavily armed and dressed in old, out of date battle harness. Knocked out by the Bester grenade, they were slumbering peacefully. The same grenade that knocked them out also impacted their brains. The thirty seconds that proceeded the attack would be erased from their memory forever.

"We've got about fifteen minutes before the Bester wears off," Sten said, "so we'd better move fast."

At the gravtruck, Kilgour gave an astonished whistle. "Weel, wood ya lookit here," he said, and gave one of the canvas covers a yank. It fell to the floor.

There were murmurs of, "What the clot?"

Kilgour peeled the rest of covers away revealing a self-propelled particle cannon. It was a immense tube, with a bulbous rear end and a mouth wide enough to engulf a gravcar. It had stubby wings for in atmosphere work and on top was a clear plas canopy for the pilot.

This was a big time weapon. Restricted to Imperial fleets. If it fell into the hands of pirates, the result could be disastrous.

"How in clot did Chinen security let this through?" Corporal Pegatha said. "If the pirates get their hands on it a lot of our friends could end up being crispy crittered."

That was no exaggeration. If a fleet ship protecting a merchant convoy tried to block a pirate attack met up with one these, the ship would more than likely be turned into atomic dust.

Mk'wolf, who was unpacking his explosives kit, said, "We can blow it in place, but what will we do with these people?"

Sten, meanwhile, was scanning the cannon with his comm and transmitting the images back to Ida and Doc on the *Jo'l Cash*.

In his ear, Ida said, "I wouldn't want to be the clotting base CO when Mahoney takes a look at this baby."

Sten said, "If we blow it, it'll expose our entire mission."

"The wee bomb will also kill aw of these fowk," Alex said, indicating the slumbering humans. He shrugged. "Ah dornt min killin' pirates, but some ay em ur jist engineers."

A Scotsman through and through, Sten knew his friend had a soft spot for engineers.

Ida said, "Hang on, I've got an idea." There was a brief silence, then she was back. "Okay, I've downloaded some software from my bag of nasty tricks. After you plant the explosives, we can load the software into the cannon's memory. First time some smeg head tickles the trigger it'll blow so high and wide that it will give the nearest star a good case of sunspots."

"I like it," Sten said. "Preserves the mission and sets up a nice surprise for the bad guys."

They didn't waste any time. Alex and Mk'wolf exposed the panels enclosing the cannon's computer, while Sten used his comm to download Ida's bit of nastiness.

Ten minutes later they were done and the drapes were back in place. Sten turned to Jonsey, who was slumped dispiritedly on the floor, Kruger standing over him.

"Now show us the back way out," he said. "We don't want to go up in the exec elevator."

Jonsey moaned, but Kruger shook him like a dog and hauled him to his feet, barking for him to "get moving."

Jonsey showed them an alternate elevator, a small car that ran alongside the massive lift that had carried the gravtruck to the bottom of the mine.

"It'll be a tight squeeze," Sten said. "But we can do it."

Doc spoke up from afar: "Remember what I said about leaving the pirates something to puzzle over."

"Sure, but I'm fresh out of ideas," Sten said.

Just then Jonsey started weeping again. "You have to protect me when we get topside," he said. "Skink will cut my throat."

"I hope he does worse'n that," Kruger said. "After what yer done to Battaria's and all those poor folks."

Doc said, "There's your answer, Sten. Leave them Jonsey."

Sten didn't have to ponder what Doc was driving at. He knew his blood thirsty companion all too well.

He grabbed Jonsey by the collar. "Come on, you," he said.

He dragged him over to the exec elevator and shoved him inside.

"What're you doin' to me?" Jonsey wailed.

Sten ignored him. Instead, he grabbed a sidearm off one of the slumbering bodies and tossed it to Jonsey.

"Here," he said. "A little protection when the time comes."

"What time?" Jonsey wailed. "What're you talkin' about." Realization dawned. "Yer not gonna leave me here, are yer?"

By way of an answer Sten popped him with a narco-dart. He caught Jonsey before he hit the floor.

"Give me a hand, Alex," he said.

The two of them propped Jonsey on a bench, hitched him in place with a line through his harness and secured the gun in place.

Next, Sten got Ida to hack the elevator computer so that the doors would pop open automatically in five minutes.

"Now let's get," Sten said.

They rushed to the other elevator, crammed inside, and pushed the topside button. As the doors closed, Sten thought he heard one of the men groaning awake.

And then the elevator lurched, the doors closed and they began their journey.

A few minutes later, the group of engineers and guards came awake. Yawning. Looking about. Puzzling over how they found themselves on the floor.

Just then there was pinging sound, as the exec elevator doors came open. A man came tumbling out, a sidearm in his hand.

Someone shouted, "Gun!"

A barrage of gunfire slammed into the unconscious Jonsey, tearing him to shreds.

Aboard the elevator, Sten and the others made themselves as comfortable as possible as they began the long trip to the surface.

Nobody felt the least bit guilty about Jonsey.

CHAPTER THIRTEEN

THE MISSION

In a darkened room deep in the bowels of Chinen's security section, Sten and his three comrades in spookery were awe-stricken as they watched the vid camera speed across the miraculous landscape that was *Demeter*.

Forests and mountains, booming seas, wide rivers, vast plains filled with golden grain and robo-tended farms and orchards overflowing with ripening crops. All that, plus an amazing variety of herd animals, birds and aquatic life.

When it came to an end, the lights came up and Mahoney's holo-image flickered into life. He was perched on the desktop of his office on Prime World, half the galaxy away.

"That's our bait," Mahoney said. "Now, it's up to you to lure them into the trap."

"Ah'm thinkin' ay grabbin' er fur myself," Alex said. "It's a bloomin' paradise."

"Literally," Ida said. "Did you see all those crops just begging to be harvested?"

"I'm not one for vegetables," Doc said. "But all those animals. Filled with lovely bubbling corpuscles." He smacked his lips.

"We almost choked, so we did," Mahoney said, "when we learned how much Fehrle is willing to shell out for an agplanet snatch-and-grab. Obviously, the Tahn want to reverse engineer *Demeter* and stamp out hundreds more."

Sten nodded. "Makes sense from their point of view," he said. "If there's ever a war and they have enough agplanets they'll be able to dodge the food shortage bullet."

"Oh, there's going to be a war, lad, so there will," Mahoney said. "I have no doubt about that." He grimaced. "The Emp and his diplomatic boyos have been working night and day to prevent a conflict. Not that the boss has any doubt about the outcome. But the Tahn won't go down easily. And the cost in credits and lives would be astronomical."

Ida said, "Looks like Lord Wichman is sitting in the cat bird's seat, ready to collect a fortune as the middleman."

"We hae tae dae somethin' abit 'at son ay a spavined joygirl," Kilgour said. "Make heem pay. Skin heem alive, alang wi' his wee weepin' willie who goes by th' name of Gregor."

Sten frowned. "Speaking of Gregor, we haven't heard from Mitzi lately. I'm getting worried."

"Never mind Mitzi," Mahoney said. "The lass can take care of herself. Smart lass, our Mitzi. She guessed Fehrle would want Gregor for a hostage so he can keep tabs on Wichman and the pirates at the same time. When Skink makes his move Fehrle will be close by to collect his prize and avoid a Wichman double cross."

Ida chuckled. "And our Mitzi will be right there to tip us off when it happens."

"Obviously, Skink is going to ambush the *Demeter* convoy," Sten said. He grinned at Mahoney. "So, I suppose the boss wants us to ambush the ambushers, right, General?"

"Aye, so he does, lad," Mahoney said. "So he does."

Sten said, "With that valuable a prize, aren't you worried that other villains might get word and join in on the fun? We could end up with a crowd of bad guys out there."

"We made sure to confine the leak to one person," Mahoney said. "Wichman's new right hand man is an ex Guards officer, with an ax to grind over forced retirement.

"On top of that, we plotted a deliberately circuitous route, which is why the trip has taken so long. It's a small convoy—low profile all the way."

Mahoney beamed. "Better still, we have Commander Thema running the operation," he said. "I've always had a soft spot for that lass. She's as tough as they come, so she is."

Sten nodded approvingly. Michele Thema, affectionately known by her people as "Little Mike," was a noted hard ass of the first order.

He said, "The main question is when and where Skink will strike."

Kilgour said, "If Ah was a wee pirate playin' yo-ho-ho an' a bottle ay narcobeer, eh'd want tae ambush 'er jist afore she reached 'er new haem away from haem." He tipped a wink at Mahoney. ""So, whaur micht 'at be, me fine wee general?"

For an answer, Mahoney called up a chart of the Possnet Sector, which looked a bit like a dog's leg. Two yellow dots flashed down near the paw.

"The most vulnerable, and therefore the most likely spots are in these two places. Either the KeplerCr5, or the SaganGx6," he said, indicating each yellow orb in turn. "There's some rather odd black holes and other anomalies in each of those areas that travelers tend to avoid."

Sten snorted. "Begging your pardon, General sir," he said with undisguised skepticism. "But we'll still be trying to cover millions of square kilometers. We either need to narrow that down more, or get more help."

"Good point," Ida said. "Which raises the question—why are you sending just us? Why not copper your bets with a few more Mantis teams?"

Mahoney chuckled. "Objections noted and rejected," he said. "And I'll tell you why. The boss sees things differently. For example, the Emperor loves to tell a little story about an ancient group of lawmen known as the Texas Rangers. The boss said they were as 'tough as nails,' and whenever there was big trouble the locals would call for the Rangers.

"Legend has it that one time there was a particular nasty uprising in a frontier town known as Deadwood, or some such. Help was urgently requested. The captain of Rangers telegraphed that help was on the way. But when the train arrived in Deadwood, only a single, solitary Ranger stepped off the car.

"The Deadwood mayor and sheriff were aghast. 'Didn't your boss understand our message?' the mayor said. 'There are hundreds of rioters. But there is only one of you.'

"Well, the Ranger just grinned at the mayor and replied, 'My boss figures one riot, one Ranger.' And sure enough, that single Ranger stopped the riot."

Sten and the others laughed. "In other words," Sten said, "one assault by hundreds of pirates, means one Mantis team?"

Mahoney nodded. "The way the bean counters look at is that we've spent more money training you four than several hundred Guardsmen. So, from their viewpoint one Mantis team should be more than enough. For a change, our boss agrees with the bean counters."

"We're aw honored at yer braw opinion of us," Alex said. "But nae matter how ye swatch at it, th' four ay us ur nae match fur hundreds of pirates an' aw their fightin' ships."

"That's why I'm giving you something special to even the odds," Mahoney said. "We have a brand new ship that's just come off the line. It has the very latest in stealth technology and armaments."

Ida, who was always plugged into Imperial gossip, spoke up. "You don't mean the HMS Gessel?" she asked.

"None other," Mahoney said.

Sten whistled. Admiral Gessel had died recently. He was a much honored veteran of the Mueller Wars who was loved by all who served under him and worked with him. It was said that the Emperor was going to do something special to pay homage to him. And here it was. A new ship, bearing his name.

"Even so," Sten said. "A lot of things can go wrong."

"Oh, don't you worry about that," Mahoney said. "If you screw the pooch—which you've never done before—we'll still have Little Mike standing by.

"The Emperor thinks this would be a good time and place to remove Wichman and his pirate buddies once and for all. And to do that, you need to draw them in then cut them off at the knees."

"I'll cut off more than that," Ida said.

"In short," Sten said, "it's the same old mission, with a new spin. You want the pirates gone, plus you want Wichman and Gregor dead and discredited and you want to blame the whole clotting thing on the Tahn, right?"

"That's the job," Mahoney said.

Sten hesitated. Perhaps a little too long. Then he asked, "What about Venatora? Is she back on the kill list?"

Mahoney shrugged. "She's supposed to be out of the *Demeter* business right now," he said. "But I doubt she'll be able to resist sticking her pretty nose into the whole mess.

"When she does, I suggest you use your... ahem... special relationship to achieve our ends."

He fixed Sten with a hard look and added, "Then kill her."

Doc chuckled. "Typical human hypocrisy," he said. "At least I keep mine alive," he said.

"For the second course," Ida said.

Doc shrugged. "Waste not, want not," he said.

Mahoney chuckled. "Funny, that's what the Emperor said. Ideally, what he'd like to see is a truel—which would solve all of the above in one fell swoop, so it would."

"A truel?" Sten said. "Begging your pardon, sir, but what in clot is a truel?"

"A three-way duel," Mahoney said.

There was silence in room as this soaked in. Then Sten said, "In other words, they all get it. Wichman and Gregor. The pirates. And Venatora."

"Exactly so," Mahoney said. "Now, off to the wars, my friends. There's no time to waste."

He rose from his far way desk and tossed them a rare salute.

"Fair winds and following seas to you all," he said.

And his hologram vanished.

CHAPTER FOURTEEN

NIGHTSWEATS

Sten wrestled with his pillow. After the day's events he was exhausted. On top of that, he couldn't remember when he'd last enjoyed a full night's sleep.

Mahoney's briefing had disturbed him. To be sure, his "one riot one Ranger" story was amusing. In his early days his chest would have popped the fasteners on his tunic when Mahoney applied that little tale to his Mantis team. One crisis, one Mantis team.

Although Sten was still on the far side of thirty, he'd survived so many murderous attempts that he'd used up more lives than a fleet of cats. Even so, instead of pride, he had a nagging sense that his luck might soon give out. Underscored by his confused feelings for Venatora. An enemy of the Emperor.

Hells, she was Sten's enemy as well. But kill her? If it came down to it he wasn't confident he could pull the trigger. Which would give her the edge in any confrontation.

Unless she had her own doubts.

Sten thumped his pillow. The single sheet was wet from adrenalin-charged perspiration. Finally, he gave up and rolled out of his bunk. He fetched his kitbag and dug out his comm, thinking he'd read a little.

What few possessions he had were in the kit bag, or stowed in his locker aboard the *Jo'l Cash*. Piled all together, it wouldn't weigh more than ten kilos, or so. That, and the little money he had in his Imperial bank account was all that he could call his own. For him home consisted of whatever bunk he was assigned, or temporary safehouse quarters and hotel rooms when on a mission.

There was certainly no room for a family, a wife, or even a girlfriend. The last woman who met that definition dumped him before their last mission in the Wolf Worlds. She was a Mantis beast handler now and a damned good one. Wherever she was, Bet was sure to be giving the local bad guys hell.

In weak moments he missed the shabby quarters he and his family shared on Vulcan. Like all Migs they'd been poor, living from pay period to pay period and borrowing against future wages by adding more years to his father and mother's Company contracts.

They'd both been dirt scrabble farm kids on some backwater planet and were sitting ducks for the Company recruiters who came around extolling the wonderful lives they would enjoy on Vulcan. Regular raises in pay and advancement in rank were practically guaranteed. Plus, they'd have their own home, plenty of good food, marvelous recreational activities, like the Feelies where famous Prime World stars graced the big screens.

The biggest draw was the promised educational opportunities for their children. Considering how smart the members of the Sten family were, the recruiter said, their kids would leave school to get great jobs as techs, or even engineers.

All lies, of course. The moment they landed on Vulcan they learned the hard truth. Migs—pejorative slang for untrained migrant workers—were so low on the totem pole of Vulcan's hierarchy, that factory 'bots were considered more important. And pay was so miniscule that there was never enough money to pay for their housing unit, or to put decent food on the table.

The Company made it easy for Migs to add time to their contracts, and easier still to spend those credits. Joygirls and Joyboys, gambling machines, and cheap booze and narcotics were featured in all the rec areas. Bleak as life for a Mig was, those inducements were hard to resist.

Sten would be there still, slaving away at a lathe or some other lowly job, if the Company CEO, Baron Thoresen, hadn't made the wrong choice when a rec hall accident threatened to expose a highly illegal project aimed at undercutting the Emperor's AM2 monopoly. That choice had cost the lives of hundreds of Migs, including Sten's family.

When Sten revolted against the Company and tried to sneak aboard a ship that would carry him away from Vulcan, he was sentenced to hard labor in Vulcan's Exotics Section. Known by his fellow prisoners as "Hellworld." This was not an exaggeration. The materials they handled were so deadly, their equipment and protective gear so shoddy, that few lived more than six months.

Sten had survived in Work Area 35 thanks to his friendship with a mystery man known only as Hite. His friend's rough manner disguised a remarkable intellect. Hite was killed by a guard before Sten learned anything about his background.

He was an expert street fighter many times over and he'd taught Sten so well, that he never really faced a challenge in the military until he started training in Mantis Section, where you learned as many ways to kill as there elements on the periodic table.

He also infected Sten with his bleak sense of humor, which shook the young man out of his doldrums so he could start fending for himself, instead constantly mourning the loss of his family.

Hite was also a skilled back alley surgeon. Thanks to him Sten had a secret weapon that no one outside of the Mercury Corps shrink, Rykor, and his closest friends like Kilgour and Ida and Doc knew about. Oh, yeah. And Mahoney. But Mahoney knew about everything.

Sten had built the ultimate knife from a stolen bit of a crystalline substance so rare and valuable that a few grams were worth more than what even an engineer earned in a year. It was unbreakable and couldn't be found by even the best snooping devices.

It was a slim double-edged dagger with a skeleton handle custom fit for Sten's fingers to curl around in the deadly knife-fighter's grip Hite had taught him. There was no guard, just serrated lateral grooves between the haft and blade that tapered from 5 cm width down to a needle tip. The knife was 15 cm long and only .39 cm thick. It was possibly the deadliest fighting blade ever made.

The crystal tapered to a hair-edge barely 15 molecules wide, and the weight of the blade alone was enough pressure to dice a diamond. The knife was housed in a fleshy sheath Hite had surgically constructed in Sten's arm. If he curled his fingers a certain way, the knife instantly shot into his hand. One swipe could remove a enemy's arm. Another could cut through tempered steel. Lock Sten in a room and he'd cut his way free as soon as his enemy was out of sight.

And so, after all these years working for the Eternal Emperor the only thing of true value that he owned was that knife.

Sten sighed, got himself a drink of water, then crawled back into his bunk. Pulled his covers up and found a likely book to read on his comm. It didn't hold his interest long. In the nostalgic mood that had overtaken him, he wished he had access to his only other prized possessions. Two real books. Printed on real paper with real ink. Protected by battered cardboard covers.

Each book had cost him a month's wages. The first was Mr. Midshipman Hornblower, by an ancient author whose name was C.S. Forester. It was a marvelous novel about a young naval officer back during what were known as the Napoleonic Wars. Instead of rocket ships, Hornblower sailed his world in wooden ships whose source of power was the wind, not AM2. The book traced his days as a midshipman—basically a boot camp private—to lieutenant.

There was very little known about Mr. Forester or his books, but Sten had ferreted out the fact that there were eleven books in the series, tracing Hornblower's rise from midshipman to fleet admiral. A knowledgeable and friendly rare book seller had promised to alert Sten the moment any of the other books surfaced.

The other book was The Stars My Destination, by Alfred Bester. The hero was Gully Foyle, a spaceship engineer who had been betrayed by his bosses and left for dead in uttermost space.

Through a remarkable series of events Foyle remade himself into a man of royal bearing possessed with a wealth of knowledge. He used those abilities to revenge himself on the men who had betrayed him. There was a lot more to it than that. An ability called "jaunting," in which a human could teleport himself to any location. Of course, even in modern times true teleportation of something the size of a man, was impossible, but it was an interesting idea.

Hite had loved that book and had memorized large portions of it, including the poem that opened the novel. To this day the words were fixed in Sten's mind:

> *"Gully Foyle is my name*
> *And Terra is my nation.*
> *Deep space is my dwelling place,*
> *The stars my destination."*

Bester said he based the book on another famous novel—The Count Of Monte Cristo, written hundreds of years before by a Alexander Dumas, a French author of African descent. Dumas was also the grandson of General Dumas, a legendary figure in the Napoleonic wars who was said to be so strong that he could sit astride a horse, wrap his long legs around its belly, grasp the overhead beams in a barn and lift himself and the horse off the ground.

Sten grinned at the memory of that little factoid, which was most likely apocryphal. He recalled wondering if the general was a heavy worlder like Alex Kilgour. That was nonsense, of course. In Dumas' days the only world inhabited by human beings was the planet Earth.

His mind wandered on that track for a half an hour or more. Then slowly, his eyes closed and he finally fell into a deep restful sleep.

CHAPTER FIFTEEN

THE PATSY

Gregor burst into his cabin, practically floating on air. "He likes me," he burbled. "Lord Fehrle really likes me."

Mitzi sat up in bed, letting the sheet drift artfully down so that it barely covered her snowy white bosom.

They bounced enticingly, as she clapped her hands, exclaiming, "How wonderful, sweetie. It's like I said. He just needed time to see your true worth."

"You were so right, Mitzi," Gregor said, as he strode to the bar, inset beneath a faux porthole which showed a vid display of starry space. "He even said that I was like the son he never had."

"You see," Mitzi exclaimed. "You've just been sick all this time, sweetie. And who wouldn't have been? Stuck on dreary old Wichlandia with nothing to do but think about the nasty old days with mutineers."

"I blame father for that," Gregor said, as he poured himself a hefty shot of Pulinka, that heady, highly addictive liqueur made from a poisonous New Brovarian fruit tree.

"Want some?" he absently asked Mitzi, displaying the bottle of clear liquid that shimmered under the cabin lights.

Suppressing a shudder, she shook her head. It took twenty distillations to make Pulinka drinkable and although it would no longer kill you, the stuff ate away at the brain, separating the real from the fanciful. In the end stages, Pulinka addiction led to constant nightmares and suicidal obsessions.

"No, you go ahead sweetie," she said. "I'll stick with my usual."

She came off the bed, noting Gregor's lustful reactions as she slipped on a sheer, rose-colored robe.

He tried to embrace her, but Mitzi slipped under his reaching arms, giggling like a little girl.

"Not now, silly," she admonished him. "First, I want to hear all about your meeting with Lord Fehrle."

Gregor was so full of his imagined victory over the cold, forbidding Tahn overlord, that he was only mildly disappointed. He downed his drink, poured another, then plopped on the bed.

"Father has always kept me far away from his business dealings," Gregor said, as Mitzi fetched a red clay bottle from the fresher.

It contained nothing more than lemon infused water that Gregor thought was a special cognac from Mitzi's homeworld.

"When mother died he shipped me off to military school," he continued. "And then, when I was falsely accused of stealing from my roomie, he talked me into joining the Guard. Saying service to the Empire would repair my reputation, so I could hold up my head when I joined him in business someday."

He shook his head. "But that day just never seemed to come," he said. "There was always some technical reason or another that kept me from taking my rightful place in his businesses."

Mitzi sat beside him, sipping her drink. All rapt attention. "Why anyone would believe you'd steal is beyond me," she said. "I mean, you're rich. You can have anything you want. What reason would you have to steal?"

The shift of Gregor's eyes gave away his guilt. The item in question had been a pearl-handled hunting knife his roommate had won in a shooting competition. A competition that saw Gregor come in last. The reasons for the theft were jealousy and greed. But Gregor would never admit to that.

"That's exactly what I told the headmaster," Gregor said. "But he wouldn't listen. He said it was proof that I was no gentleman because I wouldn't admit I was in the wrong. And take my medicine."

Gregor downed yet another drink and Mitzi didn't make him wait for more. She had the bottle handy and quickly poured another shot.

She bent low as she poured, so he'd be captivated by her breasts spilling from the robe. Meanwhile, she flipped open the lid of an antique Borgia ring and dumped its contents into the glass.

Gregor drank and smacked its lips, then said. "Pulinka always tastes so much better when you pour it for me." He frowned. "I wonder why that is?"

Mitzi giggled her most charming giggle. "It's just love, silly," she said. "Things always taste better when its offered by someone you love."

Gregor's frown vanished. After another sip, he said, "Father didn't even bother to defend me, much less hear my side of the story." He wiped away a stray tear. "Father just took their word for it."

He thumped his chest. "Me. His own son."

"That was so unfair," Mitzi said, nudging his elbow so he'd remember to drink more Pulinka. "And then those dirty smeg heads in the Guard treated you any better."

"They all acted like I was just an ordinary person," Gregor said, voice shaking with outrage. "Especially Sten. He was the worst of the lot. He said I was no better than anyone else. Me! Gregor Wichman. Son of the great

Lord Wichman. Confidant of the Emperor."

"I'll bet Lord Fehrle didn't treat you that way," Mitzi said.

"Just the opposite," Gregor said. "When I entered his cabin he got up and shook my hand. And then he apologized for seeming to ignore me during the journey. He said Skink and the other pirate captains were meeting crazy. Every time he turns around they want another meeting to discuss the mission. And then they quarrel with one another and it takes all the energy and tact that he possesses to keep them from killing each other."

Gregor took another hit of Pulinka. "I swear, the man has the patience of a saint. I don't know how he puts up with them." He shook his head. "Especially Skink. He's such a barbarian."

He lapsed into silence, reflecting on the meeting, a smile playing at the edges of his lips as he remembered the warm handshake, the lovely dinner Fehrle's servants laid out for them and the intimate talk that they'd had.

"Lord Fehrle even told me about his own childhood," Gregor said. "About how his father had underestimated him as well. And he advised me to be patient. That the day would soon come when I'd replace my dad as the CEO of Wichman Enterprises. Just like he'd replaced his own father when the right time came."

It was Mitzi's guess that Fehrle had probably assassinated his old man. She'd never know how right she was. The senior Fehrle had caught his son plotting a takeover with other discontented young Tahn. But before he could act, the young Fehrle had cut his throat and then paid a fortune to have the body disposed of. To the rest of the Tahn world the old man had tragically vanished while vacationing in the mountains.

Gregor said, "Lord Fehrle told me that now they were nearing our destination he'd be busier than ever and to forgive him if he seemed to be neglectful in the coming days and weeks."

Mitzi's eyebrows rose. She said, "Oh. Near the end are we?"

Gregor shot her a suspicious look. "What do you care?" he asked. "Not getting bored are you?"

"Oh, Sweetie," she exclaimed, throwing her arms around him. "How could I ever be bored when I'm with my lover boy?" She pursed her lips in a lovely pout. "But you did promise that you'd buy me some new clothes and jewelry when we got to a place with shops and stuff."

She ran her hands down the silken robe, which cost more than most working folk made in a year.

"Everything is getting worn out," she said. "And pretty soon you're going to get tired of seeing me in the same old things."

Appeased, Gregor laughed. "Women!" he said. "You're all addicted to shopping. It must come with the extra X chromosome."

He polished off his drink. Mitzi quickly helped him to another.

"Sorry to disappoint you, honey," he said, "but I don't think they have very many glamorous shops where we're going. In fact, I doubt if there are any.

"They'll be setting up the ambush at old pirates' lair. A place called Punta Royal, in the SaganGx6 sector. Wherever the clot that is."

* * * *

Later, when the drug took effect and Gregor passed out on the bed, Mitzi got a little device from her stash of sex toys. It had two leads, which she attached to his temples. Soon as she pressed a little button Gregor began squirming and moaning in ecstasy. In his mind, he was enjoying a marathon sexual bout with Mitzi, where nothing was forbidden and all was welcome.

She'd kept him happy this way for months now, without ever having to actually allow a real sexual act to take place. She shuddered. He was such a creep that it made her sick just to think about it.

Tucked into another toy was a remarkable little comm device just out of the Mantis labs. She keyed it, then slipped it into her ear.

Static. Then a voice.

It was Ida.

"Punta Royal," Mitzi said. "In the SaganGx6 sector."

Gregor moaned.

"What was that noise?" Ida asked.

"Oh, just another satisfied customer," Mitzi said with a laugh.

CHAPTER SIXTEEN

ON THE STALK

"We'd better ease off," Venatora said. "Skink's a cunning devil and he'll be watching his backtrail like a hungry raptor."

"Yes, Your Highness," Marta said, relaying the order to Palsonia, who was at the helm.

Immediately, the holoimage on the deck-to-ceiling monitor reflected the change and the tiny ship representing the *Takeo* slowed its forward momentum. The pirate fleet, led by Skink's own *Swagman*, moved ahead.

Palsonia chuckled. "Anthofelia's playing it safe as always," she said, indicating the position of the *Gunakada*.

It was tucked safely among the other vessels that made up Skink's main force.

"Begging your pardon, Ma'am, but she never was the bravest bitch in the kennel," Marta said.

"Skink is certainly risking it all in this operation," Clew said. "Bar talk is that he's spent several stolen fortunes getting the *Swagman* in top fighting shape."

Her yellow eyes glowed in the dim light of the command center. "Me and some of my nest mates got his purser drunk one night," Clew continued, "and she said Skink is also underwriting the cost of upgrading the ships of the other captains."

Venatora made a cynical smile. "I'll bet he's charging his fellow captains usurious interest rates for his largesse," she said. "To be paid out of their share of the booty."

"The purser said something similar," Clew agreed, her reptilian features stretching into what Venatora presumed was a smile. "Of course, if he doesn't pull this off the captains will skin him, then space him. Love to be a fly on the wall to witness it."

On the surface, Skink's ship and his entourage appeared to be a motley force, consisting mostly of mothballed Imperial ships.

The *Swagman*, a decommissioned leftover from the Mueller Wars, was the deadliest. Creaky as the ship was, she was bristling with every weapon Skink could lay his thieving hands on, including a recently pilfered particle cannon.

Venatora and her little fleet had hidden in the shadow of a gas giant, watching Skink's people mount the weapon beneath the nose of the *Swagman*. It was too big to fit into the ship for launching. To use the weapon a pilot would have to traverse the exterior of the *Swagman* and fumble awkwardly with the canopy to get in. Then he'd have to release the clamps holding the cannon in place.

But from that moment on the pilot would rule the roost, operating the cannon as if it were an independent fighting ship.

The other pirate ships, mostly frigates, were also well armed, but Venatora was confident that with a little care and a heavy helping of cunning, she could take them. But only if she had to. Venatora planned to seize *Demeter* without ever engaging another ship in battle.

Thanks to Clew, she knew all about Skink's plan to ambush the *Demeter* and her entourage at Punta Royal. He'd vaporize the most formidable Imperial ships with the particle cannon, while the other captains swarmed the agworld's support and took them out of action.

Then, he'd board *Demeter* and personally take control.

At that point Venatora planned to spring a surprise of her own. Her force was smaller than Skink's. But her women, especially the Zabanyas, were so fierce, loyal, and well-trained that she was confident they'd overpower any force Skink threw at them.

Out of the corner of her eye she watched Marta and Palsonia go about their business. They were both capable and dedicated, with plenty of combat experience. Ideal aides to help lead the raiding party.

Clew would be another plus for Venatora's raiding party. She was a legendary pirate captain, twenty years Venatora's senior, with more successful boardings under her belt than a dozen of Skink's pirate pals.

But could she be trusted? Sure, she'd believably explained her defection from Skink. Clew said she'd coldly calculated the odds and had quickly come to the conclusion that she stood a better chance aligning herself with Venatora.

As if reading her thoughts, Clew sighed and gave a sad shake of her head. "Skink is going to lead them all down the path to perdition," she said. "I'd feel sorry for them if they weren't being so stubbornly ignorant. I showed them in black and white how much they've gained since you brought us all together years ago to act in unison.

"But all they could see is that you have become so much richer than they are. Never mind that you invest a good portion of your loot in expanding and modernizing your ships.

"Or the tremendous expense you bear training all your people to act with military precision, with clear cut chains of commands. With regular pay and benefits and assistance in old age and infirmity. Like a real country, with a real leader, instead of just a bunch of crazy perpetually drunken pirates running around making fools of themselves."

Venatora asked, "Don't you worry for the safety of your friends and nest mates now that you've abandoned Skink?"

Clew's yellow eyes narrowed in apprehension. "I prepared for the blowback before I announced my intentions," she said. "Everyone was sent to a safe place with plenty of supplies and credits to last until this is over. And thanks to your generosity, they are all well defended. Even so—yes, I worry."

During her preparations for the *Demeter* operation, Venatora had sent a contingent of some of her best warriors aboard several well-armed ships to guard Clew's people.

"I won't be telling you not to worry," Venatora said. "And I won't lie to you and say everything will be okay. And nothing will go wrong. How could I guarantee something like that? Besides, in my experience, something always goes wrong. My only hope is that I can keep the mistakes down to a minimum and surprise our enemies more times than they surprise us."

Clew chuckled. "My mother always said that whoever springs the last surprise will win."

"Your mother was certainly a wise woman," Venatora said.

"I'm sure yours gave equally good advice," Clew said. "Otherwise you wouldn't be sitting here, queen of the most successful pirate operation in memory."

Venatora returned the chuckle and nodded as if in agreement. But the fact was, she was the product of not one—but many mothers.

And had never met a single one of them.

CHAPTER SEVENTEEN

THE COUNCIL OF FATHERS

Father Huber spiraled down the glittering stalactite like a great dark serpent, slowly arranging and rearranging his disparate parts until he reached his desired humanoid form just as his booted heels touched the floor.

He was early and had time to shuffle molecules around to create the look he desired for the meeting of the Fathers. He was tall, well-formed and wore a long black cloak that billowed when he moved, showing off flashes of red velvet.

His face was long and sharp with a beaked nose and looked vaguely like that of a predatory insect, the effect heightened by his dark, overly large eyes. Large hands with tapered fingers and sharp nails were almost clawlike when he flexed them. His face was a translucent green.

Father Huber moved gracefully to a long, highly polished mahogany table set up in the center of the immense cavern. There were a dozen high-backed chairs, with soft red-leather upholstery arranged around the table. One chair was larger and more regal than the others.

A golden tray with twelve golden goblets was set in front of that chair, the goblets were arranged around a large golden pitcher that was artfully carved with exotic forms that seemed to move in the dim flickering light that appeared to have no center. The light came from nowhere and everywhere.

The only sound in the room was water slowly dripping in some distant corner of the chamber. That, and the constant low insect-like buzz which emanated from a ceiling so high that it was nearly invisible in the gloom. Although it seemed to be in constant motion as if millions of small things were moving about.

Huber went around the table, stopping behind the tallest chair. He put his hands on the back, fingers clawing to get a grip and he pulled it back with a loud, scraping sound that made his internal fluids run cold.

A harsh voice came from the shadows: "You're early, Father Huber."

A shuffle of boots and a broad, squat shape followed the voice and Father Raggio stepped from behind a crystalline stalagmite.

Raggio's fleshy mouth made what Huber assumed was an attempt at a smile as he added: "Here to vie for the Emanator's Chair, I presume?"

"Presume what you like, Raggio," Huber said, noisily dragging the chair the rest of the way and sliding into it.

Raggio winced at the sound. "Must you?" he said.

He took a seat on the far side of the table. Why Raggio chose such an ugly form, then draped it in a less than stylish Roman tunic over baggy cotton trousers was beyond Huber's understanding.

His oily green face was streaked with red, as if it belonged to a heavy drinker. Like Father Huber, his hemolymph was yellow, not red. And, unlike Huber, Raggio wasn't a heavy imbiber so the broken blood vessels were purely for effect. Huber supposed he wanted to give the appearance of a jolly fat man, rather than a member of the dour, bitter Cyndarian race who hid themselves well out of the view of the Emperor and his legion of spies.

That the Cyndarians were few in number made the subterfuge much easier. Of even greater help was their mastery of the camouflage sciences. They could take the form of practically any being in the Empire—including a few that never existed.

They had three things going for them: high intelligence, the ability to disguise themselves from their enemies, and the ability to reproduce by cloning.

The Cyndarians hailed from a planet where they were at the bottom of the predator totem pole. And yet over time, they were able to take charge of the mechanics of evolution to win the mantle of Top Predator.

Little by little they eliminated the competition by simply outfoxing them—changing their colors and shape, and then ambushing their enemies and making a meal of them. Over the eons they progressed to the point where they could take the first hesitant steps off their homeworld.

And that was nearly the end of Cyndarian race.

The first intelligent beings they met were the Gulos—a race far more technically superior and avaricious than the Cyndarians. They were nearly wiped out as the Gulos swarmed their homeworld, hunting down and killing every Cyndarian they could find.

The Gulos drove the numbers down so low that only a handful of Cyndarians were left. And that was when the group known as "The Fathers" began. They weren't real fathers, of course. There were no male and female Cyndarians. Or any other sex.

To ensure their survival the Fathers determined to create an entirely new race. They would take the best genetic material from other life forms and mix and match until they had an unbeatable species of warriors who would drive the Gulos from the planet and then reach beyond.

And that was when Himmenops came into being. It was a species consisting entirely of females gathered in enormous hives. And at their center of these females there was a queen who ruled over her sisters and daughters with an iron hand and the ability to produce powerful pheromones that bent her subjects to her will.

Self cloning was no longer desirable—new genetic material was constantly required to keep the Himmenops from hitting an evolutionary dead end. And so the Fathers were always on the hunt for suitable males from different life forms to supercharge the new species.

Naturally, the Fathers intended to rule over all—but behind the scenes. Manipulating the Queen and her elite personal handmaidens—the Zabanya guardswomen. They also intended to keep their own Cyndarian genes in reserve, waiting for the day when they could safely emerge again—shedding the Himmenops chrysalis like a metamorphosing butterfly.

There were only two dozen or so Fathers in existence at one time. Periodically they induced the Himmenops to produce a special fetus, who would then be taken away to be raised and educated by the other Fathers.

The underlying problem with all this—the great weakness—was that it all had to be accomplished slowly and in great secrecy. To begin with, they had to deal with Gulos. Several centuries were required to not just defeat, but to eliminate the entire species.

Then, when the Fathers came blinking into the cold reality of the Empire and the Eternal Emperor they immediately saw that their genetic dreams of achieving the crown of Top Predator for once and forever were impossible against the forces of the Emperor—and his stranglehold over the ultimate energy source—AM2.

Once again the Fathers went underground. Setting up shop in shattered ruins that made up the center of the Possnet Sector, where an ancient cosmic disaster had destroyed a dozen planetary bodies or more.

Here they bided their time while the number of Himmenops grew. This worked well under several queens, but their latest queen—Venatora—had been so successful that birth rates had soared. Population pressures were such that the Fathers were considering bringing a new queen online to rule over a new colony.

This had only happened one time before and instead of becoming like-minded royal sisters ruling side by side, a civil war had erupted. Countless Himmenops were killed, driving the population back down to dangerous levels.

And now it was about to happen again. Princess Anthofelia had come to the fore. In Raggio's view she was the worst possible person to set up shop in a neighboring colony. She was too greedy, too egocentric and if truth be told, not very intelligent. Raggio had no idea what had gone wrong when she had been snipped and pasted together.

But she had been Father Huber's project since the beginning and it was

Raggio's opinion that he had made a hash of it. Her cell should have been broken into long before she reached attainment and the mewling worm inside killed and thrown out with the other genetic trash.

Raggio suspected Huber was sticking with his princess because he didn't want to admit weakness or error to the other Fathers. The Fathers were not a forgiving, brotherly group. Just the opposite. There were always candidates—with supporters—waiting in the wings and the slightest hint of weakness and the knives would come out.

This had also happened before.

Raggio shuddered at the memory.

That time only sheer luck and betrayal had kept him wary enough so that he'd turned, just as the blow was struck. The knife scraping along his ribs.

And he'd turned… and kept turning… capturing the knife hand.

Turning it inward.

Then upward.

And a minute later his foe had been lying on the deck of Raggio's stateroom, breathing his last while his life's blood spilled out on the floor.

The sound of a distant gong brought him out of his reverie. And then the other Fathers entered the chamber. Drifting down from on high, or slipping from dark corners.

They moved toward the big table, each taking on the form they favored for meetings like this. Some chatting amicably. Others maintaining a grim silence.

But they all had one thing in common: glittering eyes that were constantly on the move, sweeping left to right and back again.

Watching for the knife.

When they were all seated, Raggio lifted the pitcher of wine and filled a goblet to the brim. He passed it to his right and filled another.

When all had been served he raised his goblet.

"Blessings upon us all brothers," he said. "And let the emanations begin."

"Blessings," the others murmured, and they all drank deeply.

Huber made a face as he finished. "Really, Raggio," he said, "we must do something about the quality of the sacramental wine."

He ostentatiously gulped water, swished it around his mouth and swallowed. "Tastes like old blood," he said.

Next to him, Jesop, the clown of the group, laughed.

"Good going, Huber," he said. "The meeting hasn't even started and we're already arguing over the wine. This ought to be fun."

The other Fathers laughed. Raggio saw his enemy wince.

With growing confidence, and no little pleasure, he brought the meeting to order.

"The first order of business is rather urgent," he said. "We need to end this rebellion Princess Anthofelia has launched. It not only endangers our long range plans, but in the short run it may ruin our chances to capture a vital asset."

"You are making some rather large assumptions, Brother mine," Huber said. "To begin with, you are assuming we all see the princess as an upstart. That she's calling for rebellion, when to some of us her actions are the natural order of things."

"Natural?" Jesop said, his face twisted in mock outrage. "There's nothing natural about this whole shebang. Anthofelia—like all the other women—is a compilation of snips and bits of DNA from so many sources only our best computers can keep track of them."

Huber looked so outraged, that for a moment Raggio thought it was sincere, and not an act.

"I'm shocked our brother should feel this way about our creations," Huber said. "True, the bodies they walk around in were not achieved through recognized biological practices. But at the heart of every Himmenops is a kernel that is pure Cyndarian. Our true species."

He leaned forward for effect, his voice rising dramatically.

"I, for one, am sick to my heart at the cynicism displayed by our brother. When the Fathers before us launched this holy mission, they pledged that someday there will be a holy metamorphosis and the great Cyndarian race would throw off their fleshy bonds and emerge onto the Galaxy's stage as the greatest race that has ever existed."

Father Raggio was stunned when several Fathers responded with "Hear Hear." And "Well said."

He looked around the table. Only Jesop seemed to be unmoved by Huber's little speech.

"There's no arguing with a man on a holy mission," Raggio said in his most mocking tones. "But we are dealing with practicalities here. Not sanctified speech. If we allow this rebellion to continue it will dangerously divide our Himmenops daughters.

"We've seen it happen before. The palace intrigue will quicken. The knives will come out. And soon it will be sister against sister.

"In Queen Venatora we have a wise and stable leader. Under her we have experienced slow, but steady growth. And we have all become stronger and richer without rousing the suspicions or attention of the Eternal Emperor."

There were mutters of agreement, but to Raggio's dismay, they lacked conviction.

Huber caught this and rushed in to say, "I think we should call for a vote of confidence. It's clear to me that our dear Raggio has lost his way.

There is a great opportunity just before us and strong action is needed.

"Captain Skink and his colleagues have chosen to support Princess Anthofelia. And she in turn has the strong support of the Tahn's own Lord Fehrle. If we help them snatch *Demeter* from under the very nose of the Emperor and hand it over to the Tahn they will be forever in our debt."

Jesop laughed. "Pirates in our debt?" he said. "An oxymoron if I heard one. As for the Tahn—" Jesop made a rude noise. "With that and a pot of beans all we'll get is a blast of very smelly hot air."

"Brothers, brothers," Raggio pleaded. "We mustn't divide ourselves over this. A great war is coming. Perhaps the bloodiest and most costly war in centuries. The Eternal Emperor versus the Tahn. And any being foolish enough to stand between them will be destroyed.

"Like Father Huber I see great opportunity. But not in the way he portrays it. When this is over the Empire will be on its knees. With millions, perhaps billions dead. Starvation and disease will rule then. Beings will be looking for leaders. Begging for help.

"It is then that the great metamorphosis will begin. And the time of the Cyndarians will begin, just as it was foretold."

Silence.

Father Raggio's eyes swept the table, looking for signs of support. Which way was the wind blowing? It was difficult to tell.

Seeking a compromise, he said, "Perhaps there is a kernel of truth to Father Huber's complaints. Perhaps Venatora's time has passed."

There were murmurs of surprise. No one had expected Raggio to retreat one centimeter. Of course, retreat, was not what Raggio had in mind.

"Venatora has become more independent lately," he said. "Sometimes dangerously so. I'd be willing to contemplate installing a new queen. Someone more biddable. Someone willing to follow our every order.

"In my view Anthofelia is not that woman. She is not fit to be queen. If we are to keep the Himmenops under our thumbs, we need someone the women will follow even without the aid of our pheromone treatments. To find someone like that will take time and training. And it will have to be carried out in complete secrecy so Venatora doesn't get wind of it and put paid to our plans."

Jesop said, "That sounds reasonable to me. All of us agree we must have a strong queen. And all of us also agree that queen must be willing to follow our every order without question."

Huber said, "We have that queen in Anthofelia. There's no need for a search or for training. I've trained Anthofelia myself. If I say 'Jump' the only question she'll ask is 'How high."

Raggio snorted. "How kind of you to sacrifice your valuable time to train a new queen without troubling the rest of us."

Huber got his back up. "I say we should rid ourselves of Venatora right this minute and install Anthofelia to the throne."

Raggio started to argue, but Jesop raised a hand. "Brothers. Brothers. There is no need to quarrel. Besides, what is the great hurry? Why must a decision be made now? Why not wait a small while and see how the game plays out?

"What was it that great human bard said about being too hasty? 'They stumble that run fast.'"

Huber snorted derision. "Must you always play the clown, Father Jesop? Speak plainly, man. I have a motion on the table. I called for a yea or nay vote. Which shall it be? Anthofelia? Or Venatora?"

"I move that we vote to delay the vote," Jesop said.

Huber laughed. "That's nonsense."

Raggio said, "I second Father Jesop's motion."

A few minutes later he banged the gavel and brought the meeting to a close.

* * * *

Venatora paced the deck of the *Takeo* waiting to hear from Father Raggio.

She glanced up at the monitor and saw Skink's little fleet poised at the edge of the jump point.

Next stop: Punta Royal.

Should she stay or should she follow?

There was a crackling sound in her ear. And then came the voice.

"I bought us time," Raggio said. "It's all up to you, now, daughter mine."

CHAPTER EIGHTEEN

THE AMBUSHERS

ABOARD THE *GUNAKADA*

"For clot's sake, Princess," Skink said, "How in hell can you expect a full share? Only thing you're kickin' in is a dinky fighter and a crew of twenty five."

Anthofelia drew herself up to her haughtiest pose. "You forget, Captain," she said in her most regal voice, "that I am also offering my position. When we have brought this operation to a successful conclusion there is nothing standing in my way to becoming queen of all the Himmenops. And then you will have a whole fleet of top level fighting ships and hundreds of warrior women that I can bring into play with a single word."

Skink wrinkled his snout. "No matter what happens here," he said, "you'll still have Venatora to handle. I've been dealing with her for years and I can tell you from experience she isn't gonna keel over and play dead."

"You're forgetting I have Lord Fehrle's support," Anthofelia said.

Skink snorted. "See how long that lasts once he gets what he's after," he said. "Only reason he backed your play is because he wanted Venatora out the way. After that fiasco with the mutineers he doesn't trust her."

Anthofelia sniffed. "That's because she's afraid of the Emperor," she said. "She'd rather nibble at the edges and live off his scraps. Whereas I am ready, willing and more than able to hit him hard and then sit back and let him try to take on the Himmenops on their home ground. Just to take an inch of our territory would cost him more in blood and money than even he can afford."

Skink rapped on the console with his claws. "See, that's where me and you part company. You say you're not scared of the Eternal Emperor? Well, if that's not just big talk, you're either crazy, or stupid."

He thumped his scaly chest. "I'm not crazy, and I'm not stupid either. The Emp scares the clot out of me."

"If you're so scared, why are you doing this?" Anthofelia asked.

Skink shrugged. "Because Fehrle's paying us through the nose," he said. "Enough so me and the other captains can pick up and run like hell.

There's plenty of places to hide and live high on the hog if you've got enough of the old filthy lucre.

"But you and your girls are stuck in one place. You can't run. If you did, the Himmenops would fall apart and you'd be queen of nothing but a race of freaks."

Anthofelia was furious. Skink's insults were almost more than she could bear. Making it worse, everything he said was true. Her right hand drifted to her left sleeve, where she kept a minigun. The rounds were small, but she was close enough to Skink that the bullets would penetrate even his scaly hide.

In the corner, Nalene coughed. Anthofelia caught her warning look. She raised her hand and brought it slowly down palm first. Cool it, Nalene was saying. Calm down.

Anthofelia forced a smile and leaned back. If she killed Skink the whole deal would collapse.

She sighed. "You drive a hard bargain, Captain Skink," she said. "But I'm willing to negotiate. You and the others are offering me half a share. But really, that's embarrassing, don't you think? How can I hold up my head with that kind of an offer? How about if we make it eight tenths of a share?"

Skink thrust out a claw. "Make it three quarters of a share and you have yourself a deal," he said.

Anthofelia shook his scaly claw, forcing herself not to shudder.

"Deal," she said.

Later, she paced the cabin of the *Gunakada*, frantically trying to reach Father Huber.

Finally, his voice crackled in her ear. "You did well, daughter," he said. "The timing was perfect. At the moment the High Council is evenly divided on who should wear the crown."

"They are fools and cowards," Anthofelia said. "Can't they see that we represent the future of the Himmenops?"

"Patience, daughter. Patience," Huber said. "A year ago—nay, only a few months ago—no one would have thought this division was possible. Venatora was clearly everyone's favorite. Now, we have a fifty-fifty shot at the crown.

"The odds will tip completely to our side once we have *Demeter*. Then all the fathers will see things our way."

"Even Father Raggio?" Anthofelia said.

Huber chuckled. "Highly unlikely," he said. "But that won't matter. Because after the *Demeter*, the knives will come out. And you will be queen."

Skink was feeling pleased with himself. "Fetch me some of the good stuff," he told his steward. "I feel like celebrating."

By "good stuff" he meant a bottle of expensive cognac that the pirates had got off a partyship they'd run across on the way to Punta Royal.

He could see the ship—the *Jubilee*—on his secondary monitor now and when the steward brought him the crusty bottle and poured a hefty measure he toasted the screen.

"To the *Jubilee*," he said and downed his drink.

He held it up for the steward to refill. He didn't make it easy, waving his drinking hand around as he spoke, the steward chasing the glass and trying not to spill. A day ago he was steward on the *Jubilee*. But he'd been shanghaied to perform his duties aboard the *Swagman* and he was visibly terrified.

"Talk about luck," Skink said to his people. "Here we are in the middle of nowhere and we run across enough goodies to stock one of those holiday cruise liners that charge a thousand credits a minute."

He paused long enough to drink deeply and held his glass out for more, the steward racing to keep up.

His first mate snickered. "Stupid captain was lost," Raynor said. "How you can get lost because of a little old solar storm beats me. If he'd a joined a convoy he'd have been fine. But the cheap clot wanted to save a couple of credits and headed off on his own."

"Boy, was that stupid piece of drakh glad to see us," Skink chortled. "Thanking the gods that we ran across him. Said he'd reward us handsomely for saving his behind."

More laughter. More drinking. More waving of hands. Expensive cognac spilling onto the deck as the steward raced to keep up.

"Must'a soiled his drawers when we fired that shot across his bows," Raynor said. "Squealed like a little girl."

"Why, you're nothing but pirates," Raynor squeaked in imitation of the captain.

"Pirates! Eek, eek!" Skink squealed. He downed his drink and held out his glass so the steward could pour another. "'Don't shoot. Don't shoot. We'll give you anything. Anything!'"

Skink drained his glass. "Damn right he'll give us anything," he growled.

The steward missed the glass entirely in his next attempt to keep it full. Skink frowned at him. Then looked at the mess on the deck.

He snorted. "Son," he said, "if you can't do better than that we'll have to space you."

The poor man turned white. "Space me," he squeaked. "Please sir. I'm doing my best. Really I am."

"Please sir, please sir," mocked Raynor. Then: "Better clean that up before somebody slips and falls."

"Yessir. Right away, sir. Just let me get a cloth—"

"You don't need a cloth," Skink said. "Get down on your knees and lick it up like the lapdog that you are."

The steward looked horrified. "Lick it up, sir? I mean, really, that's—"

"You heard the Captain," Raynor roared, kicking the man's feet out from under him. He fell on his behind, grunting in pain.

"Start licking," Raynor said and the poor man bent down and tentatively licked the pool of booze on the floor.

"Do it like you mean it," Raynor snarled, putting his boot into the steward's butt. Sobbing, the man did as he was told. Licking and sucking the deck.

Skink leaned back, amused. He was feeling pretty good about himself. He grabbed the bottle where the steward had left it and poured himself another measure. Offered it Raynor, who accepted. Drank a little. Smacked his lips.

"Clottin' A, that's good," Raynor said.

Skink became serious. Frowning, he said, "One thing, Raynor. We've gotta watch it with that partyship. Keep the visits to a minimum until after we're done with the *Demeter*.

"Otherwise everybody's gonna get so stinking drunk they won't be able to do the job properly. We have to keep our wits about us."

"Damn straight, boss," Raynor said, downing his drink and pouring another. "Those Imperials won't go easy. Even if we do catch them with their drawers down."

Skink nodded agreement. "You've got that right," he said, holding his glass out for Raynor to pour another.

There was a retching sound. He looked down to see the steward hunched over, spewing his guts.

"Oh, man," he said. "You just made it worse, you stupid scrote."

He kicked him in the ribs, knocking him onto his belly.

"Got get a mop, or something," Skink said. "Do the job proper."

Groaning, the steward climbed to his feet and scurried away.

When he was gone, Raynor said, "You know, for a minute there I though the Princess was gonna do something stupid and try to shoot you."

Skink chuckled. "For a minute there, I thought the same thing," he said.

He knuckle-rapped his chest. There was the hollow sound of armor."That's why I came prepared. I don't want to kill her just yet. I mean, the whole thing could blow up in our faces."

"But I figured that in the end, greed would win out. That's one thing we all have in common with the trumped up princess bitch. Only difference is we just want money to burn. And she wants a crown."

"Still, we better keep a close eye on her," Raynor said.

"Sure," said Skink. "Then, when the job is done, we'll geek her. And we'll make up with Venatora by sending her the princess's pretty head on a platter."

The comm line buzzed. It was the bridge.

"Yeah?" Skink said.

"Five minutes to the Punta Royal gate, skipper," his navigator said.

"Very well," Skink said, heaving his bulk from the chair. "I'll come."

Six hours later, after jumping his ship and the others and securing the *Jubilee* so she couldn't run, he had his ambush set up. Captain Manzil and his ships were on his left flank. Barnid and his people on the right. Skink and the *Swagman* were in the middle, along with Anthofelia and her Himmenops followers.

Fehrle's *Rapier* was stationed behind the Princess. Presumably, he'd have Gregor stashed close by. Lord Wichman had his insisted that his son accompany any boarding party.

They were arrayed in a loose pincer formation that would close on the Imperial ships the moment they appeared. Then Skink would cut the *Demeter* loose from the tugs binding her to the Imperial convoy and seize her.

Unfortunately they couldn't just lash *Demeter* and her tugs to the *Swagman* and haul her away. The agworld was governed by a cutting edge AI system that someone would have to manually override. That could only be done on *Demeter* itself, so he'd have to go there, locate the entry port, then travel a hundred and fifty klicks or so to the Command Center.

Finding it should be no problem. Fehrle had assured him that Wichman had provided him with detailed maps of the agworld. The only problem, from Skink's point of view, would be if Fehrle insisted that he and his people accompany the boarding party.

Skink didn't like the idea of having Fehrle dogging him during the whole expedition, but he was paying a pretty price for the privilege, so if he insisted, there was nothing that could be done about it.

Raynor caught his attention. "Boss, what about the drones? Think we'll need to deploy them?"

Skink thought a minute. He had twenty five of the little suckers. They could zip around and patrol the area, making sure nobody slipped up on them. On the other hand, when the shooting started, they'd be the first to go and they were clotting expensive.

As if guessing his thoughts, Raynor spoke up. "Better safe than sorry, boss," he said.

"Yeah, yeah," Skink said. "Go ahead and launch them."

Soon, a silvery stream of torpedo shaped drones poured out of the *Swagman* and started patrolling the sector.

CHAPTER NINETEEN

THE GESSEL GOES BANANAS

As stealthy as the *Gessel* was, Sten didn't want to take a chance that they'd be spotted. He had the skipper park the *Gessel* in the shadows of the twin black holes that were the most notable features of the Phrygia region.

It was what had made Punta Royal so attractive to privateers. Tucked in a corner of SaganGx6, the now abandoned planet had once been infamous for its anything goes debauchery.

But that was all distant memory. These days the only thing that marked SaganGx6 was that it was named for an ancient scientist.

Now Sten and his crew were stuck in the middle of the mind-numbing task of staking out a position no one was quite sure of.

Intelligence and common sense said that Punta Royal was the most logical place for Skink and his fellow pirates to waylay the *Demeter*.

When they began their stakeout everyone was boiling with adrenaline and high spirits in anticipation of the action that could erupt at any moment.

But the excitement soon died down and the long process of waiting and watching began. The *Gessel* crewmembers found themselves with nothing to do but routine maintenance and drills. On top of that was Sten's insistence that everything be at hand when Skink and started setting up his ambush.

And so every weapon was counted, cleaned and fine-tuned to the nth degree. And he drilled them without mercy. Adding to the boredom was the fact that recreation facilities were at the barest minimum.

This was the *Gessel's* first mission and she was only a few weeks out of the drydocks. Gym equipment was sparse, and the few livees they had in the library had been screened so many times that people were ready to mutiny if they had to watch them one more time.

In short, morale-sapping boredom became as much a danger as a misfired missile.

Since their escapades on the Wolf Worlds, Sten, Alex, Doc and Ida had spent many weeks and months on mind-numbing jobs such as this and so were better prepared mentally. And even they were occasionally close to going around the bend.

But the others had yet to form the psychological calluses required for long stakeout missions.

Sten knew things were rocky, but he didn't know just how rocky they were getting until he was passing the messhall one shift and heard Alex say, "This reminds me ay th' time when me auld 'sarn't major took ower our tropical unit on the wee isle ay Borneo. An his whole platoon came doon wi' th' dreaded spotted snake disease."

The moment Sten heard the words "spotted snake" his heart gave a jump and he froze in place. Surely things hadn't gotten so bad that Kilgour was resorting to the spotted snake story. No, he was just imagining it. Alex wouldn't stoop that low.

Would he?

And then he heard Corporal Pegatha take the bait, hook line and sinker. "Spotted snake?" she said. "What the clot is a spotted snake?"

Sten raced in the messhall, shouting, "Stop right there, Kilgour. There will be no spotted snake stories on this ship. I absolutely forbid it."

"Oh, come on me wee mucker," Kilgour protested. "Surely ye won't deny uir shipmates th' vital knowledge ay hoo tae deal wi' spotted snakes."

Sten stood firm. "Nope," he said. "Not happening. There will be no spotted snakes. You'll have to kill me, first."

But before he could go on, Pegatha whirled on him. "No disrespect intended, Captain," she said, eyes blazing. "But some of us are wondering why you are being unfair to Mr. Kilgour. And to the rest of us."

Sten gobbled. "Unfair? Unfair? You don't know the meaning of the word, Corporal. Someday you'll thank me for this. I'm saving you from a fate worse than a thousand deaths."

"You already spoiled the banana story," Pegatha said. "Mr. Kilgour was just getting started telling us about that marvelous adventure. And you wouldn't let him continue."

"That's true, Sir," Mk'wolf said. "We never did hear what happened to that poor gravtrain conductor and his bananas."

Other members of the crew chimed in. They were all so bored that any cause could unite them.

"Come on, Captain," they were pleading. "Play fair."

They started chanting: "Bananas. Bananas. We want bananas." They looked like a class of kindergarten mutineers.

Faced with the prospect of a revolt, Sten backed down. "Okay," he said. "But don't say later that I didn't warn you. On your heads be it."

A broad grin splitting his mug, the Scotsman rose to his less than imposing height and cracking his thick fingers said, "Very weel. By popular demand Ah weel continue th' tale ay th' gravtrain conductor an' his escape from death by electric chair."

Turning to Sten he added, "Ain weel sae th' spotted snake fur desert." But when he saw the fierce glare on his friend's face, he changed his mind. "Okay. Mebbe it's best if we give th' spotted snake story a wee rest.

"Naw, if ye will recalect by some miracle th' gravtrain conductor escaped execution by electric chair. Nae only 'at, but he got his auld job back.

"An' soo, now he's daein' th' same thin', over and over again. Blowin' th' whistle fur arrivals an' departures. Th' gravtrains comin' an' gang. An he's getting' mighty bored like you puir wee bairns here on th' *Gessel*.

"Then one bonny day aw' th' passengers hud gotten oan board an' he blew his whistle reit quick just as a wee laddie dropped his books.

An th' little bairn went to retrieve them from th' platf'rm when Bam! he was caught atween th' doors and he was sliced in half."

Pegatha and the others gasped. "Oh, no," she cried, "not again. The poor kid."

Kilgour gave a sigh. "Och, aye, lassie, once again.

"An', once again he goes to trial an' once again he's foond guilty of murder an' once again he's sent straecht tae prison tae be electrocuted th' very next day.

"So, the pure gravtrain conductor was sittin' in cell waitin' t' die when alang came the warden, who said, 'Weel, it's yer last meal again. Whit dae ye want this time?'

"Th' gravtrain conductor says, 'weel, since yoo're askin', Ah'd loch 50 kilos ay bananas please.'

"The warden shakes his head in disbelief. 'If ye say yet wants bananas, then bananas ye'll git."

"A little later he returns wi' th' bananas an' the ravenous cheil lobs them doon his throat. Peelin' an' eatin'. Peelin' an' eatin. Until he's not chewin' any more, but just lobin' doon his throat fast as he can. Afore long he's eatin' all 50 kilos a bananas.

"Soon as he's finished they take heem to the chamber an' he's strapped in the chair. An' the electrodes are attached.

"An once again th' executioner grips the handle 'at weel end the gravconductor's life. An' he yells, 'Three... two... one...' An he yanks th' handle down.

"But to his bewilderment, nothin' happens. They check th' wires. Then the power. And they pull down the handle again. An' again nothing happens. An the warden cannae believe his peeps for the gravtrain conductor is perfectly braw.

"An' the executioner cries, 'This is an act ay god. Clearly, yet aren't meant tae die.'

"An' so once again the gravtrain conductor is released and is frae to go.

An once again, the court decrees that th' gravtrain conductor should get his auld job back.

"An' there he is, daein' th' same thin', over and over again. Blowin' th' whistle fur arrivals an' departures. Th' gravtrains comin' an' gang. Th' braw doors openin' and closin'. An he's gettin' mighty bored.

"An then one bonny day—"

At that moment every alarm on the *Gessel* began to blare. Alex stopped mid story and everybody shot Sten accusing looks, as if the alarms were his fault.

The comline came to life and it crackled with the skipper's voice. "All hands! All hands! Enemy in sight. This is not a drill.

"I repeat, this is not a drill…"

CHAPTER TWENTY

LITTLE MIKE

It was all Mahoney's fault.

At any other time in her long and distinguished career, Commander Michele Thema would have been walking on air and singing praises to the gods.

Her years of effort were finally paying off. She'd worked her way up the long ladder of succession, going from the rust buckets of her youth to commanding fighting ships. And now she'd landed the plum assignment as the handpicked leader of a special, top secret Imperial mission.

So why was her mood so far down she'd forgotten which was up?

That drakh head Mahoney had assured her that she was the personal choice of the Eternal Emperor himself to take charge of the convoy escorting a multi-trillion credit agworld named *Demeter* to its new home in the pirate-riddled frontier zone.

She was a small woman, not much over one and a half meters high and maybe 50 kilos in her bare feet. But she had more nerve than most beings twice her size and was so fierce in battle that she was known far and wide as Little Mike.

She was instinctively suspicious of Mahoney's offer and tried to pass on the job, saying that others were surely more qualified than she was for such a task.

"Don't be so humble," Ian said over dinner at a posh Prime World restaurant.

"There are only two or three people who could come even close to taking charge of this mission and bringing it to a successful conclusion."

"That's very flattering, general," she'd replied, "but I'm happy where I am now."

"Please, lass," Mahoney said. "Call me Ian."

Then he'd raised a hand summoning a waiter for another bottle of that Old World wine that must've cost a king's ransom.

Commander Thema groaned at the memory of that boozy wooing session. The scene played in her mind now so clearly it was if she'd boarded one of those time machines of fiction and was transported back to that night of soft lights, obsequious servers, exotic dishes, and heady wines.

* * * *

"Look, Ian. I've got a new ship—a top of the line battlecruiser—and a dream crew. I personally picked every swinging scrote on board from the lowest engineroom swamper to my first mate, someone I've been grooming for five years."

"That's exactly the kind of expertise we need, so it is," Ian said, filling her glass to the brim. "I can't stress the importance of this mission enough. There isn't a thing on my platter—or the Emperor's platter for that matter—that matches this in importance.

"We've already committed so many bloody resources that if it goes wrong and blows up in our gobs we'll be the laughing stock of the Empire, so we will. Our enemies will dine out for centuries bragging about the fast one they pulled on our boss."

Thema frowned. "But from what you've told me it's just a convoy assignment," she said. "A newly minted skipper could handle the job."

"It's not any old convoy job, lass," Ian pressed. He glanced around, as if checking for snoops, and leaned forward.

In a lowered voice he said, "This is the clotting Project *Demeter* we're talking about, here. We've already sunk a couple of trillion credits into the sucker, so we have."

The name definitely stirred Commander Thema's interest. She'd heard it whispered in the hallowed halls of the Naval Institute. And each time there'd been hissed warnings and nasty looks at the underling who had made so bold.

"What the clot is Project *Demeter*?" she asked. "Some kind of super weapon?"

Again, Ian made with the quick looks for snoops.

"You've hit the nail square, so you have, lass," he said. "It's the ultimate weapon. And that's why we need the likes of you, Little Mike."

Then he leaned close and whispered, "It's the stuff that armies march on, he said. "It's food, we're talking about, lass. Food."

* * * *

Now, as the HMS *Salamis* approached Punta Royal, Commander Thema was grinding her teeth in frustration.

How could she been such a fool to fall into the sweet-talking Irishman's trap? She should have said no. Capital N. Capital O. NO! Clot you, mate, and the Emerald Isle pony you rode in on. Over my dead body. No—over YOUR dead body.

"I hate this," Commander Thema said to no one in particular. "Hate it, hate it, hate it."

Jumbe, her first mate, gave her a pitying look. Glowing red eyes gleaming in his dark face.

"Maybe not so bad, bosi," he said. "We go quick like. Samu. Samu. You give order. We get out of here and go the clot home. Tomorrow have a nice drinki and forget about it. What you say, bossi?"

Thema sighed. "I know, I know," she said. "But it's just not my nature, Jumbe. This is going to be the hardest thing I've ever done in my professional life.

"Come now, bossi," Jumbe said. "What about that time on Zeta 6? The Watki had us big time surrounded. No way out, the skipper said. He wanted to run, such a coward he. You only first lieutenant then. Me, a warrant nobody. But you busted his face. Took command and then we busted the Watki. Big time, we busted them, bossi. Big time."

Thema couldn't help but laugh. She thought she'd end up in the brig over that little escapade. Instead they gave her a medal and a promotion.

But memory's joy was short lived as the reality of her present circumstances piled back on.

"Yeah, but now I've gotta eat drakh and bark at the moon, Jumbe. Gotta do what that skipper wanted to do. What the clot was that drakh head's name?"

"Rogan, he name, bossi. Captain Rogan."

"Rogan! That's it. Rogan."

She glared up at the monitor as the pirate formation came into view. She snorted at the unprofessional pincer they'd set up. Sure, there were a lot of them. She was outnumbered big time.

So what?

Any other time and place she'd have blown them all out of existence. Turned those motley group of ships into comet dust so fast it'd be like bacon through a starved Xypaca.

Instead she had to do a Rogan.

And turn tail and run.

And as Little Mike—veteran of many a bloody battle—ordered retreat she thought: "Clottin' Mahoney!"

CHAPTER TWENTY ONE

SETTING THE TRAP

Skink chortled when he saw the Imperial convoy appear on the monitor. First two little scout ships, then a medium-sized cruiser, followed by half-a-dozen squat tugs.

The 'bot controlled tugs were strategically arrayed to haul their precious cargo, using powerful tractor beams whose particles glowed eerily in the reflected light of one of Punta Royal's moons.

He knew from Fehrle's charts and specs that they in turn were controlled by the agworld's guidance system. That was also unmanned. The Imperial command ship, which had yet to appear, operated the tugs and their burden remotely. In the battle's aftermath he'd make the tugs his own and slave them to his ship, the *Swagman*.

The agworld's beauty was so astounding that it affected even Skink's calloused senses. He was caught up in the shimmering blue of *Demeter* as if it had been a warming campfire.

"Uh, you okay, Captain?" came Raynor's voice.

Skink snapped out of his reverie in time to see his main adversary come into view.

It was the battlecruiser, *Salamis*. A formidable sight. He knew from his copy of Jane's Fighting Ships that it was bristling with arms.

In ordinary circumstances he would have turned tail and run when he saw the *Salamis*. Especially since it was normally accompanied by half-a-dozen smaller warships, ranging from Avenger class to Frigates.

But the only thing accompanying the *Salamis* was an insignificant supply ship. Fehrle had said the Emperor was deliberately using a small convoy to avoid attention, but this was ridiculous. Some underling had obviously gotten his orders wrong and sent out the *Salamis* with no backup.

His hand hovered over the button that would signal his force to attack. Waiting to see if something else would appear. He checked the bank of side monitors that showed what the drones were seeing. Each screen showed emptiness. No other Imperials were coming.

Was it a trick? Something the commander of the *Salamis* had up her sleeve?

He did another drone search. The little suckers zipped about the area, checking possible ambush sites.

Nothing.

He did it again.

The drones kept beeping all clear.

Raynor spoke up: "Uh, skipper. If we don't make our move soon they might twig to us."

"Just making sure," Skink said.

He slapped the button.

"Launch," he said.

CHAPTER TWENTY TWO

THE VANISHING

ABOARD THE *SALAMIS*

Commander Thema saw the pirate fleet sweep into view. Their pincer formation was so clumsy it was ludicrous. She could have engaged them and blown them to kingdom come with little effort.

Instead: "Fire a few warning shots, Jumbe. But be careful. We don't want to scare our little pirates."

"Sure, sure, bossi," her number two said. "We shoot a little then home we go, samu, samu."

Jumbe gave the orders and the *Salamis'* offside plasma tubes spat out a weak stream of sickly yellow plasma. The engineers had restricted the flow to the barest minimum.

The target was the middle ship, an old refurbished battlewagon that Imperial spies had identified as the one captained by a notorious drakh head known as Skink.

She groaned as the plasma spattered harmlessly against the antiquated shield, running down it like the yolk of an old egg.

She said, "If I could just adjust the nozzle a bit Captain Skink would meet whatever black-hearted thing he calls his Maker."

Jumbe commiserated. "I know, bossi. I know. Make him squeal like little piggy, we would. But orders—"

"Are clotting orders," Thema finished for him. "Give him a couple of more shots to make him think we're serious."

Another feeble stream of plasma spasamed out. Then one more. Both shots were useless, except for the display of egg-yolk-yellow when they spattered against the shield.

Then the *Swagman* opened up, chainguns ripping through the void. The *Salamis'* shields easily deflected them, except for one small area which had been deliberately weakened by Thema's engineers.

ABOARD THE *SWAGMAN*

Skink's mottled green hide lit up with sparks of pleasure when he saw his guns bore through what he had been told were among the most invulnerable shields in the Empire.

The chaingun rounds hit just to the left of the cargo doors, molten metal spraying and leaving a black scorch mark.

Raynor and the other crewmembers cheered, while Skink laughed uproariously.

"Gottcha, bitch," he shouted. "Give her another go, Raynor!"

Raynor gave the order and chainguns opened up again. And once more a few of the rounds blasted through the shield.

There were more cheers and shouts of congratulations. Raynor pounded Skink on the back.

"We're gettin' them, Captain, and we're gettin' them good," he cried.

No one noticed that the penetrating bullets hit the same area as before and with practically no effect. Once again the *Salamis* fired and once again, the weak stream of plasma did little damage to the *Swagman*.

Skink's euphoria was such that he thought he'd be able to destroy a major Imperial warship with impunity.

"Launch the particle cannon, Raynor," he cried. "Let's hit 'em with the big stuff."

Raynor relayed the order and there was a jolt as the bolts holding the big particle cannon in place fired and the restraints dropped away.

The grin on Skink's face widened to the size of a quarter moon, his big eyeteeth glittering in the overhead lights.

"Oh, this is gonna be good," he chortled. "This is gonna be really, really good."

ABOARD THE *SALAMIS*

"Watch it, bossi," Jumbe cried. "We got big trouble coming on."

Thema cursed when she saw the particle cannon. In an actual one-on-one confrontation it would be only a minor threat. With her guns and shielding the cannon would need to be accompanied with better ships than the pirates had at their command to do any serious damage.

But Mahoney had warned her that the particle cannon had been booby trapped by a Mantis team early in the game. And that if the cannon opened up it would explode with such force that it would destroy all the pirate ships in its vicinity.

"Maybe I'm losing what little is left of my wits, Ian," she'd said. "But wouldn't that be a good thing."

"Not in this case, lass," Ian had replied. "If that happens it would spoil our game. So if they come at you with the cannon cut and run, lass. Cut and run."

And so—against all her instincts and pride—that is what she did.

Commander Thema, holder of the Imperial Legion Of Honor, veteran of countless wars and skirmishes, cut and ran.

ABOARD THE *SWAGMAN*

Skink blinked in amazement as the *Salamis* vanished right before his eyes.

"Wha-what happened?" he said.

"She's gone, Captain," an equally amazed Raynor said. "The *Salamis* is gone."

"Well, I can clotting see that, can't I?" Skink roared. "I've got clotting eyes in my clotting face, don't I?"

Raynor jumped back as he thrust his ugly face forward, the bulging turret eyes burning with anger.

"What I clotting want to know is where they clotting went."

Panic flickered.

He looked over at the bank of monitors hooked to the drones.

Nothing.

Nothing.

Clotting nothing!

Unconsciously he glanced over his shoulder, as if the ship could be in the same room.

Then he looked back at the main monitor. The tugs were still moving along, mindlessly performing their little 'bot task of towing the *Demeter*.

He stared at the scene, transfixed. Eventually, one by one, the tugs stopped. Soon the *Demeter* was hanging in space, beautiful and beckoning with promises of fabulous wealth.

The only conclusion: The Imperials must have fled.

Raynor broke in. "Uh, skipper, what do we do now?"

Skink waved, shutting him up. The problem was that deep inside he never really expected success. Especially not success that came so easily.

Then the com hookup to Fehrle buzzed. Absently, Skink keyed in and Fehrle's holo form swam into view.

He wore an uncharacteristic smile.

"Congratulations, Captain," he said. "It looks like all your hard work paid off."

Skink blinked, as if suddenly coming awake. "Uh, ye-yeah," he stuttered. "It did, didn't it."

"What next, Captain?" Fehrle said, prodding the bemused pirate into action.

"Oh, well... uh... we board the *Demeter* just like we planned."

"Excellent," Fehrle said. He paused a moment, then added, "There will be a slight change of plans on my end," he said.

Skink frowned. What was this Tahn devil up to now? "Yes, my Lord?"

"I'm going to retire to our rendezvous point so I can report fully and completely to my colleagues and superiors."

Skink was relieved to hear that. Last thing he needed was that drakh head second-guessing his every move.

"But I require you to take charge of Lord Wichman's son, Gregor," Fehrle said. "He'll want to see what is happening so he can report to his father later on."

Skink blinked. He didn't want or need that little piece of drakh hanging around. But if it meant he'd be free of Fehrle so be it.

"No problem, my Lord," he said. "Send him over."

"Good," Fehrle said. "He'll be accompanied by his female companion. She is more of a therapist, actually. The young man has been ill."

Skink nodded. "Sure, sure," he said. "One more body won't be any trouble."

"Thank you for a magnificent job thus far," Fehrle said.

Skink preened a little from this rare and unexpected praise.

Fehrle's smile vanished. His eyes bored into Skink.

"Just make sure that you don't spoil your success now," he said.

"You know full well that the Imperials will be back within a few days with reinforcements. So you had best get busy."

"I was thinking the same thing, my Lord," Skink said. "We'll get right on it. I don't see any difficulty. There's nobody on *Demeter* to stop us. It's all 'bot controlled."

"Very well," Fehrle said. Then his tone and manner changed, as he shed his diplomatic cloak. "Now I want to burn what I have to say into that little thing you call a brain."

Skink bristled at this. But there was nothing he could do but to take it.

Fehrle said, "From experience, beings like you and your piratical colleagues tend to be your own worst enemies. A recent example is your stupid decision to stop in the middle of the operation to seize a party ship."

Skink's mottle green coloring turned a deeper shade of green. "There was no delay," he said. "Besides, it practically fell in our hands."

"It was a ridiculous loss of focus," Fehrle said. "Plus, you now have the temptation of all that booze and sex workers."

"You don't have to worry about us," Skink said, insulted. "We know there is a right time and place for everything. Besides that, when we're done with *Demeter* we don't have to worry about drawing attention to ourselves on one of those rec worlds. We've got our own partyship to let off steam."

"See that you keep it that way," Fehrle said. "Tell your fellow captains to mind the business at hand. And to put the partyship off limits for everyone."

"Already did that," Skink lied. At that moment there were probably fifty or sixty pirates enjoying the pleasure of the *Jubilee*.

"Very well," Fehrle said, in tones that showed thought every clotting word out of Skink's mouth had been pure drakh.

"Now, listen to me closely, Skink. I want *Demeter* delivered to me as agreed," Fehrle continued. A pause for effect, then: "No ifs, ands, or buts. Do you understand me , Captain?"

Skink straightened. "Yes. Yes I do. I understand completely."

"Good," Fehrle said. "Because if you fail me in this matter you will rue the day that your mother gave birth to your stinking hide."

And then he was gone.

Skink breathed a sigh of relief. Turned to Raynor, who was standing there with his mouth open. Humiliated by Fehrle, Skink badly wanted to rip that sagging fool's jaw off with one of his claws.

"You heard the man," he snapped. "Get on the horn to Manzil and Barnid and tell them to get their people off the *Jubilee* and back where they belong. Same with our people. But leave a good guard."

"Su-su-sure, Skink. Sure." Raynor stuttered. "Right away."

ABOARD THE *GUNAKADA*

Anthofelia had hung back in the attack on the *Salamis*. Her plan was to let Skink and the pirates test their mettle against the Imperials.

If they succeeded, she would be more than happy to join in the glory and riches.

If they failed, she'd take to her heels and run. She already had a place picked out where she could hide and nurture her small force for when Venatora came for her. And she had no doubt that the Himmenops queen would be hunting for her head.

She was thrilled when Skink's guns had penetrated *Salamis'* armor. Laughed along with Nalene and the rest of her crew, when the Imperial commander's feeble efforts failed so miserably.

Even then, she half expected a devastating counter from the Imperials. All her life she'd heard just how invulnerable the Imperial forces were.

The Eternal Emperor was the monster under the bed the creche mothers used to frightened disobedient little girls. He was the evil god whose handsome face hid his malevolent intent.

He was the reason the Himmenops were in hiding, making their living by scooping up his crumbs and scurrying for cover like little rodents.

Then all those stories were turned on their head when the *Salamis* fled the scene of battle, disappearing into the star jump void.

"Did you see that, Nalene?" she cried. "They ran! They clotting ran!"

Nalene laughed. "We didn't even have to fire a shot," she said.

Anthofelia rubbed her hands together. "Now all we have to do is take possession of the prize."

"We have to be extra careful, Princess," her navigator, Yatola said. "Skink will try to cheat us."

"I'm aware of that," Anthofelia said. "But when all this is over with, he's going to need us as a foil against Venatora. He can't afford to have the Himmenops as enemies."

Nalene and Yatola looked at their princess with glowing, hero worship eyes. And they both trembled with lust. The blood red and gold Sharkwire tattoos on their biceps glowed under the ceiling lights.

"Soon," Yatola said, voice husky and low, "you will be our queen."

Anthofelia smiled, but did not reply. In her heart of hearts she knew what she was seeing was Father Huber's work. And nothing more.

Since the mission started he had been gradually increasing her pheromone output until it was dangerously in the red.

"We must keep them under your thrall so completely that there is no chance Venatora can sway them," he'd said.

"But Father," she'd protested, "all my women are my sworn acolytes. They worship me like a goddess."

She was shocked when her comment drew raucous laughter from Huber. And what he went on to say and do was now seared into memory so deeply that whenever she recalled the words that followed it was if they were happening now—in real time—Instead of several days before.

Drawing herself up to her full regal height, she retorted: "How dare you laugh at me? I am royal born. And a princess. Fated to lead my people"

"Nonsense," Huber said in a tone so denigrating that it shocked her. "They are slaves to biology, nothing more. Don't fool yourself by imagining that you are a great leader."

"But Venatora—" she began, but Huber cut her off. "Get this through your pretty head. You are not Venatora. And you never will be. Yes, she uses her biology to keep her women in line. But with her it is natural. She possesses more pheromonal powers than any other queen in the history of the Himmenops.

"To be sure, Father Raggio enhances those powers, but only a little and only when she is weary and her energy is flagging. She is a true queen, Anthofelia. Something you are not."

Shocked as she was, Anthofelia began to get angry. "If that's true, then why are you even bothering with me? Why aren't you running to Venatora and begging her forgiveness?"

Father Huber laughed. "Because I can't control Venatora, girl," he said. "For some years now the other fathers and I have been along for the ride. Nothing more. Sure, she takes advice, especially from that toady Raggio. But it's always been Venatora's show. And none other.

"When I found you in your creche I had been alerted by a nurse in my employ that you had higher levels of natural pheromones than most Himmenops. It wasn't much. Nothing like Venatora. But I saw my chance to finally take control and to assume the leadership of the Fathers. So I took charge of your upbringing and your biological care."

Anthofelia broke down. "You treat me as if I am nothing," she wailed. "Like I was a nobody, instead of royally born."

"You *are* nothing," Huber growled. "Nothing except for an interesting experiment in a petri dish that worked better than I'd supposed.

"Now, get yourself together, woman. And for god's sake quit fooling yourself that you are better than you truly are.

"Because if you fail, you will be cast out. Excommunicated. Then killed.

"Do you understand me, Anthofelia?"

She nodded and wiped her eyes.

"I understand," she said. But inside she thought—if I fail, I won't be the only one to suffer that fate.

Nalene spoke up, pulling her back from that awful memory.

"Princess?" she said. "Are you all right?"

Anthofelia covered her mouth and coughed. "Yes," she said. "I'm fine."

"What are your orders, Ma'am?" Yatola asked.

Anthofelia hesitated. Her confidence shaken.

And then there was a buzz in her ear and that awful voice of Father Huber intruded. "Be quick, woman," he said. "It is an absolute necessity that we be part of Skink's boarding operation."

As if in anticipation the comline buzzed.

It was Skink.

ABOARD THE *TAKEO*

"That was unexpected, Majesty," Clew said. She scratched her graying locks. "I've never heard of that sort of behavior exhibited by an Imperial battleship."

Venatora was just as puzzled. "Nor I," she said. "Do you suppose it was some kind of a malfunction—or a trick?"

"In either case," Clew said, "they are sure to be back with reinforcements. If they don't wait and court martial the commander first."

Thinking of her encounters with Sten and his fighters Venatora was certain that the Imperials would be back.

"They'll return—of that I have no doubt," she said. "But bureaucracy will slow them down. First, the commander will have to report to her superiors. Then, whether she's removed from duty or not, they'll still have to discuss the situation with the various levels of brass. Then, after assessing the matter, they'll have to gather a sufficient number of ships to take on the pirates."

"That might cause even more of a delay, Your Highness," Marta said. "Our spies in Fort Chinen have told us that there aren't that many Imperial ships in the region and those are stretched pretty thin."

Venatora chewed on that a minute, then made up her mind. She was an ardent gambler, but also an intelligent one. Right now the odds seemed to be weighed in her favor.

"If we don't dally, we have more than enough time to do this," she said. "Gather up our very best warriors, Nalene. Twenty should suffice. Make sure we have supplies and ammunition for five or six cycles."

She turned to Palsonia. "We'll use the cutter. It has jump drive so if the drakh really hits the fan we can make our way back home on it."

"I anticipated something like this," Palsonia said. "So our own little *Royal Fancy* is already fueled and her computers are fired up. We can leave in thirty minutes."

"Thank you, Palsonia," Venatora said.

"Yes, Majesty," Palsonia said and started away.

She paused. The next part was going to be difficult. But Father Raggio had been insistent. As always, however, his logic was impeccable. Her overall duty was to ensure the survival of the Himmenops.

Finally, she said:"One other thing, Palsonia. Who in your judgment is our best navigator? After you, of course?"

Without hesitation, Palsonia said, "Joolie. My number two. She's also levelheaded and doesn't panic under pressure. In fact, the crazier it get, the calmer she becomes."

"Call her," Venatora said.

A few minutes later Joolie was standing before her. She was tall with auburn hair and penetrating eyes.

"Yes, Majesty?" Joolie said, voice trembling. She'd never been called before her queen before and didn't know what to expect.

Venatora said, "Joolie I am about to place a tremendous burden on your shoulders."

Joolie straightened. To Venatora's delight her nervousness had vanished. Now she was the portrait of calm confidence.

"What do you require of me, Majesty?" she asked.

Without preamble, Venatora said, "The moment we depart I want you to assume command of the *Takeo*."

Joolie was so surprised, she took a step back. And she looked disappointed. Venatora remembered that she had been on the select list of warriors who were supposed to accompany Venatora on the *Demeter* expedition.

"But, ma'am. You need me," Joolie pleaded. "I'd never forgive myself if something happened to you and I wasn't there to prevent it."

Venatora held up a hand, stopping her. "There's more, Joolie," she said. "After we leave, I want you to immediately return home without us."

Joolie gasped. Marta, Palsonia and Clew were equally aghast. Staring at her with unbelieving eyes.

"Pardon, ma'am," Joolie said. "But that makes no sense. You'll be stranded."

"Far from it," Venatora said. "After we kill Skink and Anthofelia I'll slave *Demeter* and her tugs to the cutter and jump home.

"Meanwhile, I want you to prepare our people at home for an all out assault. The Tahn won't forgive us for stealing their thunder and are sure to seek revenge. As will our former pirate friends.

"As for the Emperor—I don't know how he'll react. He's much more cunning than the others. He may wait for an opening. Or he might even send a fleet.

"Whatever the case we have to be ready to hold them off and find ourselves a new home. Our days in the Possnet Sector are over. I have an excellent candidate for a new home.

"With *Demeter* supplying all our needs for food and drink we will finally be free from outsiders. And our days as pirates will be over."

When she was done not a word was spoken. The command center was so silent she could hear her helmswoman's fingers move over the control board.

She could also feel an up-swelling of intense love and respect. For a change it was not induced by her hormonal powers. It was as pure and unadulterated as any she had ever felt before.

Tears were running down the cheeks of her companions.

"Thank you, Majesty," she said. "I won't fail you."

"I know you won't," Venatora said.

Overcome by emotion, Joolie hurried away. Venatora turned back to the others.

"Thirty minutes, Palsonia," she said.

Palsonia saluted, like the soldier she was.

"Yes, Majesty," she said and hurried away.

CHAPTER TWENTY THREE

THE MICKEY

ABOARD THE *GESSEL*

"I've always had a soft spot for pirates," Ida said, as she adjusted the image on the monitor and it zoomed in on Venatora's ship.

"Ah kin why," Kilgour said. "Yoo're practically a clottin' thief yerself."

Ida sniffed. "I don't steal. I merely move certain things from the overstuffed pockets of greedy beings into the empty pockets of more deserving people. You three have certainly benefited from my ways."

Kilgour grimaced at the well-aimed blow. She'd been more than generous with her teammates, freely sharing the fruits of her "investments."

Still, they all enjoyed the repartee, picking on one another's perceived weaknesses and faults.

Ida shrugged. She said, "Besides, even if I was stealing I'm a Rom. What they used to call Gypsies. And it's an historical fact that we have a God-given right to steal."

Doc snorted. "Why do you humans insist on bringing deities into every conversation? Is there something in your genetic makeup that insists on having a big bearded old man in the sky watching over everything?"

"Who are you to talk, Doc?" Ida sneered. "Your entire species has survived by conning people into thinking you are warm and cuddly teddy bears, when in fact you are nothing but vicious little blood-sucking vampires who hate every cognizant being in the Universe."

"At least I don't claim that God made me do it," Doc retorted. "For a Blyrchynaus the taking of blood is a species imperative."

Sten said, "Ida, no offense, but I never did understand why the Rom people believe some god gave them the right to steal."

Ida said, "I learned the story at my mother's knee. And she was told by her mother and so on and so forth all the way back in time to the days on ancient Earth when the Romans ruled the world.

"Legend has it that the son of a little known deity was being punished for rabble-rousing and offending the local priesthood. To make an example of him, the Romans nailed him to a wooden cross with three copper nails.

One for each hand and one for the feet. There was supposed to be a fourth nail that would be driven through his heart, but a young gypsy lass took pity on the guy and stole that nail. For that act of charity, the father figure gave her and all her kin the right to steal without fear of sin until the end of time, or Judgment Day, whichever came first."

Sten frowned at Ida. "And you actually believe that tale."

Ida shrugged. "More than likely the girl stole the nail for the copper. It was a valuable commodity in those days. Even so, it makes a pretty story."

She glared at Doc. "Better than anything that hemoglobin horror has to offer."

Ida caught something out of the corner of her eye.

"What's this?" she said. They all turned to see and Sten's heart gave a bump.

"Looks like Venatora is sending her own landing party to *Demeter*," Ida said.

A moment later they saw the *Takeo* shift its position. It moved slightly forward and then vanished, leaving a rainbow of star-jumping colors in its wake.

"Wonder what's 'at aw abit?" Alex said. "Is she leavin' 'er landin' party behin'?"

"Not likely," Sten said. "Venatora leads from the front. And that little cutter has its own star drive. My bet is that she's heading for *Demeter* and got the *Takeo* out of harm's way in case the *Salamis* comes back."

"That's my call," Ida said. "That woman has a bigger sack of scrotes than a herd of East Taurus bulls."

"Speaking of which," Sten said. "Give Commander Thema a shout. Time for a bit of revenge, Little Mike style."

He indicated the little partyship floating in the middle of the pirate fleet.

"But warn her that there are innocents in the line of fire," he said.

"Hang on a mo," Ida said. "I've been poking around the *Jubilee's* comcenter. Pretty sure I can hack into her and warn the captain, without tipping our hand."

"Do that," Sten said.

ABOARD THE *JUBILEE*

Captain Sully cut off the comm and glanced around. The pirates onboard were too busy partaking of the pleasure of the ship to have witnessed his conversation with the woman who had identified herself as an Imperial spy.

In the main rec hall twenty some pirates—a so-called skeleton crew to supposedly maintain ship security—were barely in control of themselves.

Instead of working, they were shouting and dancing and pawing the joyboys and joygirls. Even the 'bot servers were mauled as if they were living beings. What made matters worse was that the *Jubilee's* security personnel had been locked in the hold so there was no one to keep the pirate's appetite for violence in check.

Thankfully, Sully's people were old hands at the pleasure game and had so far managed to avoid any serious injuries.

Sully was a grizzled ship's captain with years of experience, mostly as a freighter captain. He'd reluctantly taken the job on the *Jubilee* because the company he'd worked for went bankrupt and he had a large family to feed. He despised the type of passengers who frequented partyships, and was prepared to think the same of the crew.

To his surprise most of them were generous, good-humored, highly intelligent beings, whose choice of careers were limited by the circumstances of life. Also, tips far outweighed wages as a source of income and several had confessed to Sully that always having ready cash at hand was as addictive as any narcotic.

He caught the eye of the ship's emcee—Charly Chine—and tipped him the wink. Charly came sidling over. He was tall—even for a Pintar—two-and-a half meters high and so thin he looked like a stiff breeze would blow him over. His form was humanoid, with long muscular tentacles instead of arms. He had a wide, lipless mouth and his eyes were black with green, quarter moon pupils.

Despite his almost skeletal figure he was tremendously strong. And as he moved toward Sully two pirates who were wrestling over a joygirl slammed into him.

Charly caught them by the waist and effortlessly lifted them and pulled them apart. He freed the joygirl and got the burly pirates back on their feet. It was done so smoothly that the men barely noticed. They looked blankly around, grinned at one another and raced to the bar to slop down more drinks.

Finally, Charly was close enough for a whispered conversation.

"It's getting pretty bad, boss," he said. "They're pouring it down by the barrel. If they get any drunker they'll lose all control. I've already talked one smeg brain out of carving his initials on Burthagene."

"Never mind that," Sully said. "Looks like we're about to be rescued by the cavalry."

And then he went on to tell him about his conversation with Ida. Charly's eyes and smile grew wider as Sully spoke.

"They asked if we could slip these drakh heads some Mickeys so they'll be out of action when the time comes."

"No problem, boss," Charly said. "I'll tell the others and get some kind of drinking game going."

"Beautiful," Sully said. "I've got to have a few words with the helmsman and navigator and we should be all set."

And so the captain and his emcee went to war with the weapons they knew best—entertainment.

After a whispered conversation with the pleasure personnel, Charly took up position at his media center, played with a few dials, then hit it.

There was a loud drum roll that reverberated throughout the ship and he bellowed:

"Ladies and gentlebeings… Pirates of all ages… it's show time aboard the *Jubilee!*"

All the joyboys and joygirls shrieked with glee and applauded as music swelled, colorful lights flashed and erotic images played over the walls and deck.

The pirates were dumbfounded at first. Some were even suspicious, their hands going to belted weapons.

But the pleasure workers rushed to embrace them, tickling and giggling and filling their hands with luscious flesh instead of knives and guns.

The bar 'bots went into high gear, spiking drinks with knockout drops and racing to ply every pirate with drink.

Meanwhile, Sully huddled with his navigator and helmsman. They made the necessary calculations, primed the computers and kept their eyes on the central monitor.

"What exactly are we waiting for, Captain?" the navigator asked.

"All that Ida woman said was to watch for a big clotting ship, called the *Salamis*."

ABOARD THE *SALAMIS*

Command Thema grinned when Sten's message came through.

"About clotting time," she said.

"Jumbe, set a course for the Punta Royal jump gate. We're going to kick some pirate behind."

CHAPTER TWENTY FOUR

LITTLE MIKE COMES ROARING BACK

ABOARD THE *BLADE/SHARK*

"You know me, Manzil," Barnid said, "I'm not one to talk behind a shipmate's back, but I don't like this setup one clottin' bit. Skink's out there doin' who knows what while we sit here diddlin' around."

"Been thinkin' the same thing me own self," Manzil said. When it comes to cuttin' up loot, Skink's been known to put his thumb on the scales."

"He claims it's to cover expenses for Tortooga," Barnid said, "but we already kick in fifteen percent for that."

The two captains were talking via a holo hookup, looking as if they were sitting side by side in their command centers. Their first mates, Ranzid and Orkney hovered nearby, supposedly keeping an eye on the monitors, but mainly keeping their captains' glasses full, as well as their own as they big-eared the conversation.

"Thing that ticks me off the clottin' most," Barnid said, "is that old Crocface refused to take any of our crew along. Said his guys were more experienced."

"He's full of drakh," Manzil said. "I'd put any of my people against his any day, any time and any place."

"You got that right, brother," Barnid said, so indignant that he spilled his drink and his first mate had to hurry to top up the glass again.

"We've been piratin' as long as Skink," he continued, "and have boarded as many ships and got our hands on just as much loot as he ever has."

Manzil raised a finger. "Except when Captain Crocface gets his claws on the loot first," he said. "Then it never seems to be as much as we figured."

Barnid stirred in his seat. "That is so clottin' true," he said. "Remember that time when we jumped that convoy in the Hanilla Sector and—"

At that moment, Ranzid—Barnid's first mate—stepped back, as if he'd been hit in the gut.

"Holy clot," he said, "where'd that come from?"

They all looked up at their monitors and were nearly blown out of their boots when they saw the *Salamis* filling the screens. Rushing down on them full speed, weapons bristling, silvery flak shooting out of her bows.

The two captains hit their alarm buttons at the same time. Horns shrilled and weapons' officers bellowed, "All hands! All hands!"

Just before his holo image vanished, Manzil cried, "Barnid! Remember, you've got the particle cannon!"

For a moment Barnid just stared at the space where Manzil had been. Eyes glazed over with booze. He shook himself, adrenalin battling the amount of narcotics-laced booze he'd taken on.

"Oh, yeah," he said. "The particle cannon. Gotta get the particle cannon."

He looked up at Ranzid, who was almost as drunk as his captain.

"You know how to run that thing, Ranzid?"

Ranzid looked up at the monitor again. So scared that he was about to foul his drawers.

"Uh, I think so, boss."

"Well, get to it, man," Barnid shouted.

Ranzid raced from the room, while Barnid called up his weapons board.

ABOARD THE *JUBILEE*

The pirates were all either passed out, or on their knees spewing their guts. Joyboys and joygirls were loading the unconscious ones onto gravskids to transport them to a secure hold.

Meanwhile, Charly moved from one still conscious pirate to another, smacking them on their heads with the balled up ends of his tentacles. At the same time the bar 'bots were swabbing the decks, cleaning up the reeking mess the pirates had left behind.

In the command center Sully was huddled with his navigator and helmsman, eyes on the main monitor. Waiting and praying for the promised signal.

All of a sudden the magnificent sight of an Imperial warship filled the screen.

"It's the *Salamis*," Sully cried. "Just like Ida said."

Then he slapped his helmsman on the back. "Hit it, Arney," he said.

And Arney hit it.

If any of the pirate captains had been watching their secondary screens they would have seen the *Jubilee* drop from her position. Then race away, full speed.

ABOARD THE *SALAMIS*

Normally, Commander Thema took no pleasure in killing her fellow beings. Her every molecule was imbued with cold, calculated professionalism.

But now for the first time in her long and hallowed career, she took the greatest pleasure when she said: "Fire!

A split second later the first missile shot out of its tube and sped toward the pirate fleet. A moment later a dozen more followed.

She thrilled as that first missile exploded against an enemy shield. Then another. And another. The shields were giving away. Cracking.

Thema slammed her fist on the board.

"Hit 'em again," she chortled. "More! More!"

And her weapons officer gave her more.

ABOARD THE *BLADE*

Captain Barnid checked the port monitor and saw a suited up Ranzid exit the ship and head for the particle cannon, which Skink's crew had moved to his ship. It was just beneath the vessel, held by sturdy clamps.

Another missile barrage hit his shield and the force was so great that it rocked the ship, nearly throwing Barnid to the deck.

He steadied himself, then watched, terror-stricken, as Ranzid locked his magboots onto the body of the particle cannon and slowly made his way to the pilot's canopy.

Barnid wanted to scream for Ranzid to hurry, for clot's sake, but in his haste Ranzid neglected to set up a com link.

Not that it would do any good. Although Barnid was sweating bullets, he knew Ranzid was going as fast he could, lifting up one magboot after another and setting down, as if moving through thick mud.

Finally, he got to the canopy. Agonizing minutes were lost as he fumbled with the locks. Barnid groaned when he saw Ranzid lose the locking tool and it drifted away on its tether.

Ranzid struggled to reel it in, then finally caught it, swiveled back to the canopy and fumbled with the locking mechanism. It popped open and Ranzid pulled himself inside.

More precious minutes were lost as Ranzid fumbled with unfamiliar controls and the *Salamis* continued hammering the pirate fleet.

ABOARD THE *SHARK*

The shields protecting Manzil and his ships cracked first. A missile got through the silvery flak intact and hit the *Shark,* ripping an enormous hole in her guts.

Manzil was slammed against his comcenter, then crashed to the floor, his head smashing against a chair.

He fell to his hands and knees, dazed. Blood pouring from the wound in his scalp.

Desperately he looked up at the monitor, praying that Barnid had gotten the particle cannon operational.

Manzil cursed Skink for refusing to give him, or any of the other captains more than a cursory look at the cannon and its controls.

Orkney tried to help him to his feet, but Manzil slapped his hands away.

"I wanna see, dammit," he shouted.

Then he spotted one of Manzil's people unlock the canopy and hoist himself inside.

"It's Ranzid," Orkney said. "He got more time on that particle cannon than any of us."

"Well, thank his lordship for no favors what-so-clottin-ever," Barnid said.

Manzil had never been a praying man, but now he wished he'd paid more attention to his mother's bedtime ritual.

Then he saw puffs of air as explosive bolts fired and the straps holding the cannon in place released their grip.

A moment later the cannon was free and moving slowly away.

"God," he moaned. "God. God. God. God."

ABOARD THE *SALAMIS*

Commander Thema smiled as she saw the particle cannon head for her ship. The pirates were all bunched up where the *Jubilee* had been a few minutes before. But she wanted them closer together.

What she was looking for was the ultimate Cluster Clot.

And she was getting it.

"Hit them with the chainguns," Thema ordered Jumbe. "Squeeze them in from the sides."

"Gotcha, bossi," Jumbe chortled. "We give it to 'em big time."

The chainguns chewed up the smaller ships on the edges of the pirate fleet. Instinctively, the captains of the other ships moved closer together in a fruitless effort to escape the withering fire.

"Now show them our behind," she ordered.

"Oh, I love it, bossi," Jumbe said, turning the ship about. "It's so pretty too."

ABOARD THE *PARTICLE CANNON*

Ranzid sweated over unfamiliar controls. Incoming missile fire rattled his senses as his gloved hands moved unsurely from one bank of dials and buttons to another.

It was a major victory when he got the cannon to start moving forward. Through the canopy he had a clear view of the approaching Imperial ship.

His heart leaped in joy when the ship turned, presenting its stern to the cannon.

Ranzid pinged the ship and to his supreme delight the echo showed a great absence of any sort of shield whatsoever.

"The bitch doesn't know I'm here," he chortled, his right hand going to the firing trigger.

In a minute it would be over. The cannon would rip the *Salamis* to pieces. He'd be many times a hero. His name would be sung at the drunken parties on Tortooga for years to come. Visions of bonuses danced in his head. Skink would have to give him a bigger share.

Clot, he'd be able to buy his own captaincy and tell Barnid to stick his second-mate's job where the sun don't shine.

Laughing, he jabbed a finger at the firing trigger.

"Here it comes," he chortled. "A big damned kaboom!"

ABOARD THE *SALAMIS*

"Oh, what a joke," Commander Thema chuckled, as the particle cannon spit a shower of harmless sparks. "What a glorious joke."

"I don't see the funny, bossi," Jumbe said.

"Just wait, Jumbe," Thema advised. "Just wait."

ABOARD THE *PARTICLE CANNON*

Ranzid cursed at the cannon's feeble effort. In his ear Barnid was shouting, "Come on, you idiot! Come on!"

"For drakh's sake," Ranzid said under his breath. "I'm trying. I'm trying."

He dialed the cannon to its greatest force level, sighted on the *Salamis* and hit the trigger.

"Now kaboom me, for clot's sake," he shouted.

ABOARD THE *SALAMIS*

Thema stepped back from the monitor, hands going to her face, as the cannon went nova. The flare of white light was so intense that it burned her retinas.

"Oh, bossi," Jumbe said. "Lookee that!"

Thema pulled her hands away and where the particle cannon and the entire fleet of ships that surrounded it had been was now a gigantic many-colored cloud of particles shooting away into uttermost space.

"Can you believe that?" Thema said. "In all my days I've never seen…"

ABOARD THE *GESSEL*

The Mantis A-Team looked on in amazement as the entire pirate fleet turned into star dust.

"Loch the bloke said oan 'at old livee—ah loove it when a plan comes together," Kilgour chortled.

Sten turned to his friends. "Now for the hard part," he said. "On to *Demeter*."

"I have everything loaded and ready to go," Mk'wolf said.

"I want Ripley and Lancer with us," Sten aid. "I have a feeling we made need some expert trackers."

Corporals Ripley and Lancers were two Suzdals, canine-like refugees from the always contentious Altaic Cluster.

"Do you still want me and Doc to supervise from here?" Ida asked. "I wouldn't mind a little exercise."

"Leave me out of it," Doc said, wrinkling his button nose in disgust. "Nothing but vegetable matter down there."

"From my understanding," Sten said, "there's all kinds of wildlife on *Demeter*. Everything from birds and insects to deer and big cats. And then there are all the herd animals. Cattle, sheep…"

"Stop it," Doc said. "You're making me hungry. A little venison tartare will go very well just about now."

Alex laughed. "If there's onie left ower I'll bring ye backa wee gram ay two," he said.

The red line buzzed.

"That can't be good," Ida said. "It's Mahoney."

She palmed a button and a holo image of Mahoney appeared.

Without preamble Ian said, "We're got ourselves a smallish problem, lads and lassie, so we do."

Sten grimaced. In his experience there was no such thing as a "smallish" Mahoney problem.

But he only shrugged and said, "What's up, boss?"

"An AI difficulty has popped up at the agworld proving grounds," he said.

Sten and the other looked at each other. This could not be good news. Problems with artificial intelligence in modern times were rare. But when they occurred they were almost never easily solvable and were frequently catastrophic.

"And what exactly would that difficulty, be, General?" Doc asked.

"It seems they're going rogue on us," Mahoney said. "After a period of time, just when everything seems settled in and all the biological activity is up to speed, some of the critters and the AI mainframe start communicating with each other in earnest. And then they bond together for self protection."

"How the clot is that possible?" Sten asked. The others were as equally confounded.

"Apparently it starts with the trees," Mahoney said.

They just all goggled at him. "Trees?"

Mahoney raised at hand. "I'm just a mere soldier boy, so I am," he said. "This is all a bit above me. The bio boyos are telling us it started with forests way back on old Earth. The trees communicate with each other, through what the science guys call—" He raised a hand. "... And I swear I'm not joking... They call it the Wood Wide Network."

Only Doc was nonplussed. He nodded, catching on immediately.

"This isn't limited to just life from old Earth," Doc said. "It's a phenomenon natural to all planetary systems with tree-like organisms. It has to do with the roots and fibers they send out to communicate with other trees.

"They warn each other about insect attacks and other blights. In a well-developed forest they even feed each other, and share chemicals to ward off disease and insects."

Mahoney said, "That's the gist of it, near as I can understand the problem. Except in our case it ends up involving not just trees—but all plant life. Eventually, they join up with the AI mainframe to really wreak havoc. And now there are even reports that the animals are getting involved. Don't ask me how. It's just so."

"What do they do that has everyone so upset?" Sten asked.

"They attack anything they come to believe is a threat, is what they do," Mahoney said. "Only only one person has been killed at this point. But there have been a lot of injuries and any number of close calls."

Sten sighed. "I suppose that's the end of the *Demeter* Project," he said.

In every case Sten had heard of the AI project was scrapped and everything was not just destroyed, but burned to a molecular crisp before the problem spread.

"It hasn't been decided yet," Mahoney said. "It doesn't happen in every instance. At least not yet. Besides, it's such a grand idea. Fresh, infinitely transportable food for those that need it most."

"Put another way," Sten said, "while we're down there dealing with pirates and nasty warrior women the little agworld might try to bite us as well."

"That's the size of it," Mahoney said.

Ida broke in. "Pity we can't sit back and let *Demeter* do the job for us. Because she may—or may not—go rogue."

Mahoney nodded. "The purpose of this mission remains unchanged..." And his eyes cut to Sten. "Except for yourselves, no one is to leave *Demeter* alive."

Inwardly Sten gulped. Outwardly, his features remained blank.

"Yessir," he said.

And Mahoney was gone.

Everyone was silent. Kilgour squeezed Sten's shoulder.

"Sorry, mate," he said.

Sten shrugged. "It is what it is," he said.

But already his mental wheels were turning.

CHAPTER TWENTY FIVE

THE BLUE DIAMOND

Sten's first close up view of *Demeter* was so spectacular that he almost lost the ability to focus on the task before him.

The others must have felt the same way, for the usual pre-mission banter cut off in mid insult.

The little agworld reminded Sten of a ring he saw on the finger of a noblewoman at Parral's royal court during his sojourn on the Wolf Worlds.

She had worn a diamond of incomparable beauty. Ida told him later that it was a rare blue diamond. The gem was as blue as the deepest tropical sea, with hints of emerald green flowing through it. It was so beautiful that at the time it took all of Sten's willpower to not approach the woman for a closer look. If he had made so bold, one of Parral's bravos would have slit his throat at the first opportunity.

Demeter was that same blue diamond again, but magnified thousands of times over. It was a deep blue, like the fabulous inland sea of Caribola, where he and Alex had partied after one of their early missions.

Running through the blue were streaks of iridescent green that seemed to move like fantastic rivers. As he gazed upon the marvel he could see fluffy white clouds scudding through the fabulous skies, with what he thought were flocks of birds swooping in and out of marshmallow clouds.

For a moment he imagined standing on the shores of a marvelous sea, air perfumed with the flowers of exotic plants blowing across his face.

As he gazed upon *Demeter*, Sten fell in love with the precious little world and was sorry to his core that what he had come to accomplish would soil it with beingkind's nastiest sins. In his heart of hearts he wanted to seize the little planet and race away to hide it from further depredations.

Ida's rough voice on the comm intruded on his reverie: "I'm picking up signs of sentient life about fifteen klicks from the landing port," she said. "I estimate about fifty beings."

Silence, then she spoke again: "There's another group about ten klicks behind them. Not quite so many. Maybe twenty or so. My guess is that Skink is in the first group. And Venatora is leading the second."

"How fast are they moving?" Sten asked.

"That's what has me puzzled," Ida said. "As near as I can tell neither group is moving much faster than a walk."

Kilgour said, "Wonder why they're afoot? Plenty ay transport oan *Demeter* frae whit Mahoney said."

"Maybe they've already come to blows," Mk'wolf said. "And they're getting set to fight it out."

"Makes sense to me," Corporal Pegatha—Mk'wolf's number two—opined.

"Don't think so," Ida said from her command seat on the *Gessel*. "They are moving steadily in one direction. And that would be north, toward the Command Center."

Besides Kilgour, Mk'wolf and Pegatha, Sten's team consisted of Ripley, Lancer, and five other fighters. If for some unforeseen reason Skink and Venatora joined forces that would be seventy against ten. But Sten's ten were all Mantis trained, which would more than equal the odds. Of course, Sten had no intention of letting his enemies join forces.

In Mahoney's words, this would be a truel. A three-way duel. And Sten had every intention of coming out on top.

On Sten's monitor, *Demeter's* overlaid chart took the form of a compass rose. It was 180 kilometers in diameter and looked like a ball cut in half. The top half was the agworld proper. The bottom, a flat plate. One edge of the plate—where the main entry port was located—was designated as South. North was where the Command Center had been built. It was in a dome on top of a mountain a hundred and twenty six kilometers to the north. The agworld's solar-style arclights moved from east to west, with a sufficient period of darkness—night—for the plants to complete their photosynthesis cycle.

"Let's find the entry port," Sten told Mk'wolf, who was piloting their transport. "But come at it from an off angle, in case they have people watching their ships."

"Aye, boss," Mk'wolf said and got busy with the controls.

The bottom of the flat plate that *Demeter* sat upon was so black that it was difficult to see who or what was parked there.

Then they spotted a circle of lights flashing on the southern tip, where he guessed the entry port was located.

"There be th' pirate ships," Alex said, indicating shadowy shapes near the flashing lights.

A large, sleek little ship was parked nearby. "Venatora," Sten guessed. After studying it a minute he added, "Just like we thought, it has star jump capabilities."

"Th' wee lass has somethin' tricky in her noggin," Kilgour said.

"Indeed," Sten said.

A few minutes later Mk'wolf found a nice hidey-hole behind some girders and brought their little vessel to a halt. They clamped on, suited up, and exited the ship. Moving cautiously toward the entry port.

Mk'wolf, along with Ripley and Lancer, went ahead, battlerifles locked and loaded. A moment later they gave the "clear" signal and the others joined them and they followed signs pointing to the Transport Center.

But when they got there, they found a mess. An impatient someone had sheared off the entry port's locking mechanism and it almost fell open at Sten's touch. Not good. This sort of damage could lead to atmosphere leaks.

They went inside and pulled the lock shut.

"Better fix at sae it doesn't bite us in the arse later when we're wanderin' abit," Alex said.

"I'll get it," Pegatha said, getting a little tool kit out of her pack. She had proven to be as talented with her hands as she was a fighter.

Alex and Mk'wolf took up position on either side of the second door. This lock was undamaged—probably because the mechanism was so simple and didn't require a pass code, or bioscan.

"How are we doing, Ida?" Sten whispered into his comm.

"No life signs in the chamber beyond," Ida reported.

Even so, Sten cautiously eased up the unlocking lever, heard a soft, satisfying "click" and slowly pushed the door open, bit by bit.

He saw light. Waited. Pushing his senses forward. Nothing.

Sten went through fast, jumping to his right, and swinging his battlerifle from side to side, ready to fire at the slightest movement. Kilgour and Mk'wolf were right behind him. Mk'wolf going left, Kilgour joining Sten.

They looked about the Transport Center. The huge chamber they stood in was dimly lit. A large console stood several meters away. The monitor bank didn't seem to be fully operational. The screens were blank and a few computer lights flashed on and off.

A half-a-dozen small gravsleds sat idle on one side of the chamber. They were all out of place, sitting askew of the bays that had once held them. Those bays were crowded with transports.

Scaffolding climbed three of the walls and Sten could see 'bots standing inactive on the different levels. A variety of other 'bots were scattered around the Transport Center, but all of them were inactive.

To Mk'wolf, Sten said, "See if you can get any of those gravsleds running."

Mk'wolf set off, accompanied by Pegatha and the two Suzdals to investigate the transports. Meanwhile Sten and Alex led the others across the chamber to a wide alcove, with an unlit "Entry" sign above it.

One again they found damage caused by an impatient intruder. The alcove led to a large decontamination chamber. Signs warned of the dangers of foreign bugs and bacteria invading the agworld. Framed directions outlined the steps that needed to be taken before anyone was permitted to enter *Demeter*.

As near as Sten could figure, the process took about half-an-hour. Not long, even for a large party, considering the size of the decontamination chamber. It had room for several vehicles and twenty or more beings.

The big doors that had once closed off the chamber were buckled and sagging on their hinges. From the charred floor and drips of molten metal it looked like someone had slapped a blast charge on the doors and blew them apart.

Sten thought it was probably the work of Skink and his pirates. Venatora was not one to bull her way through an obstacle.

Mk'wolf came trotting up. "No joy there, boss," he said.

Pegatha said, "Not a single one is operational. Can't see why. They appear to be in top running order. Tried running juice through them, but it was like the cables and wires had been turned into non-conducting material. Not one speck of electricity could get through."

"Curiouser and curiouser," Sten said. "Well, I guess we'll all have to walk. Fortunately, the others are in the same fix. I'd bet good money none of the pirates have walked further than one end of a bar to the other, so they'll not only be slow, but they'll get winded easily and have to rest a lot."

"Bit uir lassies will nae hae at trouble," Ales said. "They aw probably run five klicks a day affair sittin' down to a braw breakfast ay steel-cut oatmeal an' eggs."

"We'll soon find out," Sten said, shouldering his pack and moving across the chamber toward a far door.

A moment later he was standing in the bright Demeter sunlight, a dark green forest of tall oaks before him and a wide silver metal roadway leading through the trees.

There was green grass all around them, with yellow and blue flowers popping up here and there.

A large sign had been kicked over onto the lawn. It read:

WARNING!
ALL UNAUTHORIZED LIFEFORMS
MUST STAY ON THE ROADWAY

"Ah ken thae means us," Kilgour said.

"Indeed," Sten said and set off down the roadway, leading his little army into the unknown.

CHAPTER TWENTY SIX

UNAUHORIZED LIFEFORMS

Skink was furious. Nothing had gone right from the moment they'd docked at *Demeter*. First, Raynor had bumbled the controls at the entry port. And when Skink had yelled at him to hurry the clot up, he'd drawn his sidearm and shot the lock off.

It must've been booby-trapped, because the lock had exploded, metal pieces barely missing Skink. He'd drawn back his booted foot to give Raynor a well-deserved kick in the rear, except his chief-aide and right-hand man for lo these many had a metal spear sticking out of his face plate.

It had hit him square between the eyes.

His death ticked Skink off to no end because now he was stuck with Gurnsey as his number two. Gurnsey was a native of the Paludicar system. Tall, burly, humanoid in form, he had two long eyestalks that moved restlessly, a mouth like a crab's and one large claw that could cut a steel-bar in two, and a smaller arm with finger-like appendages.

Gurnsey wasn't exactly stupid, but he had no imagination and a violent temper that exploded at the slightest provocation. A sick feeling rose in Skink's belly as he looked at him now.

The real pity of it was that Gurnsey was by far the best being to take over for Raynor. The others weren't good for much beyond killing of the simplest kind.

And now here Skink was, exhausted after walking for nearly thirty klicks with at least another hundred or so to go before he reached his goal. He was also thirsty as hell.

Like his troops, he'd foolishly gone through all the water he'd brought along. His map showed a river six or seven klicks beyond, but at the moment he didn't have the energy to hoist himself off the tree stump he'd squatted upon when he'd called a halt.

Gurnsey rattled his claw to get his attention. He looked up at his new second and noted with disgust that he looked as fresh as when they'd started out. Skink came from a hardy race, but it took a lot longer for a second wind to cut in. Even so, he was resentful of Gurnsey's cheerful display of energy.

"Yeah, Gurnsey. What'cha got on that little bean you call a mind?"

"I was thinkin', Skipper, that ever'body looked pretty thirsty," Gurnsey said. "Me, I don't mind. Paludicarians don't use up as much water as other folks."

"So?" Skink said, almost spitting.

"So, what if I was to go on ahead to that river and fetch water back?" He held up a couple of knapsacks with his smaller arm and rattled it. "I already collected a bunch'a empty canteens."

Skink's eyes widened. It never occurred to him that Gurnsey had enough smarts to come up with a plan of any sort that required thinking beyond the next fifteen minutes.

"Good idea, Gurnsey," he said. "You go on ahead. We'll rest here a bit more, then set off after you."

"Sure thing, Skipper."

He started off, but Skink called to him. "I'm warning you, Gurnsey, if you lose your temper like you did last time I'll rip your head off and drakh in your neck."

Gurnsey's crab-like mouth drooped, as did his eyestalks.

"I'm sorry, Skip," he said. "But that 'bot was disrespectin' me. And one thing I can't abide is disrespect."

"For clot's sake," Skink said, almost losing his temper. "It was just a stupid 'bot spouting programmed directions. How could it possible disrespect you?"

Gurnsey's non-existent chin came up defiantly. "It called me an unauthorized life form, is what it done," he said. "Us Paludicarians are as authorized as anybody else and I won't hear nobody say otherwise."

"But that's not what it meant, Gurnsey," Skink said. "All it was doing was—" He stopped midsentence. What was the use? "Go on," he said. "Get the clottin' water and come back."

"Yessir, Skipper," Gurnsey said, and strode off for the river.

Skink stared after him. It was Gurnsey's fault they were all afoot. He should have killed him then, but necessity intervened. He thought back to the incidents that had set off a very unfunny comedy of errors.

After dealing with Raynor's body—by giving it a kick and sending it sailing off into space—Skink and his party had entered *Demeter's* main chamber. At first there were only a few winking lights over by a bank of monitors, but they'd gone no more than a few steps when the whole chamber came alive.

Lights blazed on every wall, computers beeped into life and 'bots began scrambling about. Moving along the main floor to tinker with machinery, including the array of transports parked in their bays.

Some scrambled along the catwalks that climbed the walls, doing what, Skink didn't know. He also heard a myriad of whispering voices, but couldn't make out what they were saying, or even what language they were using.

"Here, you, Bonser," he said to one of his people. "Get some of those transports going." He looked around, mentally calculating. "We'll need eight, maybe ten."

"Aye, Cap," Bonser said and set off with several other pirates.

About then Anthofelia made her entrance, along with a squad of her warrior women, their arms bared to show off their Sharkwire tattoos.

She planted herself in front of Skink, two of her women—Nalene and Yatola at her side.

"What happened out there?" she demanded, nodding in the direction of the spoiled lock.

Skink shrugged. "An accident," he said.

"Humph," Anthofelia said. "I hope you spoke harshly to the incompetent who caused that. We don't want any more accidents."

"He's dead," Skink, said and started to turn away.

Anthofelia's eyes widened. "Oh," she said. Then she regained her composure. "We'll be requiring at least three transports for me and my warriors and their gear," she said.

"No problem," Skink said. "Looks there's plenty to go around. Pick what you like."

Nodding at Gurnsey to follow, he turned on his heels and headed over to an alcove with an "Entrance" sign overhead.

To his surprise, he found Gregor and Mitzi already there, looking over the posters mounted on the wall.

Immense double doors barred their entrance to the agworld. A large sign read:

DECONTAMINATION CHAMBER

All Non-native Lifeforms And Objects
Must Undergo Type R676 Decontamination.

"I wonder what Type R676 means?" Mitzi asked.

Gregor said, "I don't know about this. "I'm allergic to a lot of stuff. I could go into anaphylactic shock or something."

Gurnsey's eyestalks wriggled nervously. "What kind of shock is ana-phyl—well, whatever you were talkin' about?"

"It can cause all kinds of things," Mitzi said. "I had a girlfriend who was allergic to peanuts. One day it got into her food somehow, and she started wheezing, and sneezing and an ugly rash broke out all over her. She vomited a couple of times, then she just sort of keeled over and fell on the floor."

Gurnsey's took an involuntary step back. "She passed out?"

Mitzi shook her head. "No, she was dead."

"Peanuts killed her?" he almost squeaked.

Mitzi snapped her fingers. "Just like that." She shook her head. "Folks can be allergic to all sorts of things and never know it until they stumble on something they never bumped into before. Food. Makeup. Perfume. You never can tell. There's tests you can do to check it out, but they're kind of involved."

Gurnsey's eyestalks swept the various posters. "Don't see nothin' about no tests," he said. "Or what that R676 drakh is."

"I'm sure we'll be fine," Skink said.

"Yeah, but my mom had a lot of allergies," Gurnsey said. "And I got sick once when I was a kid just eatin' a couple of eggs." He rubbed his belly. "It was awful."

Skink ignored him. He turned a wheel set into the wall next to the doors. As they slid soundlessly aside, Gurnsey took a big step back.

The doors revealed a large empty chamber with nozzles set into the walls, ceiling and deck.

"Looks like some kind of spraying system," Skink said.

A large wheel was set into the wall. Above it were posters with printed directions.

"To start the process," he said, "it looks like we just turn this."

He looked back. Bonser and the others were rolling out several transports. Some were already fired up and lifting off the deck. Anthofelia's people were boarding one of the vehicles.

"Let's get started," Skink said, reaching for the wheel.

"Maybe not so fast, Cap," he said. "Let's check it out."

"Oh, nonsense," Skink said. "Come on, we gotta get going."

But as he reached for the wheel, Gurnsey's big claw blocked his hand.

"Just let me get a gander for a sec," he pleaded. "I don't want any of that antha shock stuff happen' to me."

Skink sighed. "GA" he said. "But make it snappy."

Gurnsey strode to the other side of the chamber where a large steel lever controlled a second set of immense doors. He tugged at it with his big claw . Nothing happened. He gave it another mighty tug, this time bending the lever.

A voice boomed from a speaker set into the ceiling: "You are an unauthorized life form. Please step back from the door."

Gurnsey looked up at the speaker. His mottled green-gray face with was twisted in fury. His crab-like mouth gnashed its teeth.

"Who you callin' a unauthorized life form, you dirty clot?" he yelled.

Again he yanked at the lever, bending it more.

Alarms started to blare. More speakers buzzed into life.

"Warning, warning," they cried. "*Demeter* is under attack by unauthorized life forms."

"That's it," Gurnsey said. "I won't be disrespected like that. I'm as good a life form as anybody else."

"Stop it, Gurnsey," Skink shouted. "That's just a—"

But Gurnsey didn't stop. Instead he took a firm hold of the lever with his massive claw, set his feet, and ripped it off its mounts. He muscled the doors open and light exploded into the chamber.

Then another, louder voice called out, "Initiate security procedure Zebra Echo Charlie 355."

Then a countdown began: "5, 4, 3, 2—Initiate security procedure."

And with that all but a few of the lights in the main chamber winked off. All the 'bots came to a halt, freezing in the middle of whatever task they had been performing.

Worst of all, the engines of the vehicles went silent, sinking slowly to the ground. Their grav units inoperable.

"Ah drakh!" Skink said.

In one smooth motion, he drew his sidearm and aimed it at Gurnsey. "You just can't seem to listen," he said.

But before he could shoot, Gurnsey said, "Please, boss. I messed up. I admit it. But that thing was disrespectin' me."

"Damn, you are stupid," Skink said.

Then he hesitated. Gurnsey might be stupid, but he was the best fighter among his troop. And now that the drakh had hit the fan, he might very well need him. And he thought, *I can always kill him later.*

He sighed and lowered his pistol. "Okay," he said. "But if you screw up again, you are a dead son of a scrote."

"Gotcha, Cap," a relieved Gurnsey said.

"Now now get those doors open the rest of the way," Skink ordered.

Gurnsey hurried to the doors and with much grunting and groaning he got them open.

Anthofelia came hurrying over, flanked by her aides.

"What the clot is going on?" she said. "All the transports are inoperable."

Skink's belly did a flip flop and his heart started racing like crazy. With a great deal of effort he brought himself under control. Skink was pathologically incapable of admitting error. And if he ever were to admit such a thing, he'd never do it front of this trumped up princess.

"I guess we'll have to walk," he said.

Anthofelia was aghast. "Walk?" she cried. "It is a hundred and forty kilometers to the Command Center."

"Guess we'd best be going then," Skink said.

And he grabbed his knapsack and weapons and headed into the bright arclight.

* * * *

Skink closed his eyes. He was in a tough spot and didn't have all that much time. There was no telling when the Imperial ship would return with reinforcements.

Much as he hated to admit weakness to his fellow captains he needed to speed things up. He had several old ground transports stowed on his ship. Barnid and Manzil likely had a few of their own. The problem was that they'd insist on joining him, which would lead to arguments over larger shares.

After a brief inner war between greed and pragmatism, he finally gave in. Slid his comm from its holster on his belt.

He'd start with his own ship, the *Swagman*. He tapped the entry. There was slight buzzing sound, but nothing more. Frowning, he tried again. Still nothing. What the clot? Were they all off partying on the *Jubilee*?

His blood started to boil. He'd left strict orders that not one member of the crew—other than the ones assigned to the security pool—was to set foot on that ship until the mission was over. When he got back he'd line them all up and then…

He broke off. This was a useless exercise. Skink tried Manzil next. He was a hard nose and kept a firm grip on his crew. But when he tapped the entry all he got was the same buzzing sound.

His heart started to hammer. What the clot was going on here? Okay. Calm down. Surely Barnid would answer.

Once again there was no reply.

Desperate, he broke all of his own security rules and entered in a special "All Ships" security code. This number was unshielded, so anyone could overhear his communication. And they'd also get a fix on his location. But he was so desperate he ignored his own rules.

There was a click. He smiled. Another click. The smile grew. He was getting through.

And then he yanked the unit away as an earthly howl blasted his ear. It was so loud that the others turned their heads to see. He chopped it off.

Anthofelia called over to him. "What's wrong Skink? What was that noise?"

He opened his mouth to lie. To tell her nothing was clotting wrong and to mind her own clotting business.

But just then Mitzi and Gregor strolled up. "Say, Skink," Gregor said, "I've been meaning to ask. Why don't we call the other captains and have them send down a few transports? It'd save us a long walk."

"I was thinking the same thing," Anthofelia said. "Here, hang on. Let me call my ship."

She tapped her comm. Listened. Then frowned.

""Nobody's answering," she said. "What could be wrong?"

"There's nobody there, is what's wrong," Skink growled. He held up his own comm.

"I tried every swinging scrote," he said. "And nobody answered. It's like they all vanished."

"What'll we do?" Gregor wailed.

Disgusted, Skink lumbered to his feet. "The only thing we can do," he said, "is to take control of *Demeter* before the Imperials do show up. We'll lash her to the tugs and get the clot out of here just as fast as we clotting can."

There were shouted protests and confused noises, but Skink paid them no mind.

"Let's go," he said, shouldering his pack and heading off toward the river.

Anthofelia tapped her comm again, hoping to get Father Huber. He'd know what to do. Her eyes widened as a small robotic-type voice buzzed in her ear.

"You are an unauthorized life form. Please disconnect your unit and return to the Transport Center." She stared at her comm. Tried again. The same voice, with the same message repeated itself.

She looked around. The others, including her own Nalene and Yatola were staring at their comms, bewildered looks on their faces.

A short distance away Gregor was talking to Mitzi.

"I can't get through to Dad," he said. "And I'm using that special unit he gave me. It can get through anything. But all I'm getting is some creepy message saying I'm an unauthorized life form."

Mitzi lowered her own comm and stuffed it into her pocket.

"How about you?" he asked.

Mitzi sighed and shook her head. "Dead as dead can be," she lied.

CHAPTER TWENTY SEVEN

THE BANANA WAR

With a laugh, Sten cut the connection. "Mitzi says they're freaking and peeking in the worst way," he said. "They're not only afoot, but their comm systems are all out."

"Tsk. Th' puir wee pirates," Kilgour said in mock mournful tones. "Went knockin' oan th' door an' nobody was at haem."

Mk'wolf laughed. "Thanks to Commander Thema," he said, "there's no home for anybody to go to."

"I'm still having trouble believing what happened," Corporal Pegatha said. "One minute we were looking at a fleet of pirate ships, the next nothing but space."

"Apparently there's more to it than a mere absence of their ships," Sten said. "It seems *Demeter* has declared them unauthorized lifeforms. Paybacks for all that damage they caused back at the Transport Center. Besides sidelining all ground transport, all communications have been blocked."

"Other than putting us afoot as well," Mk'wolf said, "it doesn't seem to have affected our communication."

Indicating his comm, Sten said, "These are hot off the Mantis tech bench. Nothing short of complete destruction can interfere with them."

Ida broke in. Speaking from the *Gessel*, she said, "Doc's been running progs on all this rogue world drakh Mahoney told us about. There's a good chance that *Demeter* won't be differentiating between you and Skink's load of drakh for brains."

"Meaning?" Sten said.

Ida snorted. "Meaning, watch your arses. She's just as likely to strike out at you as she is Skink."

"Or Venatora," Alex said. "Let's nae forgit uir wee Venatora."

Sten buried a sigh. He fished out an energy chew and nipped off a bite. The road they were standing on meandered through a wide field of golden grain.

A series of thick cables were strung across the field, attached to tall towers spaced about a half-a-klick apart. Wide platforms near the top encircled the towers and he could see 'bots moving about. There were two levels of cables. The lowest was about two meters above the ground. The others ran just beneath the platforms. Cars moving back forth at the highest levels seemed to be carrying equipment and supplies for the 'bots.

Elevators cars ran from the platforms to the lowest cable and as he watched he could see 'bots traveling up and down the elevators. Some attached themselves to the lowest cables, hung from them, then started across the fields—tending the plants without ever touching the soil. Which they treated tenderly, as if dirt was a precious thing.

Some seemed to be misting the plants and the spray made scattered rainbows. Others had tools attached to long poles which they manipulated, poking and prodding the soil.

A refreshing northern breeze blew across the field, carrying the scent of spices and citrus. The grain field rippled under the breeze in a smooth wave. It was as if a large sleek animal was stretching after a long summer's nap. It was such an idyllic scene it was hard to imagine that any sort of nastiness lay in wait.

A glance at his comm's screen showed that Skink's group was on the move again. Surprisingly, they were moving at a faster pace despite many hours on the march. They had traveled about fifty klicks. Venatora's contingent was still about ten klicks behind.

He glanced up. To the west, the arc lights were closing on the distant mountains. It wouldn't be long before night descended on the agworld. From Mahoney's warning, he surmised that it would be unwise to travel at night.

His map of *Demeter* showed a secondary road off beyond the grainfield. If he got a decent start now he could make a good fifteen or so klicks before calling a halt. If all went reasonably well he should be able to catch up to the two groups before they met.

Kilgour was studying the map over his shoulder. He evidently came to the same conclusion.

"Best we get movin' now, young Sten," he said.

Sten nodded. Then he motioned to the two Suzdals who were sprawled on the roadway, basking in the sun, like two large dogs. Their fur was dark brown—almost red. The whiskers on their muzzles were black.

"Ripley, Lancer," he said, "I want you two to take point. But be careful. *Demeter* might have surprises for us."

"Sure, boss," Lancer woofed.

They got to their feet and stretched, looking a little like the undulating grainfield. The Suzdals were about Sten's height and although they walked upright, they were just as comfortable dropping to all fours.

Lancer started forward, but before he could set one paw onto the field,

Ripley pulled him back. She sniffed at the ground, then looked left and right, blowing out to clear her nostrils, then pulling in fresh air.

"We'd better stick to roads, if we can," she said. She indicated a metallic pathway a few meters distant. "Maybe start there," she added.

"You lead, we follow," Sten said.

And they all set off across the field, taking care to stay on the path.

* * * *

With nothing to see but grain fields for many kilometers, the group soon became bored. Early journey annoyances crept in. Boots fresh off the supply shelves tend to be too tight until they are broken in. Knapsack straps cut into shoulders unaccustomed to carrying weight in that position. Collars became abrasive, sweat-soaked clothing wrinkled and pinched.

Although they had all trained in a variety of terrains, it had been a long time since any of them had had to hike through empty countryside.

There were the usual gripes and complaints, but there was an edge to them, and Sten started worrying about morale. He tossed around for ideas to lighten the mood.

Alex must have been thinking along the same lines, because he raised a hand to call a boot emergency halt.

He sat on the road and pulled off his boots. Straightened his socks and wriggle his toes. The others, including Sten, took advantage of the break. Sipping a little water and getting a quick snack.

Kilgour reached into his own knapsack and pulled out a big, ripe yellow banana. He held it up for all to see.

"Thank, ye, Uncle Alban," he said, and took a big bite.

"Say, yeah, what about your Uncle Alban?" Pegatha said. "You never told us how the story ended."

Kilgour waved her away. "Nah, lass," he said. "Tisn't th' right time or place."

Mk'wolf objected. "Come on, Kilgour," he said, "you can't leave us hanging. It's not fair."

Alex indicated Sten. He said, "Sometimes Ah think wee Sten does nae loch mah stories."

Pegatha and the others turned on Sten. "Come on, boss," she said. "Don't be so tight-arsed. Let the man speak."

Sten shrugged. "On your heads be it," he said. "And don't say I didn't warn you."

The group turned to Alex, urging him to continue the tale of Uncle Alban the gravtrain conductor. He made a show of reluctance, then finally gave in.

"Weel, if ye recollect," he said, "after Uncle Alban escaped th' grim reaper he ance again got his auld job back.

"Ain jist loch afair it was borin' as clot. Th' gravtrains comin' and goin'. The doors openin' an' closin' when he blew the whistle. On and on. Day after day. But thes time he kept his wits abit heem an' didn't kill anyone.

"Until one bonny day he saw the most beautiful woman he hud ever laid his peeps oan. As she strutted by he whistled an' she turned an' gae heem a wink.

"But the gravtrain's driver thought th' whistle meant it was safe tae close the doors. And bam!—they crushed a poor sailor.

"So, for th' third time Uncle Alban was hauled afair th' court an' was tried and convicted ay murder.

"Th' judge was dain wi' him an' sentenced him tae death tha' very same day. As he was sittin' in his cell ance again, th' warden came to him.

"'50kg of bananas again?" The warden asked Uncle Alban. Uncle Alban nodded. 'Please, saiir. 50kg of bananas woods be jist fine.'

"The warden walked away, baffled at th' events of th' past two years. He returned wi' 50kg of bananas an' gae them tae Uncle Alban. Only thes time he didn't finish aw th' bananas as he hud awready eaten quite a large breakfast.

"Th' warden marched heem tae th' electric chair an' strapped heem in, curious as tae what wood happen. Th' executioner was also intrigued as tae whether ur not Alban cood cheat death again.

"He grabbed th lever and coonted down. "Three, two, one," and he pulled th' lever down.

"Once again, naethin' happened. Th' warden threw his hands up and said, It's a clottin' act of God. But, please, thes time tryst me ye won't get a job at that clotting gravtrain company. Uncle Alban refused tae tryst an' walked away a free chell.

"Th' warden caught up tae heem jist outside th' gate. He said, 'This is drivin' aw ay us bampot. Ah hae to ask. Hoo hae ye cheated th' electric chair sae many times?

"'Is it the bananas? Is 'at what's daein' it?"

"'No, it's nae the bananas,' Uncle Alban said. "'I'm jist a really bad conductor.'"

Dead silence greeted Alex's big finish. He looked around at everyone, but they all avoided his gaze.

"I think I'm going to be sick," Pegatha said.

"I'm already sick," Mk'wolf said.

Sten got to his feet.

"I'm not going to say, I told you so," he said. "But I clotting told you so."

And he marched away. A much chastened group followed him, wrung out of all complaints.

Alex trotted merrily along, whistling a happy tune.

CHAPTER TWENTY EIGHT

THE FATHER QUESTION

Venatora paused at the edge of a forest. She'd never been in a place so strange. *Demeter* was a planned wilderness. The trees, the mountains, even the rivers and waterways had the appearance of great age. And yet she knew for a fact that the agworld couldn't be more than a few years old.

The trees before her had golden leaves, but as the forest climbed the mountain they took on a deep green hue. Set against the slate gray of the rocky cliffs and the pure white snow caps of the promontory, it was a place of remarkable beauty.

A beauty that was all but lost on Venatora. At first, she was dazzled. They had passed a waterfall a few klicks back and as the water poured into a lake it kicked up a mist of lovely rainbows. But as she gazed upon the scene a feeling of dread crept up her spine. There seemed to be a malevolence lurking in the perfumed air. It was a feeling that was difficult to ignore.

Once she had stepped off the road to get a closer look at a strange bird and under her feet the ground gave a lurch and she quickly stepped back. A small leafy plant lay crushed against the earth and she could swear it moved. Stems seemed to writhe. Nothing dramatic. The movement was slight. But she could have sworn she heard something whine, as if in pain.

Clew came up beside her. "Something wrong?"

Venatora thought a moment. Good question. Was there something wrong?

"I don't know," she said. She shivered. "Except I don't trust this place."

"What's not to trust?" Clew asked. "It's an artificial world built by ordinary beings like ourselves. More of a machine than a truly living thing."

"You're right, of course," Venatora said. She rubbed her forehead. "I'm just tired," she said. "All I want to do is find Skink and kill the drakh head. Then get us to the Operation Center and then get the clot out of Dodge."

"Dodge?" a puzzled Clew asked. "Is that another word for *Demeter*?"

Venatora shrugged. It was something she'd heard Sten say once.

"Never mind," she said.

She called over Marta and Palsonia. "I don't think we have much hope of catching Skink before nightfall. I don't want to march in the dark. We might run into them and then there will be hell to pay—and it might not be a hell that is in our favor."

"I could scout ahead," Palsonia volunteered. "See what the terrain is like so we're better prepared in the morning."

"Good idea," Venatora said. "Don't get too close to them. Skink doesn't even know we're here. When the time comes we'll have surprise on our side."

Palsonia preened at being chosen for such an important task. "Yes, Your Highness," she said, voice tinged with emotion.

"What about me?" Marta said. She seemed a little jealous. "I can get a squad together and follow in case Palsonia runs into something she can't handle."

Palsonia snorted. "As if," she said, a little angry.

Marta put a hand on her hip. "It could happen," she said. "Even you are not perfect, Palsonia. No matter how much—"

"Cease and clotting desist," Venatora snapped, cutting her off. "Fighting nerves do not become either one of you. Remember your training."

The two hung their heads, mumbling apologies.

"Now, let's sync our comms," Venatora said. "Make sure everything is copacetic."

She keyed her unit, but to her surprise it remained dead in her palm.

"What's this?" she said, slapping the unit against her thigh and trying again.

Still nothing.

"Mine's dead too, Majesty," Marta said.

"And mine." This from Palsonia.

Clew had the same problem. Venatora called to her other women. "Check your comms and see if they are working properly."

After much fumbling and cursing, the other women reported the same problem.

"This probably has something to do with what we saw back at the Transport Center," Clew said. "All the gravsleds were dead. The computers and 'bots were inoperable."

"Skink must have pulled something," Venatora said. "In case he was followed."

"But how could he know that we are even here?" Marta asked.

"He couldn't have known," Venatora said. "My guess is that he doesn't trust his fellow captains. He's afraid they'll double cross him."

Clew chuckled. "And so they would, first chance they got."

Venatora thought for a minute. "We'll just have to make do," she said. "I'm sure we can straighten things out when we get to the Central Command Center."

She looked around her group. After she'd discovered the lack of transport she'd loaded up enough supplies to get them to the Center, with a little to spare. Knowing Skink's love for big guns, she'd also brought several heavy weapons to even the odds. The only drawback was that they slowed her down.

Venatora could move much faster than Skink—her women were in tip top shape, unlike the pirates whose idea of exercise was lifting a mug of spirits as many times as it took to get falling down drunk. Even so, it would take more time than she liked to catch up to Skink and remain fresh when they engaged him.

After thinking it through, she added, "We'll have to do things the old fashioned say. We'll have runners bringing messages back and forth."

She turned to her women. "Atlanta, front and center."

A young woman with amazingly long legs trotted out of the crowd and gave her a salute.

"Yes, Majesty," she said.

"You are by far the fastest runner in our group, are you not?"

Atlanta blushed. "I usually win most of the running contests," she admitted.

"She's never lost a single race since she was twelve," Marta said.

Atlanta's blush deepened.

"Very well," Venatora said. "I want you to go with Palsonia. You'll be carrying messages back and forth for us."

"I'm honored, Majesty," Atlanta said, a tremor in her voice.

Venatora studied her. The young woman was clearly overawed to be in the presence of her queen. Venatora had grown accustomed to such things, but the poor woman's knees were practically shaking.

Side glances confirmed that the others were equally affected—with the exception of Clew, who was not a member of the Himmenops race and so wouldn't be as affected as much by Venatora's pheromones.

Instinctively, Venatora worried that this might not be healthy. Passions could run amok. The women could start fighting to curry favor. Witness Marta and Palsonia's little tiff. Normally, they were competitive, but remained the best of friends.

She wished she could ask Father Raggio's advice. Maybe tone down her pheromone output—something she couldn't do on her own without so much effort it would exhaust her.

Experimentally, she touched the earbud. It was dead, just like her comm unit. Okay. So she didn't have Raggio to fall back on. She'd just have to make do without him.

Lately, she'd begun resenting Raggio and the other fathers. Why did they need them, anyway? What did they really contribute?

Venatora had lain awake the past few nights, counting the plusses and the minuses. It soon became clear that the plus column was almost non-existent.

And she began to think that with *Demeter*, she wouldn't need the Fathers at all.

"Ma'am?" This was Palsonia, who had been standing there the whole time awaiting orders.

Venatora waved an impatient hand. "What are you still doing here?" she snapped. "Get going."

Palsonia flushed, her head bobbing up and down. "Yes, ma'am," she said. "Sorry, ma'am."

And she trotted off, Atlanta at her side. Marta stared after her, a look of dislike on her face. She muttered something under her breath.

Venatora shot her a look. The woman was clearly pleased at Palsonia's discomfort.

"What are you looking at?" Venatora growled. "Get everybody up and moving."

Chastened, Marta did her bidding. Without looking behind her, Venatora set off at a blistering pace. She was moving so fast she nearly caught up to Palsonia, who looked back over her shoulder and speeded up.

This won't do, Venatora admonished herself. Get a grip woman! And she slowed down to a reasonable pace.

Just at nightfall, she found a good camping place beside a little stream.

And she settled her people in for the night.

CHAPTER TWENTY NINE

DISSENSION IN THE RANKS

Lightning split the sky and Gregor shouted in alarm and nearly jumped out of his skin.

Mitzi sat calmly by his side, counting: "A one, a two, a three…" She kept going until she reached ten and at that moment thunder boomed so loud Gregor nearly wet himself.

"Clot me, that was close," he said.

"Not that close, sweetie pie," Mitzi said. "The lighting was maybe two-and-a-half kilometers away. Maybe more."

Gregor frowned. "How do you know that?" he demanded.

"My momma was a farm girl," Mitzi said. "She said every five seconds between lightning and thunder equaled a bit more than a klick in distance. That one was over ten seconds, so that's more than two kilometers."

"Doesn't make me feel any safer," Gregor said. "Maybe the same rule doesn't apply here."

Mitzi shrugged. "Maybe."

They were deep in the forest. Skink had called a halt when it became too dark to see. They were camping on the sandy banks of a creek, surrounded by tall trees and thick foliage.

The little creek made musical sounds as it ran over its rocky bed. A few birds called, and there was rustling in the bushes by small nocturnal animals going about their business.

The pirates were grouped around lanterns, speaking in low tones. Gregor had purposely made his own camp a short distance away. He told Mitzi it was for privacy, but the fact was Skink and his pirates scared the clot out of him. They were all rough and ready beings of a half-a-dozen species and shot him nasty looks whenever he met their gaze. He could tell they despised him. They're just jealous low class slobs, he thought. My father would kill them if they dared touched me. He fingered his dead comm. Help was depressingly far away.

Anthofelia's group had also set up camp a short distance from the pirates. Gregor thought that they seemed an odd group, morosely nibbling trail rations, or tending their weapons and gear and speaking to one another in whispered asides.

Even to Gregor, who was not sensitive to the feelings of others, they seemed to be out of sorts with their leader.

There seemed to be a growing disdain. When she spoke to them there was much rolling of eyes behind her back, and barely concealed snorts of disgust. It seemed a far cry from earlier in the day at the Transport Center, when they gave her fawning looks and treated her with respect—even adulation.

Gregor didn't care about them one way or the other, but they added to the sense of unease that had descended on him after the Transport Center debacle. He knew that in theory he was perfectly safe. He was Lord Fehrle's guest, after all. Gregor refused to use the word "hostage," although he knew that was actually the case. But Fehrle had called him a guest and Gregor clung to that term with grim determination.

Making things worse, Gregor hadn't been out in the countryside since his basic training days. He'd hated it then, and hated it even more now. He felt dirty, the food was tasteless, the ground hard on his buttocks, and even with the thermal blanket around his shoulders he was cold.

He felt completely out of place on *Demeter*. An unwelcome visitor shunned by all of his companions except for Mitzi and even she had seemed not quite as respectful as before.

Nothing he could put a finger on, or even put a name to. It just seemed that… He broke off that train of thought. It was stupid to distrust the only real friend he had. His loyal and passionate lover.

It was this place that was at fault. In *Demeter* he was definitely a stranger in a very strange land. Everything was so very neat and artificial in the agworld. From the farms they'd passed where there were no houses, only shelters for the 'bots and farm equipment. To the high mountains with their snow-capped peaks that looked so perfect, as if they'd been carved with a giant hand. And here in the forest it felt particularly contrived.

The trees were so neatly spaced and there were more varieties than he'd ever seen before. Stranger still, almost all of them bore fruit or nuts. Some trees had several kinds of fruit growing from their branches. The same with the nut trees.

Cables dangled from the trees, all of them going from platform to platform and 'bots of various sizes swarmed back and forth on the cables, busily going about their tasks like insects ruled by a group mind.

The spookiest thing of all is that when Gregor looked up through the tops of trees there was only dead night to be seen. There was not one star in the sky. Logically, there wouldn't be. This was an artificial world, after all with no sun or breakaway moons.

It was also an enclosed world, with thick opaque shielding to hold the atmosphere in. So, no, there wouldn't be any stars or moons to see. But it just added to the strangeness. The feeling that crawled up Gregor's spine whenever he heard a noise.

Out of the corner of his eye he saw Anthofelia climb to her feet. Flanked by two of her women, she stalked over to Skink's group.

The pirate chieftain looked up at her when she approached. She leaned down to speak to him and a moment later he rose and followed her to a spot a short distance away.

Gregor strained to hear, but they spoke in such low tones that it was impossible to pick up a single word. From the look of things, it was not a friendly conversation.

* * * *

"I hesitated to speak my mind before, Captain Skink," Anthofelia said, "but now your decisions directly affect the safety and well being of my women. I fear it is my duty to criticize, where criticism is warranted."

Skink sighed. He'd had been waiting for a confrontation ever since Anthofelia's forces joined his group. He knew the Himmenops looked down on other species. That bitch Venatora made it plain that she thought her people were far superior to other beings.

Except Venatora, he grudgingly admitted to himself, often had reason to consider herself the brightest being in the room. But Anthofelia was definitely *not* Venatora. From the beginning, she'd done nothing to distinguish herself or her troops. In fact, whenever a conflict threatened, she tended to hang back. Like how she positioned her forces when they set up the ambush so there would be little danger to herself.

"I suppose you're referrin' to the little mix-up we had back at the Transport Center."

Anthofelia placed a hand on an outthrust hip. "I certainly am," she said. "Clearly your people rushed in without thinking and made some critical errors. Errors that have left us afoot and have threatened the success of the mission."

Skink shrugged. "Wasn't too pleased myself, the way things worked out. But none of us have been faced with drakh like that before. Mistakes happen. The trick is to swallow it up and move on. Which is what we're doin' now."

"I blame lack of leadership," Anthofelia said. "You should have investigated the Transport Center thoroughly before you let people run around like headless capons."

Skink didn't know what a capon was, but the word was clearly meant as an insult. His yellow eyes narrowed and one clawed hand rose to grip his side weapon.

"Careful what you say, lady," he said. "I won't hear my people being insulted. One of them died gettin' into this place. While you and your people lollygagged around doin' nothin' to help."

Anthofelia's temper rose. "How dare you," she said. "You're an incompetent. And I intend to tell Lord Fehrle what a fool you are the minute we see him at the rendezvous."

Skink laughed. "Listen, you trumped up crown stealer, Fehrle won't give a drakh what you or anybody else has to say when we show up. He'll have *Demeter*, and that's all he'll care about."

The princess was momentarily taken aback. Skink was right, of course. Fehrle was only interested in results.

"Very well, Captain," she finally said. "But consider my words a fair warning. If there are further mishaps I may be forced to take steps."

"I'm sure you will, Princess," Skink said.

Then he rudely turned on his heels and stalked back to his people. He said something in a low voice and everyone laughed. Anthofelia was certain it was something crude. Crudity, after all, was the last bastion of misogynists. Never mind that a good number of the pirates were female. They might as well have been male, from the way they behaved.

She walked back to her women, who were huddled around an array of lanterns.

"That didn't look like it went very well," Your Highness," Nalene said.

"Don't know why you bothered, ma'am," Yatola said. "Me and Nalene warned you that all you'd accomplish was to set them against us even more."

Anthofelia was shocked at the criticism. None of her people had spoken to her that way before.

"Mind your place, woman," she said. "I'll not be addressed that way."

To her surprise, Yatola opened her mouth, as if to make a retort. Then she stopped herself. Shrugged.

"Sorry, ma'am," she said. "I'm a little tired."

And then she turned away and stretched herself out on a sleeping mat, pulling a thermal blanket around her. Deliberately turning to face the other way.

Astounded, Anthofelia looked over at Nalene, her most ardent supporter. But Nalene wouldn't meet her gaze. Instead she covered her mouth to yawn.

"Forgive me, Highness," said. "I'm pretty tired myself."

And like Yatola she curled up on her mat, back to her superior, and acted as if she were falling asleep.

Hesitantly, Anthofelia stretched out her senses. Testing her pheromone powers over her soldiers. Normally, they would sigh and gaze on her with loving, almost lustful looks. Their skin would become flushed. Their breathing would quicken.

But this time she got very little reaction at all. Those who were awake, paused a moment, then went on with whatever they were doing. Those who were asleep, stirred a bit, then resumed their slumbers.

What was happening? She had to talk to Father Huber right away. She lifted up her comm to call, then remembered. It was dead.

Anthofelia was desperate. She didn't know what to do. A breeze picked up and she shivered. She was cold. That was the problem. Just a chill. Maybe she'd picked up some sort of bug. What she needed was warmth. The kind of warmth that a good campfire gave off.

All she required was a little wood. She'd get a big bonfire going and her women would gather around and talk about old adventures.

Anthofelia strode over to a nearby bush. Getting her knife, she grabbed a good handful of fairly dry branches and slashed down.

The branches didn't part on the first blow. So she hacked away. Then began sawing back and forth.

Suddenly the ground under her feet seemed to move. She paused. Put a hand to her forehead. My imagination, she thought. I'm just tired. A little dizzy. She took several deep breaths to steady herself, then went back to her sawing.

There was a slight whimpering sound. Almost a whisper. Above her, the leaves on the tree stirred in a non-existent wind. Almost like wagging tongues.

Ignoring it, Anthofelia made a final, heavy blow with her knife, then wrenched the branches away from the bush.

Anthofelia raised the branches over her head in the rebel pose that had served her so well. As if she were the victor in a glorious battle.

She'd show them. She'd clotting show them all.

And then everything went to hell.

CHAPTER THIRTY

IF A TREE FALLS

The ground heaved, there was a tremendous ripping sound and the earth beneath Anthofelia's feet was torn apart—hurling her across the glen.

She sprawled there, dazed and in pain. All around her there were shouts and screams as the earth groaned and shook.

Voices, a myriad of whispering voices, buzzed in the air like angry bees, crying "Unauthorized lifeforms. Unauthorized lifeforms."

She couldn't see what was happening—her vision was obscured. For a panicky moment she thought she'd been stricken blind. She put a hand to her forehead and it came back wet and sticky. Was it her blood?

There were more tearing sounds. The ground bucked and rolled. Something cold and wet and hairy pushed up under her, once again throwing her to the side.

Nalene shouted "Princess! Princess!" And then someone grabbed her collar and dragged her across the ground. She could hear people running and shouting and clods of dirt rained down on her head and shoulders.

Desperately, Anthofelia scrubbed at her face with a sleeve and her vision cleared. The ground around her was a jungle of towering roots and as she watched, more roots punched up through the earth.

Then she saw Nalene's frightened face and she was screaming for her to "Get up, get up."

There was a Crack! and she looked up to see the tree leaning forward, the trunk splitting and the crown slowly descending.

Anthofelia scrambled away on hands and knees and then the tree came down with an enormous crash barely missing her.

The little creek twisted in its course, then jumped its banks and a wave of water came rushing toward her. She got to her feet and ran, only to stumble over a heaving root.

And then more roots were waving about, lashing the ground like whips. One of them hit her thigh and she shouted from the pain as blood oozed from the wound.

A dark shape shot out of the night and slammed into her head.

Intense pain.

Then darkness.

A long time seemed to pass. She saw flashing lights and odd shapes. Images floated up and then dissolved. And she hurt. Oh, how she hurt.

Then a voice was calling her and someone was shaking her by the shoulders.

"Princess! Princess! Speak to me, Princess."

Anthofelia tried to open her eyes, but the lids were stuck together. She groaned and through swollen lips said, "I can't see."

A wet cloth was drawn across her face. Water splattered down and then the cloth came back and wiped away the stickiness. Finally, she got her eyes open.

Nalene was standing over her. Her face was smeared with dirt and her tunic was filthy with mud and debris.

Another form appeared, looking over Nalene's shoulder.

It was Skink. Yellow eyes glaring her through a mask of bloody filth.

"Get up, bitch," he snarled. "And see what you've done."

With great difficulty, Anthofelia clambered to her feet. Nalene just stood there watching. Not helping. A flash of anger. How dare she? The anger broke off. Replaced by confusion.

She looked around at what had once been an idyllic meadow. Now it was pure disaster. The ground looked like it had been raked over by an enormous machine. Huge tree roots, covered in mud and hairy with tendrils, stood as stark witnesses to what had occurred. An immense tree, trunk broken and splintered, sprawled across the glen.

Bodies were strewn here and there. Some lay still, as if in death. Others squirmed and moaned. And they were all covered with so much muddy debris it was hard to make out if they were Skink's people or her own.

As she watched, she saw Yatola and another woman lifting a groaning figure from beneath the branches of the tree. Here and there pirates were attending their own, while Anthofelia's people were washing and bandaging their wounded.

She looked at Skink. "What happened?" she said.

Skink snorted. "What happened?" Incredulous. "Woman, you are what happened." One claw swept around, taking in the scene. "This was your doing."

Anthofelia was aghast. "Me? I had nothing to do with this."

"Well, it all started when you ripped up that bush," Skink growled. "We were all just sittin' there watchin' you go nuts and hack away with your knife."

"That's ridiculous," Anthofelia said. "Obviously there was an earthquake of some sort. It happened at the same time that I was trying to get firewood."

She looked over at Nalene, almost pleading. "It was a coincidence," she said. "Surely you can see that." As she spoke she pushed hard to increase her pheromonic powers

Nalene's eyes clouded a moment and she took a step back. "Sure," she said. "A coincidence. Had to be."

"Well, where did all those 'unauthorized lifeforms' voices come from?" Skink demanded. "Last time that happened one of my people messed with things he shouldn't have. This time it was you. And after fair warnin' too. My guys had no idea what would happen if they messed about."

Anthofelia was getting her nerve back. Her confidence.

"Nonsense," she said. "It was an earthquake. Nothing more." She looked at the chaos all about them. "Now, let's do something sensible and useful," she said, "and get some order restored."

She glared at Skink. "You take care of your people and I'll take care of mine. It'll be morning soon. And we'll have to get a move on before something else happens."

Skink started to say something, but Nalene's hand rose to rest on the butt of her sidearm.

He cursed, then turned on heels and walked away.

"I think you're going to have to kill him, Majesty," she said.

Anthofelia nodded. "Yes," she said. "I was thinking the same thing."

* * * *

Many kilometers away, Venatora was dropping off to sleep, when she felt a chill run up her spine. Voices were whispering in her ear, but she couldn't make them out.

Her eyes snapped open. They seemed to be drawn to something happening north of her position. In the distance she saw a large black cloud forming low to the ground. There were flashes of light inside the cloud, but it didn't seem to be lightning and there was no sound of thunder.

The atmosphere about her seemed out of sorts somehow. Angry. If it had a voice beyond whispering, she sensed that it would growl.

The many colored lights continued flashing for several minutes. Suddenly, the cloud dissipated and was gone. A moment later she realized the whispering had stopped as well. And everything seemed to return to normal.

I'm just tired, she thought. Overwrought. Her mouth was dry, tongue thick. She got out her canteen, sipped water. Then lay back on her ground cloth.

In a few minutes, she was asleep.

* * * *

Sten and Alex were double-checking the charts of *Demeter*, going over plans for the next day.

"Ideally," Sten said, "we should probably stay out of sight as long as possible and let them fight it out. Then step in and deal with the winner."

Kilgour nodded approvingly. "Fewer chances fur our wee bairns tae gie their pinkies burned," Alex said.

Then he caught the dark look on his friend's face.

"Ah can see yer troubled by this, mah puir mucker," he said. "It's aboot th' lass, yes?"

Sten sighed. "She's got to go," he told his friend. "Those are our orders. And I can understand Mahoney's reasons."

"But it doe nae make it onie easier, does it?" Kilgour said. "When th' time comes, best lit me dae it."

"Won't make it hurt any less," Sten said.

He was about to say more, when he caught a whiff of something burning. It had an ozone smell to it, like an electrical fire.

Across from him, Alex sat up straighter. "Somethin's afire," he said.

"I smell it too," Sten said.

They both looked about.

"Over there," Alex said, pointing to the north.

Sten saw it. A burning object was arcing across the northern sky. Like a slow moving meteor.

As they watched it broke apart and fiery bits floated down, then vanished before they reached the forest below.

Suddenly, Alex slapped at his neck. He turned up his hand and reacted, surprised. He held his palm out for Sten to see in the lantern light. There was a bloody insect body lying there.

"Skeeters?" Alex said.

Sten frowned. "Why would any sensible being introduce mosquitoes in a manmade world?" he said. "It's one of the reasons I've always been an atheist. I mean, only a very stupid God would make a mosquito."

"Ah'm a religious chell, meself," Alex said. "Ah loch a guid malevolent God. It's more natural."

CHAPTER THIRTY ONE

THE ATTACK

The next morning, Skink and Anthofelia decided to leave the injured behind and strike out for the *Demeter* Command Center as fast as they could.

They barely took time to stack rocks over the corpses of two pirates and the Himmenops woman who died in the previous night's disaster. They used rocks because they were afraid if they dug into the ground *Demeter* would consider it an attack and retaliate.

Anthofelia's women were decidedly unhappy when she announced her decision. There was a good deal of discontented muttering.

One of the women made bold to speak her mind. "Venatora would never leave us behind," she said in a loud voice.

There were noises of agreement from many of the others.

Her authority questioned, she was about to come down on them hard, when Nalene stepped in.

"We don't have much of a choice," she told the group. "If we take the injured with us, we won't be able to keep up with the pirates. And they'll cut us out of the whole thing if they get to the Command Center first."

"Even so," the woman said. "Venatora would have thought of a way."

Anthofelia had enough. "I advise you to shut your mouth," she told the woman, "before I shut it for you—permanently."

And with that, she drew her sidearm. The woman's mouth snapped shut. Anthofelia glared at the others.

"Anyone else care to voice their uninformed opinions?" she said.

No one spoke.

"Good," she said, holstering her weapon. "We have wasted enough time. Let's get going."

She started off, walking swiftly and trying not to limp. Her injured thigh throbbed fiercely, but she didn't dare show weakness.

Even so, there was s definite extended moment before the women followed. To her dismay, Nalene and Yatola made no attempt to catch up to her and walk by her side, as was their custom.

She could hear them talking behind her. Their voices were too low to make out what they were saying. She doubted if they were being complimentary.

She began to get an uncomfortable itch between her shoulder blades. She kept her hand resting on her sidearm, fearing that at any moment one of them would attempt to plunge a knife in her back.

Oh, Father Huber, she thought. Where the clot are you?

* * * *

Skink was so tired he could barely think and no matter how much water he drank his thirst was never quenched. Usually, the only exercise Skink ever got was repeatedly hoisting a goblet of spirits, or carving a thick, juicy soy steak.

And yet he kept going, leading the long columns of pirates and women warriors. Periodically stopping to hasten their pace with shouted curses and boots to their lazy butts.

Skink was a Parlitas, after all—a nomadic desert world race whose bodies were uniquely suited to travel great distances in difficult terrains. Severe deprivation—like hunger or thirst—triggered special organs in his body that allowed him to carry on for weeks and months at a time without food or water.

And, so while his fellow pirates and Anthofelia's women suffered from the long march under *Demeter's* hot, merciless lights, Skink was not only able to soldier on, but in some ways he felt stronger than when they started.

It helped that they'd emerged from the forest a short time ago and were now moving past a desert-like stretch of *Demeter*. Rows of cactus pears and varieties of ground nuts grew in sandy soil that rolled onward toward the mountains in towering dunes.

Behind him, he heard Gurnsey curse as he tripped and fell. Skink glanced back to see Hasana help the burly pirate to his feet. At any other time it would have been a humorous sight. Tiny Hasana, who stood barely over a meter and half, hoisting up a fellow pirate nearly twice her size and weight.

But Skink was in no mood for joking, even when it involved his favorite type of humor—the suffering of another being.

"Pick up your feet, Gurnsey," he growled. "We have a long way to go."

"Can't we stop for just a minute, Captain?" Gurnsey pleaded. "Got a pebble in my boot that's startin' to feel like a boulder. And I'm hotter'n hell. I know the other fellers are feelin' just as poorly. A bit of rest would set us all right, it would."

"What a bunch of weaklings," Skink said. "We'll march till I say otherwise. We've gotta get some serious klicks down before it's night again."

"Just ten minutes, Skink," Gurnsey urged. "Ten minutes."

"You want to rest?" Skink said, his hand going to his sidearm. "I'll fix it so you can rest all you like."

Gurnsey flushed, getting angry. He was not one to take threats well. He was about to speak, but Hasana gave him a nudge.

"Skink's right, Gurnsey," she said. "We gotta keep moving. Come night, no tellin' what kind of trouble we'll see. Sooner we get to where we're goin', the better."

Gurnsey sighed. "Sorry, Skipper," he said. "Just feelin' out of sorts."

Skink was about to push it, but Hasana gave him a pleading look.

Relenting, he said, "Guess we're all feeling out of sorts after that bitch woman's shenanigans last night."

He resumed the march. Behind him, he heard people cursing as they once again began the arduous task of putting one boot in front of the other.

Skink thought that before long he might have to kill one them to set an example. Gurnsey? Nah. Dumb as he was, Gurnsey was popular. When he got drunk he had all kinds of amusing tricks.

Once he'd ripped off a prisoner's face and stuck it on his own. Then marched about the Gibbet's Hall making rude noises through the bloody lips.

Skink chuckled at the memory. No, he wouldn't start with Gurnsey.

As they marched onward he came upon a large cactus pear whose fleshy branches intruded over the walkway. The plant itself was well over two meters in height with a thick main trunk.

Skink's mouth watered. Cactus pears were his favorite childhood treats. He reached out with one of his claws. Hesitated, then thought, what the clot, fruit was meant to be eaten. How could there be any harm?

He plucked a particularly plump fruit from its home. It bristled with nettles, but that was no matter to Skink, whose mouth was hardened by evolution to devour such fare.

But just as he was about to bite down, the mother cactus plants stirred. Sensing the motion, Skink glanced up just as one of the cactuses wrenched its roots out of the sand.

"What the clot?" Skink said, taking a step back. He'd never seen or heard of such a thing.

To Skink's amazement, more roots were pulled free of the ground and the cactus lumbered forward on hairy root balls.

It was actually walking!

But plants can't walk—can they?

He was so amazed he just stood there, frozen, while the thick, fleshy cactus branches slowly drew back.

Then another root ball emerged, and the cactus lurched forward, spiky branches whipping out.

Skink shouted in fear and fell on his back. Several thorny branches slashed his face. Only his scaly reptilian hide kept it from being ripped off.

And now the cactus was above him. Its shadow blocking out the rays of the arc lights. Then it came smashing down with its full weight.

Skink rolled to the side, clawing his sidearm from its holster, and fired.

There was a shriek as the first shot missed and one of his pirates was smashed backward, a smoking crater in his chest.

The cactus struck again, Skink desperately trying to roll away. A thick branch slashed his belly and there was a burning pain.

He fired again and this time his aim was true and he blasted a hole in the plant. It bellowed in pain, but still came forward.

Skink held down the trigger. A stream of AM2 bullets blasted out, cutting the cactus in half. The top part fell over, but the bottom section kept coming, roots dripping clumps of sand.

Now Gurnsey was at his side, opening fire on what was left of the plant.

It kept moving, so they continued firing until there was nothing left but a steaming pool of green.

With difficulty Skink climbed to his feet. He felt drained. His mind reeled.

"What the clot?" he said.

"Uh, boss," Gurnsey said, voice breaking. "Look'it out there."

Heart thumping double time, Skink looked to see what Gurnsey was so excited about. In the desert beyond he saw other cactus plants stirring into life. There must have been fifty of sixty of them. And they were all turning in Skink's direction.

"Let's get the clot out of here," Skink said and ran as fast as his stubby legs would carry him.

The entire column of pirates and women warriors took to their heels and ran after him.

As they ran, they fired on the cactus plants with every weapon that came easily to hand. Sidearms, battlerifles, and even a few grenades, came into play.

But the big cactus pears kept coming. Pieces were ripped off. Green liquid splattered everywhere.

And somewhere high above the pirates could hear an unearthly wail.

* * * *

When Venatora emerged from the forest the heat from the unrelenting arc-lit sky fell on her like a blow. She held up a hand, bringing the column to a halt, then looked around to examine the terrain.

Ahead, a wavering, mirage-like haze rippled above mirror surface of the steel road. Yellow desert sand stretched on either side. Having just stepped into the bright light it was difficult to see more than general shapes and colors.

Then, as her vision cleared, she heard Clew exclaim, "What in the clotting world?"

And then the others were all making noises of astonishment as they looked at what appeared to be the scene of a strange sort of battle.

On both sides of the road, the desert was littered with the remains of huge cactuses. Some were whole. Most were ripped to pieces. Branches and trunks scattered everywhere. Pools of green liquid soaked into the sand. It was like the aftermath of an aerial assault.

Venatora drew her sidearm. "Clew and Marta," she said, "come with me. Palsonia—take charge."

There were murmurs of "Yes, Highness," and the three moved forward, weapons at ready.

As they drew closer to the forms sprawled on the road a hot breeze picked up, bearing the awful smell of rotting corpses.

A moment later they saw the first body. It was a Himmenops woman. From the Sharkwire tattoo on her bicep, she was one of Anthofelia's people. Her clothing and flesh were ripped to shreds, as if she had been beaten to death with a flail. She was covered with dried blood, except for her face, which was untouched. Her eyes were open and the look on her face was that of someone who had witnessed a great horror.

"I know her," Marta said. "She sat next to me in navigation class. Used to stop by her creche once in awhile. Her creche mistress made great chocolate chip cookies."

She started to say more, then stopped. She looked up at Venatora, her eyes moist. "I can't remember her name," she said, voice quivering. She leaned down as if to examine the woman's gore-covered dog tags.

Venatora stopped her. "It was Fryda," she said.

Marta frowned. "What?"

"Fryda," Venatora repeated. "Her name was Fryda."

She put an arm around Marta and pulled her close. Marta sobbed into her shoulder, while Venatora slightly increased her pheromone output.

In a moment, Marta recovered. She pulled back, eyes brimming with love and admiration.

"Thank you, Highness," she said.

Clew spoke up. "Do you really know all of your people's names?" she asked. "I thought it was just… you know… stories. Politics."

Venatora sighed. "I know them all," she said. "No politics involved. That's one reason why it hurt so much when people like Fryda deserted me for Anthofelia. It was like losing a friend. No, not just a friend. But a sister."

They moved onward. Edging around cactus remains. Examining the corpses of dead pirates and women.

"I count eleven dead," Marta said. "Three of Anthofelia's and eight pirates."

"Too bad Skink wasn't among them," Clew said.

"It's just as well," Venatora said. "I'm looking forward to doing him myself."

CHAPTER THIRTY TWO

ROGUE WORLD

Sten and the others stood well back while Ripley and Lancer investigated the carnage. They trotted from one corpse to the other, pausing to get a good whiff, then moving to the next.

Ripley snuffed a dead pirate, then sneezed. "That's nice and smelly," she said. "Wouldn't mind a good roll."

"Better not," Lancer said. "I don't think our friends would like it much. Especially Kilgore. He's got such a queasy stomach. Probably puke all over the place."

"Yum," Ripley said. "Nothing like a good slurp of vomitus to start the day. Remember that time when Alex had all that haggis?"

"Regurgitated sheep guts and oatmeal," Lancer said, voice dreamy. "A Suzdal gourmet delight. When we open our restaurant we just have to put that on the menu."

"Here noo," Alex said. "What're ye two wee pups gonnae oan about?"

"No biggie, boss," Ripley said. "We're just talking about that restaurant we wanna open one of these days."

"You know," Lancer said, "we didn't see a single Suzdal diner in the entire Possnet Sector. We could clean up."

Sten laughed. "With vomitus haggis on the menu," he said, "you can't go wrong."

Alex frowned. "You three aren't makin' fun ay th' Scots, ur ye?" he asked.

Ripley laid a paw of great sincerity across her furry chest. "Never!" she yipped.

"Furthest thing from our minds," Lancer added.

"Haggis is a serious subject, ye ken. It's ay great importance in th' Celtic culture."

While Kilgour pondered, wondering if he'd been insulted, the two Suzdals continued their examination.

Suddenly, Lancer gave a yip. "What's this?" he said, pawing at a scrap of cloth beneath the arm of one of the pirate's bodies.

Ripley trotted over to see. Sniffed at the cloth, then freed it from the corpse. Gripping it in her teeth, she trotted over to Sten and dropped it at his feet.

"I think it's something from Mitzi," she said.

Sten picked it up. The cloth turned out to be an old, faded scarf made of some filmy material and it was wrapped up like a little packet, with a string holding it together. Kneeling down, he untied the scarf then spread it out on the road. There were three objects inside: a rolled up sock, a clump of hair, and a note that read:

Dears:

A present for my puppies. Stinky sock from Skink. Dirty hair from Gregor. Pretty scarf from Anthofelia.

XOXO—

Mitzi.

"Oh, she is so nice," Ripley said.

"Always thinking of us," Lancer said.

Mk'wolf was puzzled. "What're those two going on about?" he asked. "Who cares about stinky socks and dirty hair, much less an old scarf?"

Ripley replied, "So we can track them, dear Mk'wolf. So we can track them. Once we get a good whiff we can follow them anywhere. They'll never be able to shake us."

Mk'wolf shrugged. "Maybe," he said. "As long as they stay out of water, anyway."

"Oh, water's no trouble for us," Lancer said. "As long as it isn't too deep, we can smell things under water just fine."

Ripley took a good whiff of the Skink's sock. Sneezed.

"I could follow that pirate's stink to the bottom of the deep blue sea," she whuffed.

Sten heard a loud hissing sound, then a roar. Up ahead—beyond a jumble of boulders stacked many meters high—a column of water shot into the sky.

It was a beautiful sight, rainbows forming and dissolving then forming again. A moment later the geyser subsided. A breeze brought the scent of steam.

"Smells loch a big kettle ay Earl Gray," Kilgour said.

Sten led them all forward. Coming around a sharp bend in the road, they found themselves standing in the middle of a bizarre landscape, where pillars of stone poked up like giant fingers and enormous boulders were tumbled about as if a giant's child had left his toys out.

The ground was covered with what looked like green lichen. Sten leaned down to examine it closer, but as he reached, Ripley stopped him.

"Better not, boss," she said.

Then she and Lancer dropped on all fours and padded out a few meters from the roadway. They sniffed about for a minute, then returned.

"It doesn't seem to mind us, boss," Lancer said. "But it has problems with you and the others."

"It?" Sten said, a little incredulous. "Who is It?"

"Beats me, boss," Lancer said. "But It's there just the same and It is mad as clot and getting madder by the minute."

Ripley had moved a few meters down the road to where there was a bare patch of ground. She sniffed it, then gestured to Sten.

"Over here," she said. "See for yourself."

Sten went to her, looked at the bare patch, then at Ripley.

"See what?"

Ripley spread a piece of cloth over the bare spot. She dropped down and put her ear against the cloth. After a minute she got up.

"You try it," she said.

Sten knelt, then—feeling a little foolish—he put his ear to the ground.

To his surprise, he heard a scurrying sound. And there was a definite rippling motion, as if thousands of underground creatures were moving just beneath the surface.

"What the clot," he said, getting to his feet and dusting off his trousers. Then, to Ripley and Lancer, "Do you guys have any idea what's happening?"

"We're not sure," Lancer said, "but it's like *Demeter* is making things."

"What kind of things?" Sten asked.

Ripley shrugged. "Scary things," she said.

"Hang on a sec," Sten said and got out his comm to key in Ida.

"What's up, Cap?" she asked.

"We have some strange things going on here," he said.

Then he told Ida what the two Suzdals had reported.

After hearing him out, she said, "Me and Doc will run some scans and get back to you." She paused, then said, "Before I go, Doc and I were just commenting on the situation down there. From what we can see, Skink's column went crazy for a time, breaking up formation and going like hell. Now they are all gathered in one place. Probably resting after that bit of cactus craziness."

Doc broke in. "Morale has to be at an extremely low ebb right about now," he said.

"That'd be my guess as well," Sten said, dryly. "If you were attacked by a big clotting cactus plant, I don't think you'd be singing the Blyrchynaus national anthem either."

"You wouldn't know it I did," Doc said. "The notes are beyond your poor human abilities to hear."

Kilgour laughed. "Dog whistles, are they?" he said.

"Stifle it, you walking lump of boiled haggis," Doc said. After pausing to collect himself, Doc continued: "It's not Skink's morale I'm speaking of. It's Anthofelia's group. There is something going on with them."

"How can you tell," Sten asked.

"Living things give off chemical signals when they are stressed," Doc said. "When dealing with the Himmenops, those signals include pheromone readings. In Venatora's case, the readings are high normal. She's in complete control of her people.

"That is not the case with Anthofelia. Her levels are so low they are practically nonexistent. The only thing that holds her people together now is custom. Momentum.

"They have been obeying her without question for several years. But now that momentum is slowing down. I wouldn't be surprised if she were challenged soon."

"Thanks, Doc," Sten said. "That's good to know."

Ida came back on. "Okay, Sten," she said, "I'm running tests right now and it appears that *Demeter* has seriously taken on her duties as Mother Nature. She's working with the AI to not just build defenses, but biological weapons as well."

Sten took in a deep breath. Let it out. Then asked: "What kind of biological weapons are we talking about?"

"Hard to tell," Ida said. "It's like she's got a big pot set to boil and she's whipping up a molecular soup."

Just then the ground rumbled. A split second later a huge column of steaming water shot out of a jumble of boulders about a half a klick away. So enormous was the geyser's power that It went up and up, and up. And then finally it came cascading down with an enormous crash.

"Better beat feet, boss," Ripley said and she and Lancer took off running. "It's gonna blow big time."

It was a good thing Sten and the others followed, because a moment later an enormous wave of boiling water crashed down, then spread across the ground to wash over the roadway where they had stood seconds before.

When they were safe, they paused to look back. The road was empty now, but it buckled from the intense heat of the water

"Smell's loch somethin's cookin'," Alex said.

I'm just glad it wasn't one me," Sten said.

Ripley barked laughter. "Cannibal stew," she said. "My favorite."

* * * *

Skink came upon a broad lake, surrounded by blossoming fruit trees. Little 'bots scurried about, misting the trees and sliding long metal tubes into the ground to feed nourishment directly to the trees' roots.

The lake itself was crisscrossed with thick cables that hung from strategically placed towers. Enormous buckets moved back and forth on the cables. As he wondered what they were for, a huge net filled to the overflowing with fish was cranked up from the lake, water cascading through the holes.

The net swung around to one of the pots, which paused long enough for the net to dump its pectoral cargo. Then the net was lowered again and vanished beneath the surface of the lake.

At this point the metal roadway led to the edge of the lake, then curved around it to the other side and seemed to go on from there.

Skink looked ahead. From the roadway onward was nothing but stubby grass and thick bushes that led to a woody area, which climbed to the mountains beyond.

He was tempted to take a quicker route and strike north across country. But he was wary of leaving the road. What if *Demeter* had more surprises waiting for him. No. Better stick to the road.

Skink stopped at the edge of the lake. The water looked so cool and clean and inviting. He dipped up a handful and tasted it. Delicious. It had just a hint of citrus.

"Tell everyone to fill up their water carriers," he told Gurnsey, then knelt down to fill his own.

When he was done he plunged his face into the lake, then came up shaking the water from his head. Oh, that felt so good. He did it again, then scooped up water and splashed it all over himself, washing away many weary kilometers of dust and dirt.

Shouts and laughter drew his attention and he turned to see some of his pirates and many of Anthofelia's women had made so bold as to enter the water waist deep to bathe and play, splashing and laughing.

Skink grinned. It was good to hear people laugh. It had been a long time.

He turned back to the water and got out a cloth from his knapsack to wash himself. As he dipped it into the water he heard rippling noises.

Something was moving in the water. Some of those fish escaping the nets, perhaps?

Just beneath the lake's surface, Skink spotted gray shapes wriggling along. Several of them swam towards the bathers.

Suddenly he felt slimy. The water felt oily. A disgusting smell rose to his nostrils.

Someone screamed.

Skink whirled to see a two-meter-long leech-like creature hanging from the back of one of the women. It looked like it was sucking at her, and as he watched in frozen horror the creature began to swell to many times its original size. Several more creatures leaped up to cling to the woman.

Then there were more shouts and more screams as the giant leeches attacked anyone in the water. Scores of them leaped out to cling to people, sucking the juices from them and ballooning red and belly-wrenching ugly.

Skink heard a noise and he turned to see one the creatures swimming towards him. For a moment, he couldn't move.

And then it came right out of the water, rearing above him, its ugly maw was rimmed with tiny sharp teeth. Then the creature plunged down at his face.

Skink scrambled away, pulling his sidearm. He fired as the creature fell upon him. It was greasy and filthy cold and it gasped at his face, its breath so disgusting it almost paralyzed him. He fired again, cutting it in half, then rolled away, frantically swiping at slime covering his body.

He jumped to his feet, looking wildly about and saw people clawing at the creatures, trying to get free of them. Wailing for someone, anyone, to help them.

Friends were frantically slashing the creatures with knives, or shooting them. When they pierced the beasts' flesh gouts of blood spewed out and soon the whole area was drenched with blood.

Skink joined in, shooting and cutting, desperately trying to free his people.

Finally it was over. The giant leeches were dead, leaving long slimy corpses—gray skin so thin he could see through it.

Everyone was covered with blood, but no one dared approach the lake to wash off. Instead they used the precious water in their carriers to clean themselves.

It was at this point that Skink noticed the great absence of Anthofelia. Some of her women were dead, or dying and people were crowding around them.

Why wasn't Anthofelia there? Was she injured? Dead?

Then Skink saw her on the other side of the glen. She was leaning against a tree, watching what was going on. An odd expression on her face.

Oddest of all—she was the only one without a spot of blood on her. What kind of a leader was she?

Skink shook his head, trying to clear his mind. Never mind Anthofelia. None of his concern. He had work to do. Dead and wounded to tend to. They had to hurry as fast as they could before the clotting planet ate them alive.

Night fell before they could make much progress.

They huddled together, fearful of what the night might bring. Most didn't sleep and when the morning came they were as tired as the moment they had collapsed on the road the night before.

Gurnsey made bold to approach Skink after a hasty breakfast.

"Boss," he said, "some of the fellers wonder if maybe we should just pack it in. Go on back. They're scared, and I don't mind admittin' it meself."

Skink drew in deep breath. Then he said, "You don't understand, Gurnsey," he said. We can't go back."

"Why not, boss?"

"Because there is nothing to go back to. We either go forward, or die here."

Gurnsey was so shocked he couldn't speak. Then he just nodded.

"Okay," he said. "I'll tell everybody else."

Skink didn't wait. He just strode off, trusting fear would drive the others onward.

* * * *

A little later, Venatora came upon the ghastly scene by the lake.

There were mounds of rocks stacked here and there and knew them to be the coffins of her enemies.

She counted twelve of them. Good. The odds were lessening.

But the gory scene was disturbing. All that blood drying on the ground. Swarms of flies flitting over long, gray shapes. What had happened here?

She looked at the lake. Peaceful. Almost serene. Fishing nets dipping in and out of the water, no doubt carrying away fish to distant freezers for later consumption. A feeling of dread came over her.

Marta's voice startled her. "I don't think we should stop here, Highness," she said.

Venatora didn't even have to think. "No," she said. "And tell the others to stay clear of the water."

She marched on. If they hurried they'd catch Skink before the morning was over.

CHAPTER THIRTY THREE

WHIPLASH

She caught up to him when he was more than halfway up a mountain. Here the road moved in a series of sharp switchbacks, climbing to a huge white dome on the mountaintop.

She could see the twin columns of pirates and Anthofelia's women moving up the road, like ants intent on finding prey.

Motioning for Marta and the others to stay down and out of sight, Venatora found a hiding place behind a blowdown to study the situation. The blowdown had been a large tree, so it must have taken a high wind to topple it. Thankfully, they hadn't encountered severe weather so for.

First she looked for another easier route than the road. Cables snaked from a forest of towers below, bearing cargo cars that escalated up the mountain to the dome.

It would be easy enough to dump the foodstuff the cars carried and climb aboard for a quick and easy way to the top.

Unfortunately, the cables were set too far away from the road and the cliffs were so steep that not even a mountain goat could manage them.

On top of those concerns, Venatora was feeling so uneasy about *Demeter* that she wondered if that kind of interference with the natural order of things would bring on more dangerous oddities. So far she had managed to avoid becoming one of *Demeter's* targets. She didn't know why and was reluctant to take a chance by disturbing the natural order of things.

She looked elsewhere, searching for the best way to attack Skink and Anthofelia. They had the high ground. Which was bad. They also had the numbers. Which was worse. The weapons were not quite equal—Venatora was much better equipped because of her years of looting Imperial armories. Loot that she deliberately did not share with Skink and the other pirate captains.

Behind her, Clew and Marta slipped out of the bushes.

"It doesn't look good," Clew said.

An experienced captain in her own right, Clew's opinion was to be valued.

"Maybe there's a way around the mountain," Marta said. "We can catch them on the other side. If we're quick enough, we might even be able to ambush them."

Venatora sighed. "You're right," she said. "if we hit them now we'll be giving up surprise for the dubious distinction of taking on a superior enemy on higher ground."

Suddenly there came a enormous Boom! as if someone had slammed a gigantic door. They looked up to see a cloud of dust and a jumble of the boulders cover the mountain road near the top of the column. They heard distant screams and saw people scattering.

Then they saw other people stopping to turn and take a stand. Against what, they couldn't tell. They seemed to be firing at a beast of some sort.

The creature let out a skin-peeling shriek that echoed down the mountainside.

"What the clot?" Clew said.

"Whatever it is, I wouldn't want to be in their boots right now," Marta said.

"Let's just wait a bit and see what develops," Venatora said, squatting on her haunches and fetching rations from her knapsack.

Marta signaled the others to take a break, then she and Clew settled down next to Venatora.

It was like watching a livee thriller where the life and death stakes were for real.

* * * *

Skink awoke in the pearly *Demeter* dawn with a sense of dread. His skin crawled with the feeling that a faceless something was pursing him.

Heart thumping, he came to his feet and shouted for everyone to get up and get going.

Ignoring the grumbles and curses, he hastily tended to his necessities. He swallowed a high energy ration pack without tasting it, then grabbed his knapsack and battlerifle and marched off, not looking behind him to see if anyone was following.

He moved in a half-trot, stretching his muscles until they were loose. He heard loud cursing from the columns behind him and without looking back he shouted, "I hear one more clottin' complaint and I'll skin the complainer alive.

"So shut the clot up and move your lazy behinds. We're going to lay down some kilometers today or I'll know the clotting reason why."

Adrenaline drove Skink onward. He barely noticed the fields of grain and produce he was passing. The sound of cars moving along cables and whirring harvest 'bots toiling to fill them only added to his anxiety. The feeling that he had to keep moving or all would be lost.

At one point a chattering little creature hopped out of a field and landed on the roadway a few meters in front of him. It had huge eyes, pointed little ears and it held a hunk of melon in its paws. It nibbled on the melon as Skink approached, juicy bits falling onto the road.

Skink had no intention of stopping, or trying to shoo the creature away. He swung his battlerifle around to fire and suddenly there was a bellow from the field to his left.

The little creature turned its head to see, looked back at Skink, then hopped off the road and disappeared into rows of peas in the direction of the bellowing sound.

A cold chill ran up Skink's spine. What if he had shot it? Get your wits about you, man, he admonished himself. Under no circumstances did he want to meet the owner of that bellow. It was probably its mother.

About midday the road began to climb a mountain in a series of sharp switchbacks that rose to a large white dome at the top. Cable cars snaked up the side, moving through low bushes and stubby, wind-blown trees.

Without pausing for an afternoon break, Skink kept going, settling in for the long and arduous trek to the top.

Behind him he heard Gregor's whining voice. "Really, Mitzi," he was saying, "I have to stop soon or I'm going to collapse. Someone should speak to Captain Skink. This is inhumane."

Skink was about to turn and let him have it, when he heard Mitzi's low voice shush him, then say soothing words to calm him down.

It was just as well. Gregor was Lord Fehrle's personal hostage and he had made it quite clear that if anything untoward happened to him there would be hell to pay.

Typical rich kid, Skink thought. Lord Wichman had spoiled him until he wasn't worth the drakh he emitted every day, much less the food and drink he took in to keep his miserable self going.

At any other time, Skink would have happily slit his throat and taken Mitzi for his own. Just thinking about the lovely joygirl brought his blood to a boil. Soon he was in lost in erotic visions of what he would do to her if she was his bedmate.

The real world became a hazy thing as he put one boot in front of another. On and on. At one point he started to tire and slowed down, but then the prickling sensation at the back of his neck began again, and he quickened his pace.

When he reached for a drink of water it was getting late into the afternoon. Mentally, he guessed that they'd made at least forty kilometers since morning. He was determined to reach the top well before the day's end. Then he could look over the terrain with his binocs and see what—if anything—was following.

Skink was so absorbed in his thinking that he barely noticed the trickle of dirt spilling down the mountainside onto the road ahead.

There was a rumble.

Gregor gave a terrified shout.

Skink jerked up to see a huge circle of earth studded with bushes and small trees breaking away from the mountainside above him.

There were loud ripping sounds as roots were torn away and rocks began to tumble down the side.

Then a long, hairy tendril pushed through the opening. Followed by several more until they formed an insect-like claw that was pushing against the earthen doorway.

Skink shouted for everyone to run, then sprinted ahead, Gregor and Mitzi and some of his pirates close behind. He sensed rather than saw that that the twin column had broken up and people were scattering in all directions.

But before he could clear the area, the doorway slammed open with an enormous boom that sent showers of boulders and rocks rolling down the mountain.

He heard an unearthly shriek and he swung his battlerifle up and found himself looking at an enormous insect face, with gnashing mandibles, beneath hundreds of red eyes looking out from a huge single optical organ.

Skink fired and the creature shrieked as AM2 bullets chewed into its face. Unfazed, it kept coming. Claws dragging a huge hairy many-limbed body out of the cave.

He dropped to his knees and kept firing. Some of his pirates stayed with him, opening up on the creature. Battlerifles firing streams of bullets poured into the beast. On the other side of a jumble of boulders he could see other pirates and some of Anthofelia's women doing the same.

The creature was almost all the way out now. Twin claws were reaching down and grabbing people, and stuffing them into its maw.

A moment later it was all the way out and a huge stinger emerged, dripping green venom, that sizzled and sent up smoke where it touched the ground.

Then out of nowhere he saw Gregor coming to his feet and running toward him. Blocking his aim.

Thankfully, Mitzi tackled him, but as he fell, Gregor grabbed her, twisting so that he could use her body as a shield.

Then he was out of the pirate captain's way. Skink slapped a grenade round on his battlerifle and fired as the stinger came plunging down at him, mandibles going like crazy—clackclackclack!

The grenade hit. There was an enormous explosion and then yellow gore rained down on them.

The creature was still. Except for the mandibles, which continued to clack. But slower. Clack. Clack. Clack. He watched, mesmerized, until it stopped.

He looked over at Gregor and Mitzi. She'd freed herself from him and was coming to her feet, furiously scrubbing away yellow. She paused to douse a rag with water and started to wipe her face when Gregor reached up a hand, his face like a spoiled child.

"What about me?" he whined.

Skink couldn't bear it any long. He reached out with one foot and booted Gregor so hard, that he fell on his back.

Thoroughly disgusted, the pirate got to his feet.

"What was that for?" Gregor whined, rubbing his behind.

Skink stated to tell him. To call him every kind of a coward, but realized it was pointless.

He shrugged. "Sorry," he said. "An involuntary twitch."

Then he turned and surveyed the disaster that had befallen his marching columns. But out of the corner of his eye he caught Mitzi looking at him. As if measuring him. For good or ill he could not tell.

He shouted for Gurnsey and Hasana and when they'd dragged their weary bodies to his side he gave orders to round everyone up and get moving again.

"If anyone is too injured to march, leave them," he said. "But take their food and water and spare ammo. Especially the ammo. I'm guessing we may need every bit of it before this is done."

There were no arguments. It was a good thing, because Skink would have killed anyone who balked.

Down the road, Anthofelia appeared. He waited until she found her way around the jumble of boulders and the horrible creature that lay sprawled halfway across the road.

As she came up to him, she said, "I don't think we should stop. We don't know what *Demeter* has in store for us next."

"For a change, Princess," he said, "we are in complete agreement."

Before he could turn and continue on his way, she said, "This might be one of those times when Lord Fehrle might be sorry that he got what he wished for."

Skink grimaced. "Once again, we agree," he said. Then: "Enough talk. Let's get moving."

* * * *

Venatora lowered the binocs. "I think it would be wise to avoid this next section of road," she said.

Clew and Marta were still wide-eyed over the horror they'd witnessed.

"Exactly so," Clew said. She was visibly shaken by what she had witnessed.

"I think we need to find another road Your Highness," Marta said. "Circle the mountain, like you mentioned before."

Venatora got to her feet and brushed herself off. She said, "Let's poke around and see what we find, before we just strike across country and get *Demeter* even madder at us."

Clew gave her an odd look. "It's not alive, you know," she said. "It's an artificial world built by sentient beings like ourselves."

Venatora laughed. "Tell that to *Demeter*," she said.

* * * *

Near nightfall, Ripley and Lancer came upon the place where the three women had watched Skink's battle with the monster.

They'd already checked the area where the troops had waited on their leaders and they could easily make out the place behind the blowdown where Venatora, Marta and Clew had hidden behind the dead tree.

There was a breeze blowing down the mountainside. The two Suzdals sniffed the air, catching the scent of spent AM2 rounds, exploding grenades and the bitter taste of fear.

There was also something else on the wind that was even more disturbing.

"Too big to be an insect," Lancer said, "but that's what it smells like."

"Whatever it is," Ripley said, "it's dead now."

They circled around some more, looking for signs.

"I don't think Venatora followed Skink," Ripley said.

"Where could she have gone?" Lancer wondered.

They snuffed around, then came upon a trampled over spot where another large blowdown partially obscured the road.

Climbing over it, they found a place where the road forked—this path heading to the northwest, probably circling the mountain.

More checking uncovered an area where many booted feet had followed the new path. There had been an attempt to cover the trail, but there were few beings in the Empire who had the skills to fool Ripley and Lancer.

"Should we follow Skink or Venatora?" Ripley wondered.

"Let's go get Sten," Lancer said. "Let him decide."

"I'll bet he follows his girlfriend," Ripley said.

Lancer woofed with amusement. "Do you really think Venatora is his girlfriend," he asked.

Ripley chuckled. "Just give him a sniff whenever her name is mentioned," she said. "The musk is so thick it would make a very expensive male perfume."

The two had a laugh at their boss's expense, then trotted off to find him.

CHAPTER THIRTY FOUR

THE TRUEL

When Skink reached the other side of the mountain storm clouds were knuckling under the sky. A brisk wind blew in from the snow-capped peaks in the north, biting his nostrils and bringing tears to his yellow eyes.

Behind him, Gurnsey was saying, "Better find a place to hole up, boss. Storm looks like a nasty one."

Indeed it did. Already, they could see lightning crackling from sky to ground The wind bore the heavy scent of rain as it drove the storm clouds toward them.

He hated to stop. Except for a few hours, he'd driven his people mercilessly all through the night. He'd called a halt once and everyone dropped to the ground, exhausted. But the howling of wolves kept anyone from sleeping and put them further on edge, wondering what *Demeter* had in store for them next.

So they'd marched on, their way lit by lanterns, constantly on the alert for the wolves. They never caught sight of them, but fearful yellow eyes glaring from the underbrush, and the sound of low growls and padded feet had everyone's nerves stretched to the breaking point.

When dawn arrived, Skink let them pause long enough to snatch a bite to eat and then they were on the move again, laying down kilometers at a furious pace.

Now they were coming into a rocky area cut by canyons and creeks. The road snaked past two high bluffs that would be perfect for an ambush. But Skink no longer had the feeling that he was being followed and decided that it would be a waste of time to set one up of his own and wait to see if anyone was following.

He stopped to sweep the terrain with his binocs, looking for a likely place to camp. As he did so, Anthofelia came up with Nalene and Yatola.

Without preamble she said, "We need to find shelter right away. That storm will be on us at any moment."

Anthofelia's voice was tight and she had a harried, nervous look about her. A quick glance at her bodyguards told the tale of a leader who was falling out of favor with her troops. When Anthofelia spoke they observed her with narrowed eyes.

Emboldened, Gregor spoke up. "I'm dead on my feet, Captain," he whined. "I don't know how much longer any of can continue without a little rest."

But as he spoke he was braced, as if expecting a blow and his eyes were blinking like crazy. Next to him, Mitzi was stroking his back, soothing him.

Skink almost gave them all hell for stating the obvious, but thought better of it. He needed calmness now. And he sure as clot didn't need a revolt of Anthofelia's troops.

He draped an arm over Gurnsey's shoulder, startling him. "Me and Gurnsey were thinking the exact same thing," he said with a companionable smile. He pointed at a tree-lined canyon just ahead. "That looks like a good place. Out of the wind with a nice overhang to keep the rain off."

Anthofelia blinked. She'd been expecting an argument. "Oh," she said, the wind spilling from her sails. Then she pulled herself together. "I'll get my people organized," she said, then turned on her heels and headed back to her column.

Gregor opened his mouth to speak and Skink was immediately sorry that he'd acted approachable for even a minute. The little piece of drakh would start blabbing his ear off now.

"Captain," Gregor began. "I've been meaning to—" But before he could utter another word lighting crashed down on the bluffs above them and Gregor squeaked in terror, practically wetting himself.

"Let's get moving, Gurnsey," Skink said, and started toward the mouth of the canyon."

Mitzi held Gregor back and let Gurnsey and a few others move past them. She had a feeling that things were about to come to a head.

Her comm buzzed in her ear and she stopped, stooping down as if to adjust a boot seal.

"GA," she whispered.

"To your right," Sten said. "Hill. Red blossomed tree."

She looked. Spotted the hill with the distinctive tree.

"Rendezvous there when you are done."

He clicked off. She got to her feet and raced after Gregor, who was so frightened he didn't realize Mitzi wasn't with him.

The realization hit just as she caught up to him. He turned, eyes in a panic, then he saw her and grabbed her arm.

"Don't leave me like that, Mitzi," he whined.

"Not to worry, sweetie pie," she soothed. "Mitzi's here."

* * * *

Venatora was slammed onto her back, the rocket launcher clipping her forehead. Thirty meters away the ground was smoking from where the lightning had hit.

"Clotting hell!" she snarled, dabbing at blood trickling down from a cut in her head. "I had that filthy drakh head right in my sights."

Marta rushed to her side, whipping out a cloth treated with a clotting agent from her medpack and applying it to the wound. Venatora made to push her aside, but Marta persisted.

"Hold still, Highness," she said. "In order to fight you have to see and to see you have to keep the blood out of your eyes."

Sighing, she let Marta dab at the wound. But when she was done Venatora pushed her aside and came to her knees. She was in time to see the last of the enemy disappear into the canyon.

Spatters of rain fell and she was about to order her own people to find shelter when the dark skies suddenly brightened. She looked up and to her amazement the storm clouds were dissipating as fast as they'd formed.

Clew scrambled over to her side. "Looks to me as if we have two choices," she said. "We can wait until they come out and kill them. Or, we can seal them off with a few well-placed rocket and mortar rounds and head for the Command Center lickety-split and take control."

"I suggest we kill them now," Palsonia said. "We're going to have to do it eventually."

Venatora was about to speak—she favored the killing them now choice—when there was a tremendous explosion.

Instinctively, she crouched down. There was another explosion, this one even bigger. She looked around, but there was no sign of any damage to their little fortress.

Cautiously, she peered over the boulder and caught a glimpse of a smoking crater at the mouth of Skink's canyon.

"What the clot?" she said, starting to raise her head higher.

But then Marta was shouting, "Down! Down!" and a mortar round exploded in the center of their camp. Rocks and debris crashed over them. Through ringing ears she heard screams of pain.

Another round found them, debris shrapneling everywhere. Marta and Palsonia threw themselves on Venatora, trying to shield her from the worst.

Where the clot had those mortar rounds come from? Had Skink spotted their ambush and prepared one of his own?

Frantically, Venatora pushed Marta and Palsonia aside, shouting, "Hit them back! Now! Now!"

Somehow she found her launcher and was on her feet, firing at Skink's redoubt.

All around her, women were opening up with battlerifles, rockets and grenade-launchers. Pouring fire on the enemy.

* * * *

Skink didn't know what had happened. There were two explosions. The first at the mouth of the canyon, which did little more than collapse part of the canyon's side and send debris flying everywhere.

The next hit the center of the camp, falling on the cooking detail and leaving a smoking crater where a large pot had just begun to boil. The cooking crew was sprawled on the ground, dead or groaning.

What kind of craziness was this? Those were definitely rocket rounds. Was *Demeter* armed with rockets? How could that be?

Then he heard battlerifle fire. And the distinctive sound of mortar rounds being launched.

More explosions ripped his camp. AM2 rounds were pinging everywhere. And he realized—This was not *Demeter's* doing.

Swiftly he clambered to the top of a jumble of boulders and peered out. The attack appeared to be coming from the bluffs he'd earlier marked as a good ambush site. Apparently someone else had the same idea.

As he looked he saw a tall, distinctive figure standing on top of a boulder, a rocket launcher in her hand.

It was Venatora!

How in clot did she get here?

Somehow he found his battlerifle. Pressing the stock to his shoulder he took careful aim. Slowly squeezed the trigger.

But a split second before he fired another woman rose up and swept Venatora away and his bullet pinged harmlessly on the spot where she'd stood.

Clot!

He slid back down to the canyon's floor.

"It's Venatora," he shouted.

But no one heard him, except Gregor and Mitzi.

"Oh, she caught us, she caught us," Gregor moaned in terror. He looked wildly about. "Sten!" he shouted. "Sten must be here someplace!"

Skink wanted to kick him. Take his frustration out on this whimpering coward with several well-placed boot tips.

Mitzi stepped in just in time, pulling Gregor aside, an odd smile on her face.

For a split second Skink wondered why she was smiling. And what was all this Sten business? But then there were more explosions and the AM2 fire increased.

He grabbed Gurnsey and Hasana and started issuing orders. He'd show that bitch. He'd get his people organized and clotting fight back.

He'd make her sorry she'd ever met him.

188 | ALLAN COLE

Across the way Anthofelia stood in the middle of her women, frozen in terror.

All around her women were scrambling to get into fighting position. But it was no thanks to their boss. Vaguely, she recalled Nalene shouting at her to do something. Anything! But she was so terrified, she couldn't speak.

Desperate, Nalene and Yatola took charge, working like smooth machines and barking orders.

Anthofelia knew that when this was over, no matter the outcome, they would kill her if they could.

But she couldn't help herself. Venatora, her most hated enemy, had somehow followed her to this place, appearing from nowhere to rain death and destruction upon her.

An explosion erupted nearby, jamming her against a boulder. Her ears rang from the explosion and her mind descended to a chaotic ground zero. She fought against it, grasping for sanity. For reason.

Gradually she recovered. And with recovery, came a gut-wrenching resolve. She would live, dammit. She would live and personally shoot Venatora between the eyes.

Confidence restored, she took charge of the fight. Directing her women. Joining in on the defense. But all the while she stayed carefully out of the line of fire.

On the other side of the canyon, Mitzi guided Gregor to a spot that was out of sight of the others.

All the months of coddling the little drakh for brains, tending to his every infantile need, were piling up on her. For days now it was all she could do to keep from cutting his throat.

Now, with the battle raging while he wined and hid behind her, she had reached the end of her patience. Every time there was an explosion—be it near or far—he'd squeal and jump and blubber for somebody or other. Mitzi supposed it was his mother.

Disgusted as she was at this poor excuse for a sentient being, a small part of her felt sorry for him.

Yes, he was not only a coward and a greedy manipulator of anyone in his charge, but a frightful human being who took delight in the torment of others.

When he was in his cups, which was more often than not, he'd boast of scams he had pulled on people, some of which led to their maiming, or even death. He acted like a giggling bad seed of a child pulling wings from flies.

On the other hand the months of drugged isolation ordered by his father had made him infantile. The condition was further worsened by Mitzi herself, who had added her own brew to the narcotic stewpot to keep him firmly in control.

She'd wrapped him in an imaginary world of eroticism where his every word or thought became commands that Mitzi's mental avatars followed.

It was almost humorous. Gregor believed he'd participated in wild orgies with Mitzi. That he'd done everything imaginable to her and her drug-induced avatars.

And yet, other than kisses and caresses, he'd never done a thing. Never consummated their joygirl and john pairing.

So, when she pushed him behind a boulder out of sight of the others and shot him with her little hideout gun, she only felt the smallest amount of guilt.

Just a twinge.

Then she stepped through the narrow opening that led to the trail beyond.

And was gone.

* * * *

Sten rested against a tree that grew out of the rocky surface of the peak that overlooked the gory chaos below.

He looked up at the fabulous red blossoms and wondered for a moment how the tree could even exist here.

There wasn't speck of soil to be seen, or a drop of moisture to be found and yet it had grown to a tremendous height. Its branches were thick with scarlet blossoms, which produced large, bulbous fruit. The fruit was red on the outside and black on the inside—witness the examples on the ground that had fallen, spilling black seeds across presumably barren rock.

Sten shook himself out of the brief reverie to watch the battle unfold beneath him. They'd been at it for nearly an hour. Every once in awhile there'd be a lull and then he, or Alex, would loft a rocket round into one side of the battle, or the other.

"It's loch stirrin' up a wee ant's barnie," Kilgour said as he fired yet another round.

Mk'wolf chuckled, as he handed Alex a fresh launcher.

"What did Gen. Mahoney, call it?" he asked no one in particular.

"A truel," Sten said. "A three-way duel."

Laughing at the odd word, he leaned back against the tree. He heard a cracking sound overhead and looked up to see a fruit falling from a high branch. It crashed through several other branches, and then Sten reached up and caught the fruit in midair.

He stared at it for a second. The surface was so polished he could almost see his face.

The fruit began to throb, as if it were a little animal. It was so sudden, he almost dropped it. Before his eyes it began pulsing like a beating heart.

Then he heard whispering voices and he looked around but couldn't find the source. He noticed Alex and Mk'wolf doing the same thing.

In a low voice, Kilgour said, "It's th' tree, lad. Th' bludy tree."

Sten tilted his head. Alex was right. The whispers seemed to be coming from the tree.

How could that be?

"I can't make out a clotting word they're saying," Mk'wolf said.

"Shh!" Ripley said.

Sten looked up. He hadn't realized the Suzdals were nearby. Lancer squatted on his haunches next to her. Head tilted, eyes closed in intense concentration.

"What it is?" Sten asked.

Ripley held up a paw, shushing him.

Sten shushed.

She might be a lowly corporal, but she and Lancer had proven themselves many times over in the past few days. Besides, it was *de rigueur* that rank on a Mantis team counted for nothing. Whoever knew best took the lead.

Still, he was getting impatient and about to prod her when Ripley said, "It's *Demeter*. And she's telling us—no ordering us—to leave."

Sten frowned. "Leave? Leave where?"

Lancer broke in. "Here, Captain," he said. "We have to leave here."

"*Demeter* can spik?" Kilgour said in awed tones. "Ah didne ken tress coods spick."

"This one can," Ripley pointed out.

Lancer said, "Makes me sorry for all the times I lifted my leg and— well, you know."

Sten had a flash along similar lines and almost laughed.

Instead, he said, "Tell Demet..." but he stopped when Ripley once again raised her paw.

"You don't need me to talk, Captain," she said. "Tell her yourself."

"Okay," Sten said. Then, feeling a little foolish, he raised his head and addressed the empty sky.

"*Demeter*," he said. "We only need a little longer. Then we'll get out of here. Two, no three days max. Then we'll all be gone."

Silence.

The whispering had stopped.

A cold finger traced his spine, and he shivered.

"*Demeter*," he called out again. "Can you hear me, *Demeter*?"

More silence.

"Just three days," Sten said. "I promise we'll only be here three more days. To be honest, there will be some damage. But we'll do our best to keep it at a minimum. Nothing you can't heal naturally."

He waited. Then waited some more.

"Maybe she can't hear me," Sten said, getting to his feet. "Maybe if I stand up she can hear me better."

"Oh, she heard you, Captain," Lancer said.

"What? How do you know?"

"Can't you feel it," Ripley said.

Soon as she said those words, Sten felt a strange sensation. It felt like little creatures were crawling up his skin.

He shuddered and shook his shoulders, as if to throw them off.

"Ah think our Truel jist turned intoae somethin' else," Alex said.

Sten was about to ask if anyone knew what to call a four-way duel when he heard someone call his name.

He whirled to see Mitzi bursting out of the underbrush and come running toward him.

"Damn, am I glad to see you," she cried as she closed on him, arms spreading wide for an embrace.

Then the ground opened up, and Sten plunged into a dark abyss.

Above him he could see Mitzi, arms outstretched, shouting, "Sten! Sten! Sten!"

But he kept falling and falling.

A hard blow.

Then another.

Pain.

Then blackness.

CHAPTER THIRTY FIVE

THE HIDDEN ENEMY

Venatora was starting to realize that there was another enemy at work.

Skink was reeling from her ambush and was struggling to regroup and return fire. But it was a sporadic effort and so weak that her forces should have overwhelmed them right at the beginning.

And yet she was being hammered by rocket and mortar fire that far exceeded his visible efforts at defense.

The ground shook as another round came blazing in. Once again, it didn't come directly from any of Skink's people she could observe.

And then Clew said, "What's that over there, Highness?"

She looked where Clew was pointing and saw a flash of light.

"I don't see how Skink could have flanked us," she said.

And then it came to her.

It was Sten!

It just had to be. Who else could have staged such a cunning operation? Who else would have had the sheer nerve to take this sort of risk?

Only an all-in gambler like Sten would have the *cajones* to take such a chance.

The issue became settled in her mind.

It was Sten. It could be no other.

But what did he want? What did he hope to gain?

When the answer came she shivered. This was a mission to wipe out piracy in the Empire. Obviously, it couldn't be completely destroyed. But with Skink and the other captains dead, or out of action the Emperor would be taking a big bite out of the problem.

Well, not just Skink. There was more. Much more. There was a burgeoning pirate culture that would only get deadlier and more successful as they grew.

The Himmenops.

Led by none other than Venatora herself.

A gut wrench.

Sten wanted her dead.

He was here to kill her.

But I thought—

Woman, it doesn't matter what you thought. The lover of your dreams wants you dead. And you have to act, and act fast, or all will be lost.

"Marta," she called out. "Palsonia. Get over here."

In a moment her two most trusted women and Clew were by her side.

"There isn't time to explain," she said, "so just listen very carefully and do exactly as I say."

There were murmurs of "Yes, Highness," and she went on.

"Any minute now, things are going to blow up in our faces."

"But, Majesty," Marta protested. "We've got him. Skink is all but done."

"Clot, Skink," Venatora said. "He's not the problem."

And then she laid it out for them. Told them that Sten was here with a Mantis team. When the drakh hit the fan, there was a good chance Venatora would be killed, or at the very least, taken out the action.

"If that happens," she said, "I want you all to regroup and head back to our ship. Never mind the Command Center. All that is over and done with."

"We'll never leave you here, Majesty," Palsonia objected.

"You may very well have to," Venatora said. "The important thing is our homeland. Our people. When you reach the ship get it fired up and ready to go. Wait for me for one cycle. No more. Then go."

"Majesty," Marta wailed and her love of Venatora was so strong it was almost overwhelming.

Venatora dialed her pheromones back. Felt the tension in the women ease somewhat.

"One cycle," she repeated. "No more. And if you should see the enemy before that get the clot out of here and go home."

A barrage of rocket rounds blasted into their camp and they all had to duck down to escape the raining debris.

When it stopped, Venatora raised up. "But before we do anything else," she said, "I have one thing I want to accomplish. One person I want to make sure is dead. The one who started this whole thing."

Grabbing a launcher, she went to an overlook, knelt down to sweep the forces below with her binocs.

She heard a rustling sound and she looked down to see a little green lizard scurrying along the branches of a bush that grew from the side of the cliff.

It stopped and stared at her for a moment, completely still, except for a throbbing at its throat, that revealed scarlet folds.

Venatora was captivated by the sight. The throbbing throat. Green, then skin accordioning to reveal flashes of ruby red. In and out. In and out. In and—

She shook herself. This was nonsense. Once again, she looked through the binocs. And there was Skink, plain as day.

He was such a smeg head. Yo-ho-hoing like the legendary pirates of yore. All a stupid testosterone-fueled pose.

But he was really no different than any of the other captains. Greedy clots. Short on loyalty, long on back-stabbing.

The binocs swept onward.

And there she was:

Anthofelia!

She settled her sights on the upstart princess. This would be one of the rare times Venatora would take real pleasure in snatching someone's life away.

Once again there came the rustling sound. Strangely clear over the sounds of the raging battle. And there was that little lizard staring at her again. The scarlet throat seemed to be pulsing faster.

In and out. In and out. In and—

Whispering voices came from nowhere.

Everywhere.

The voices suddenly took on an overwhelming importance. What were they saying? Who were they talking to? And who the clot were they?

Beneath her, the outcrop shuddered. Then moved. Slowly at first. She felt sick in her stomach.

There was a lurch.

Venatora shouted in alarm as she plunged from her perch. She fell a few feet, but was brought up short by the thick bush below. Somehow she'd managed to hang onto the rocket launcher.

She scrambled around until she found a good position. Pulled up the binocs, which were dangling from a thong about her neck.

She found Anthofelia again.

Excellent.

This death was not to be denied her.

She settled her sights and was about to fire, when she saw two women approach Anthofelia from behind. She recognized them immediately: Nalene and Yatola.

Very well, she'd kill all three.

But just as she about to pull the trigger she saw Nalene grab Anthofelia from behind. She had her by the hair and was pulling her head back.

And then Yatola stepped in and slit Anthofelia's throat.

A gush of blood and the would-be princess was on the ground, limbs thrashing while Nalene and Yatola held her down.

Then she was still.

And Anthofelia was no more.

A great sense of satisfaction swept over Venatora. It was right and good that Anthofelia's own people had put an end to her.

She heard Marta calling her: "Majesty? Are you all right?"

Venatora looked up and saw Marta and Palsonia standing there. Palsonia had a rope. She dropped the end down and Venatora caught it, then started to tie it about her waist.

Then somewhere far above here there was a blood-curdling SCREECH!

Venatora froze. Found herself staring into Marta's dark eyes.

Then came a crash and a roar and a flash of burning pain as a lightning bolt split the sky and it was if the gates to an enormous river had been opened and rain came torrenting down.

It was heavy. So heavy. Pounding her back and head. Then the Raid turned to hail and she was being peppered with ice that stung through her clothing.

She hid her face in one arm, tried to shelter her neck with the other. Then it was hail and rain together, slashing her flesh, while at the same time the rain was so thick that she could barely breathe.

Venatora knew that if she was going to survive she would have to get the clot off this cliff.

At first, she tried to go up, but couldn't find a handhold. So she went down, jamming a fist into a rock crevice, finding a place for her boot, then slowly…slowly…going down while the rain and hail pounded at her.

Somehow she managed to continue down and after what seemed to be an eternity, she was on the ground and finding shelter beneath several huge boulders.

She huddled there while all around her the storm raged, lightning crashing and thunder rolling and it seemed like there would never be an end to it.

* * * *

Someone was tugging at his arm, going "Boss? Boss?"

Skink raised his head and saw Hasana kneeling beside him. He was so glad to see her he nearly wept. Good and faithful Hasana staying with him no matter what.

He looked about. "Where's Gurnsey?"

"Dead boss. At least I think he is. Last I saw of him he was running, but no way could he outrun all those… those… things." She stifled a sob. "It was terrible, boss. Terrible."

Skink tried to remember. His mind was so shocked he could barely think. What was Hasana talking about? Why had Gurnsey been running?

He looked around. He could see debris. Probably from the storm.

But wait a minute.

What storm?

Then he recalled the intense downpour of rain and hail. Okay, but now the storm was clearly over. The day was bright. The sky cloudless.

He shifted his bulk, bumping up against something large and fleshy. Skink reached down and grabbed the object, pulling it up so he could see.

And then he nearly screamed. It was an arm! The bloody stump of an arm from the shoulder down to the wrist. As he looked, frozen in horror, there came a chittering noise and a little black bug came scampered out of the bloody wrist stump.

Skink shouted and hurled the arm away. His stomach clenched and he got to his knees and spewed his guts. Hacking and coughing and vomiting, Hasana holding his head and saying, "There, there, boss. You'll be fine. Everything's okay."

But he wasn't fine and nothing was okay and it would never be okay again.

Memory came flooding back. The raging storm. The rain and the hail the lightning and the thunder and suddenly it was over as quickly as it had begun.

The canyon floor was flooded with water, but then the arclights bloomed on and cracks appeared in the floor of the canyon and the water was sucked into the cracks until nothing was left but steam rising under the hot arclights.

He didn't see his people so he shouted for Gurnsey to get his behind over here they had a war to fight and where the clot was the enemy?

People started to creep out of their shelters. Blinking in the light like underground animals after a long winter's nap. There was Gurnsey, coming at a trot. Hasana just behind him. Then some of his other pirates.

Then he saw Anthofelia's people rising up and he had a sudden flash back to the moment when he saw her aides catch her and slit her throat, which was fine with him. Good riddance.

A moment later his troops started to appear, looking dazed, but coming out of it. Checking their battlerifles and gear.

Then he heard a pop! pop! pop! like firecrackers going off and he whirled to see little puffs of dirt exploding—pop! pop! pop! One went off just by his boot and a little black bug come tumbling out.

He smiled. It was a fierce little thing with tiny gnashing mandibles and clicking claws and a protruding tail with stinger on the end.

It came running toward him, as if to attack.

Stupid little thing.

"Ooh, I'm scared," he chortled and he raised a boot and smashed the bug to a yellow pulp.

There was a sudden stillness. All across the canyon people came to an abrupt halt and fell silent, looking about as if sensing something was about to happen.

Skink felt a chill run up his back.

Then the entire floor of the canyon erupted in miniature explosions and millions of little black bugs came crawling out of the ground, mandibles and claws clicking, stingers waving about. Chittering with so many little voices that the sound became a series of ear-piercing shrieks.

They swarmed the pirates and the women and the air was rent with screams and there was blood everywhere as the insects devoured every scrap of flesh until only bloody uniforms were left behind.

Skink turned and scrambled up the hillside, not daring to look back. Then he found a safe place beneath some boulders and crawled in. He got himself turned around and saw the carnage below as the little bugs swarmed anything that moved.

Then, just as quickly as it had begun, it was all over. And a long silence settled in over the dead.

And night fell so fast that it was like enormous curtains had closed on the scene.

Skink was too frightened to move and after a time he fell into a restless sleep full of screams and chittering bugs and empty, blood-soaked clothing.

And the next thing he knew, Hasana was tugging at his sleeve, going, "Boss? Boss?"

He felt a gnawing in his belly, realized he hadn't eaten for hours, and looked for his knapsack so he could grab some rations. But it was nowhere to be seen.

"Got anything to eat?" he asked Hasana.

"Sure, Boss," she said. "Right here."

He looked up and Hasana was just sitting there, staring at him. Hands empty. She grimaced and an odd look crossed her face, as if she were in pain.

"What's wrong, Hasana?" he asked.

"Wrong, Boss? What could be wrong?"

Then her mouth came open as if she were going to say something else. "Hasana?"

She lurched forward, retching. Gagging. Skink reached over to slap her on the back. To rid her of whatever was stuck in her throat.

She moaned. Gagged again. And then she vomited up hundreds of chittering black bugs that fell from her mouth into her lap and raced across her body toward Skink and he was screaming and shouting, "Get away, get away, get away," but they kept coming, wave after wave of them and he fell back, screaming and screaming and then in a moment he was entirely covered with stinging, biting insects, thrashing wildly about, but there was no escape, no way to get free of *Demeter*.

A moment later, there was nothing left but a heap of bloody clothes, a battlerifle, a holstered pistol and a pair of boots, standing side by side.

CHAPTER THIRTY SIX

REBIRTH

When Venatora awoke she felt oddly elated. She stretched and there was no stiffness in her limbs, or discomfort from lying on the hard ground.

She thought of Marta and the others, but for some reason she didn't feel worried about them, even though when she last saw them the earth split apart and *Demeter* was smashing down on them full force.

Something tickled her arm and she looked down to see a honey bee strolling across her arm. What a cute little thing, she thought. Venatora looked closer look and saw little balls of pollen on its hind legs.

She brought it closer still and the little creature's antenna twitched and she gazed at Venatora through two large eyes. They were a deep brown set between the antenna and its yellow mouth.

Venatora felt a strange kinship to the creature. Her heart quickened and she reached out and gently stroked the bee's back. It arched under her finger like a pet, staying there for long seconds.

She opened her hand and the bee crawled onto her palm and started doing a little dance. Venatora was fascinated—hypnotized by the little creature's antics.

The whispering sounds came back again. Like before, the sound came from nowhere in particular. Although she still couldn't make out what was being said, the tone was not aggressive like it was before. In fact, it was rather gentle and soothing.

She felt a tingling sensation and then—unaccountably her pheromone levels rose. As usual it began with a warmth that rose from her hips, over her abdomen and breasts, to her neck and then she felt tingly and warm all over.

As all this happened, the bee's dance became more intricate. And it moved faster and faster. It was trying to talk to her—of this she was sure. Was it trying to interpret the whispering for her?

"What do you want, Little Sister?" Venatora asked.

As if in answer, the bee flew off her palm, pausing in mid air.

Waiting.

Venatora had the feeling the bee wanted her get up. She rose to her feet, the bee rising with her. It circled her head—once, twice, three times—then it took off in a straight line.

Venatora felt compelled to follow and trotted after her new sister. They crossed a wide field filled with blossoming yellow flowers. Then across a creek and as Venatora splashed though the chilly water she saw a little crab-like animal scurrying about and then a pretty little orange and black snake moving smoothly through the water.

On the far bank a cloud of tiny birds burst from the brush and a second later a catlike creature followed. Neither the birds or the feline paid the slightest attention to Venatora. They just went about their business, the feline trying to catch the birds, while the birds dived at its head and scolded it. Venatora guessed there must be nests nearby.

Momentarily she became lost in thought about all the worlds—big and small—that existed around her. Where the creatures cared not one whit about the struggles of supposedly superior sentients.

She was so wrapped in thought that she lost sight of the bee. Her heart quickened. She looked all around, murmuring "Where did you go, Little Sister?" And then the bee was back, circling her, then taking off in the same direction as before.

Eventually, they came to a fragrant apple orchard. The blossoms were white and tinged with a blush of pink. The bee didn't stop to sup on the blossoms, but continued onward until they came upon an enormous oak standing alone in a mossy glen.

The bee vanished in the branches. Venatora felt a little anxious, but a cool breeze carrying the scent of the apple orchard picked up, fanning her face. Calming her.

She heard buzzing and her heart thumped. Was her sister returning?

Buzzing loudly, the bee flew out of the tree. It flew toward her and Venatora reached out a hand, palm open. The bee lighted there, did a little dance, buzzing all the while. Then suddenly another bee appeared and landed next to the first.

Then another.

And another.

Each adding its "voice" to the buzzing chorus.

Soon her entire hand was covered with bees and they kept coming until hundreds were attached to her hand, which became a large ball of moving insects. Still, the bees kept coming until her entire body was covered with bees.

Not only did not a single one sting her, but she felt delicious all over. A warm feeling of acceptance swept over her. No. Not just acceptance. But a joyous welcoming to the tribe.

It was if they had been waiting for her arrival for a long time.

The whispering turned to wordless singing and Venatora suddenly felt like she was blending into the world around her. The woods. The fields. The mountains. The rivers and the streams and all the creatures that crawled, walked, swam, or flew.

All this as *Demeter* enfolded Venatora into her embrace.

A voice broke the reverie.

"Venatora?"

It was Sten.

Standing across the glen staring at her, pistol in his hand. She noted that it was pointed down, away from her.

And just like that… like the snap! of a finger… the bees were gone.

At first, Venatora was frightened. Had they fled her? Was her new found acceptance gone? But then a calmness came over her.

Demeter was still here.

Inside and out and all around her.

She smiled at Sten. "I hope you're not here to kill me," she said.

The words startled him. He looked down at the gun, then back at her. His face became sad. He raised the gun until it was pointing directly at her.

"Yes, I suppose I am," Sten said, finger tightening on the trigger.

* * * *

Sten fell, and fell, Mitzi calling out, "Sten! Sten!" There was a sharp pain as he hit something hard, and then another and then everything went black.

Cold water shocked him to consciousness and he found himself thrashing about in a strong current, going under, coming up, choking for air, then going under again.

He caught something leafy, which turned into something more solid and he clung to it. Head just above the surface. The current of an underground river rushing him along.

But then the branch caught on a jagged rock and he was pulled under, the swift current driving him deep. But if he let go all would be lost.

Sten fumbled. Turned his hand. His little knife shot out of its fleshy sheathe. With one quick motion he cut the branch free. Then he was surfacing again, gasping for air, but clinging firmly to the severed branch— his knife safely back in its home.

He was swept endlessly along, a captive of the current. Then he saw light. It was just ahead. There was a roaring sound and the current moved faster still.

And then the river spit him out into the light and he was tumbling down a waterfall. He lost the branch and went under for long seconds. Clawing to get up, up, up into the air and light.

Sten fought his way to the surface. Spotted a grassy shore and struck out for it. He caught an overhanging branch, then slowly, painfully, dragged himself out of the water.

He collapsed on the bank. Vomited water. Then passed out.

Sten had no idea how long he was out. He had the feeling that night had come and gone and now it was a bright *Demeter* morning. The skies were clear, birds were singing and little animals scurried in the bushes, going about their daily tasks.

He found himself in a meadow full of yellow flowers, whose petals stretched wide to drink the nourishing light. The river that had nearly killed him burbled peacefully by, so unlike the raging torrent that had carried him away.

As he watched it flow past a fish leaped, trying to catch its breakfast and he was suddenly ravenously hungry. His stomach loudly complained that it had been many hours since he'd last filled it, and that was just a few mouthfuls of tasteless rations.

Sten sighed. It was a hunger that would have to go unsatisfied because he'd lost his knapsack and all of his gear, including his battlerifle. All he had were the clothes on his back, his pistol and the knife in his arm.

He wondered how Alex and the others had fared and then panic rose when it suddenly came to him that his comm was gone. He was cut off from everyone. Sten was torn. Should he wait here for Alex to find him? Or should he continue the trek to the Command Center?

As he contemplated, a little bee made itself known. Rising up from a pretty yellow flower, it hovered mere centimeters from his nose. He could have sworn that it was looking at him through those bulbous brown compound eyes.

Then it shot away. A moment later several other bees buzzed past. Then several more. He noticed they were all heading for a group of trees and it came to him that there must be a honey tree nearby.

During his Mantis training, when they were learning to live off the land, his instructor had stressed the necessity for calories. And there were few things in nature that offered more calories and nutrition than a honeycomb.

Honey was also a superior disinfectant and did wonders when made into a poultice and placed on a wound. A hive offered one-stop shopping—food, plus a pharmacy.

His stomach grumbled and when still another group of bees buzzed by, he got to his feet and followed them.

His heart sank when he saw they were flying into a blossoming apple orchard. To his surprise the bees flew on without stopping, which convinced him more than ever that they were heading home to their hive. So he continued on, grabbing an apple, shining it on his tunic, and biting into it. Delicious. But it would be even tastier and more filling with a little honey dribbled on it.

As he continued onward the sound of buzzing grew louder. The hive must be nearby. Ahead, bushes screened a glen, where an oak tree spread its proud branches.

He pushed through the bushes, but gently. The last thing he wanted to do was rouse *Demeter* again.

A flicker.

Why hadn't *Demeter* punished him for taking the apple?

For some reason he no longer feared retaliation. He felt at peace inside.

Sten shrugged, and took another bite.

Then he was brought up short. Beyond the foliage he could see a strange figure standing beneath the oak. It was humanoid in form, but its image seemed out of focus. And its limbs appeared to be enclosed in a constantly moving shell.

He drew his gun and moved forward. The figure turned toward him and his heart gave a bump. The figure was that of a fabulously beautiful woman. The woman gave a little shake of her shoulders, and suddenly thousands of bees were flying off her and the image became clear as if a curtain had been parted. It was—

"Venatora?" he said.

And it was indeed Venatora. She looked at him, amused. She indicated the gun.

Smiling, she said, "I hope you're not here to kill me."

His pulse quickened at those words. He wanted nothing more than to go to her and fold her in an embrace that would never end.

But then he looked down at the gun and duty, horrible duty that could not be denied, crawled up and seized his will in its thorny grasp.

There was no doubt that Venatora was a clear and present danger. She was the leader of the Himmenops, the most successful pirates in the empire. Never mind Skink or all the other clumsy outlaws that preyed on Imperial commerce large and small. The Himmenops were also a group that was fast expanding in numbers and sophistication.

With Venatora as their queen, there was no stopping them.

There was only one tragic answer to Venatora's question.

Raising the pistol, he said, "Yes, I suppose I am."

Venatora lifted a hand. "If you hear me out," she said, "you will know that killing is no longer necessary."

His finger tightened on the trigger.

"I'm sorry," he said. "There is no other way."

"Don't you understand? Sten," she said. "It's over. *Demeter* has won and it's over. Skink is dead. Anthofelia's dead. Even Gregor is dead."

Sten sighed. "Why should I believe you?" he asked. "How do I know you aren't lying?"

She just looked at him. "You know I'm not," she replied.

The gun drooped a moment, then he raised it and tightened his grip.

"My people are alive," he said. "They'll complete the mission, with or without me."

"Yes, they are alive," Venatora said. "We decided, *Demeter* and I, that it would be best so they could carry the message back to the Emperor that we are no longer a threat."

Sten gaped. "We?" he said "Meaning, *Demeter* and you? Have you gone insane? That's even more of reason to finish the job."

"Can't you see, Sten?" she said. "Can't you feel it? *Demeter* is not just close, she's standing right across from you."

Venatora took a step toward him.

"Don't," he said.

Her eyes bored into him and the scent of the apple blossoms seemed to enfold him. He was drawn to her, like a powerful magnet. And he could feel that she was drawn to him as well.

"Don't," he said again. It was almost a plea.

She took another step. So close he could feel warmth radiating from her body.

And now every bone, every muscle was atremble. His mind awhirl with confused images of trees and animals and birds and fish, mixed with the horrors of the deaths and fighting he'd witnessed—been a part of—the past few cycles.

"This is nonsense," he said.

"Your friends are waiting for you, Sten," she said. "Back at the Transport Center. But they don't have long. Nor do you."

Sten almost wept with frustration. Finger on the trigger frozen in place. He didn't have the will to fire.

Then she leaned forward and kissed him. It was a quick kiss, a gentle kiss, but it jolted him down to his very core. His heart and body ached for her.

She stepped back, releasing him.

He started to shoot. Pressed the trigger. In a split second a stream of AM2 bullets would cut her down. And Venatora, his beautiful Venatora, would be no more.

Sten shook his head. "I can't," he said. He closed his eyes. "I won't," he said.

He sensed motion and when he opened his eyes Venatora was gone.

Sten looked about. The glen was empty. Silent. Even the buzzing had stopped.

Then a little animal darted through the glen, disappearing into the bushes beyond. And he saw a flash of light on metal. Going forward, he saw it was the roadway they had been following.

Time to get going. As if in a dream, he holstered his weapon and moved through the bushes, pushing branches aside. A moment later he was standing on the roadway under *Demeter's* hot bright arclights.

Should he go north to the Command Center, or south, back to the Transport Complex. He flipped a mental coin, then turned to go north.

Sten had only taken a few steps when he heard the purr of an engine. He turned to find one of the gravcars he'd seen back at Transport Center.

Hmm. It looked like at least some things were working again.

The car stopped and a door swung open. He got in. Reached for the controls, but the car started moving without him. It wheeled about, then headed south, back to Transport.

He put a hand on the stick that guided it, but it was unmovable. The other controls didn't seem to work either.

Sten thought he'd wait until the car slowed for a bend, then he'd jump out. But when he came to a long curve a tremendous weariness settled over him and suddenly he just didn't care one way or the other.

He settled back in his seat and closed his eyes.

Clot it, he thought. Clot it all.

A hour or so later he was back where it had all begun and the gravcar was swooping past the buckled doors into the center and a moment later he was greeted with a cacophony of blaring sound and shockingly bright lights.

Alarms were howling, red and green and yellow lights blinking crazily on the comcenter. Around him, 'bots were scurrying everywhere, toting things to distant doorways that were constantly opening and closing.

Then he saw his friends near the exit and the gravcar came to a stop before them.

Alex was shouting, "There's uir wee bairn. Uir bonnie Sten. Ah tauld ye he'd show up."

Kilgour dragged him from the gravcar and Mk'wolf and Pegatha and Mitzi were all embracing him.

He tried to push them away. "What's going on?" he said. "What's happening?"

But no one paid him the slightest attention, instead they were stuffing him into a spacesuit and dragging him to the exit.

"We have to go," someone shouted in his ear. "She's gonna blow at any minute."

Then he was hustled out the exit and was practically carried to their little ship. There was a blur of activity he was too exhausted to make any sense of. And then he was strapped in and they lifted off and in no time he was back at the *Gessel*.

Ida and Doc were there, and Doc was saying, "For a minute, I thought we'd lost you," and Ida was saying, "Clot that! He's too pretty to die. Now let's get out of here before the drakh hits the turbos."

Sten craned to see *Demeter*—that beautiful blue diamond—on the screen.

"Would somebody please tell me what's going on," he demanded.

They all turned and looked at him like he was crazy.

"Didne ye hear, lad?" Alex said. "Dine ye hear *Demeter* spikn?"

Sten opened his mouth. He was about to tell them about his encounter with Venatora and all that had occurred between them. Then he decided they'd think he'd gone round the bend and send him off the Rykor to pick through his brain. He shuddered, remembering their last session.

Instead, he shook his head and said, "I was pretty much out of it until a couple of hours ago."

Alex patted his back. "That's alrecht, laddie. You've hud a hard time ay it."

Sten said, "I still don't get it. Who was speaking? Before, all I heard were nonsensical whispers."

Mk'wolf said, "This time it was one big voice, clear as could be."

"It was a woman's voice," Mitzi said. "Very loud and it seemed to come from everywhere."

"Especially in the woods," Pegatha said. "It was like the leaves of the trees had tongues. It was pretty spooky."

Sten said, "Did any of you recognize the voice?"

"Aye," Alex said. "Ah kent it." He put a hand on Sten's shoulder. "It sounded a bit like yer wee lass," he said. "Your colleen—Venatora."

Sten's heart quickened. "Wha-wha— What did she say?"

"She said she was going to bring everything to an end," Mk'wolf said. "That she was a failed experiment and she couldn't go on living knowing that."

Sten felt ill. He found it difficult to breathe. He guessed what was going to come next and totally forgot his Mantis training.

Ida reached over and felt his forehead.

"Get him a drink," she said.

A glass was pushed into his hands and he lifted it to his lips and took a long swallow. It burned all the way down. He thought it was going to come right back up, but Ida slapped a mouthpiece on him and fed him pure oxygen. After a minute or so his heart stopped racing and he could breathe again.

"Suicide?" he guessed.

"Planetcide would be more accurate," Doc said. "When *Demeter* goes she'll take every living thing with her."

Sten looked at the monitor. *Demeter* shone against the backdrop of space. A marvelous jewel set against millions of sparkling stars.

"When?" Sten asked.

The moment he spoke *Demeter*'s lights started blinking on and off. Darkness then light. Darkness then light. Faster and faster, until it climaxed in a blinding flash of blue and green.

And *Demeter* was gone.

Where she had once been was now nothing but cold, dark, empty space. Very much like the cold, dark and empty space in Sten's heart.

The place that Venatora had once occupied.

Sten sighed and said, "Set a course for home, Ida."

"We don't have a home, remember?" she said.

"Ah vote fur th' nearest pub," Alex said. "Where th' drink ur strong an' th' wee lassies ur slow afoot."

"Add a boy toy or three to that," Ida said and I'll hit the go button."

Wisely, Alex did not disagree.

But just before they made the jump Sten noticed that the tugs that had accompanied *Demeter*, were also gone.

Strange.

Originally, they were parked about fifty or sixty kilometers away from their charge, waiting for orders to clamp their tractor beams on again and carry her away. Hmm. What a curious absence.

Sten almost laughed aloud as he realized that in the end, Venatora had thrown the dice and they'd come up lucky sevens.

He buried the laugh, but inside the hurt was not so painful as before.

And he wondered if in all the wandering years to come she would ever think of him.

CHAPTER THIRTY SEVEN

THE RECKONING

Mahoney was locked and loaded with a bottle of scotch and a brace of tumblers when the Eternal Emperor came trooping into the throneroom.

Considering that he'd just returned from a meeting with a pack of industrialists and politicians, he was in a rare good mood.

Mahoney poured and the Emperor raised his glass. "Confusion to the enemy," he decreed and took it all down in a single swallow. The general followed suit, then poured them both two more.

"What's this all about, boss?" he said. "You usually come back from those meetings and start dictating a wet list, which I have to hide in the mess on your desk until you've calmed down enough to rescind the order."

His boss barked with laughter. "So that's why the political woods stay so thick," he said. "No matter how hard I try, my own people subvert my most excellent instinct to kill as many politicians as I can."

"We do our best, boss," Ian said.

"Next time, remind me to put your name at the top of the list," he said.

"Oh, I will, boss," Mahoney said. "Cross my heart and hope not to die."

The Emperor said, "The reason I'm so delighted is that not only was our little mission to *Demeter* a resounding success, but we managed to pull it off without spending one thin credit."

Mahoney was in the middle of taking another drink and choked on it.

"How the clot did you accomplish that, boss?" he said. "We not only had the cost of the Mantis team, and all that it entails, but we had several very expensive ships of war pulling extra duty, all kinds of collateral civilian damage at Chinen, plus a very expensive agworld experiment that went boobs up in the sun."

As he spoke he ran a mental calculation, but he soon lost track of the number of zeroes in the column and gave up.

"I'll be short and simple and sweet," the Emperor said. "I showed my buddy Tanz Sullamora the fine print in our agworld contract that laid out the financial responsibilities.

"If you remember, he drove a hard bargain on his commission for every agworld we sold."

Mahoney chuckled. "Oh, he laid it on thick, so the dear man did," he said. "Accused us of starving his poor wee grandchildren."

"Well, you might also recall," the Emperor said, "that I relented. Gave him a bigger future commission in return for him eating all the expenses related to the building, testing, and operation of the agworlds."

Light dawned for Mahoney. "Oh, you are devil from the hells, so you are, boss," he said. "And I'm proud to know you."

The mental calculation became easy now. In one column would go all the credits for the future sales of the agworlds. And in the other, all the expenses for *Demeter's* final field test. Which proved to be such a disaster that would be no future sales.

"Oh, the poor wee man," Ian said. "He must be down to his last trillion credits about now."

"And so," the Emperor said, "using only a single Mantis team we managed to wipe out the worst of the pirates—including the Himmenops and their queen. We stuck it to that Tahn drakh head, Lord Fehrle, who is getting behind-the—scenes blame for the debacle. And at the same time we revenged ourselves on the Wichmans."

"We're not quite done with the last bit of business, though," Mahoney said. "Gregor's gone to an early grave, so he is. However, we've yet to put paid to his old man."

"But you've spoken to his chief of staff, right?" the Emperor asked. "That Khelee fellow."

"So I did, sir," Mahoney said. "We had to wait until Fehrle got out of the line of fire."

"And rightly so," the Emperor said. "Don't need the grief of being blamed for the death of a Tahn bigwig just about now. Especially not with upcoming talks."

"Khelee told us this morning that Fehrle's gone now," Ian said. "We'll wait until he's well on his way then he'll trigger those bombs Sten planted in Wichman's bar."

"Nicely done, Ian," the Emperor said. "Meanwhile, be sure to convey my personal thanks to young captain Sten and the rest of the team."

Mahoney stirred in his seat. It seemed like the perfect time to bring forward his little idea regarding Sten.

"What's up, Ian?" the Emperor said, sensing the change in mood. Spit it out, man. You're in my good graces now. I'm not likely to bite your head off."

"It's about Captain Sten, sir," he said.

The Emperor's eyebrows rose along with his curiosity. "What about him?"

"There's a lot more to that young man then just a Mantis operative,"

Mahoney said. "I think with some seasoning, he could become one of our more valuable assets."

"In other words," the Emperor said, "you think it's time to bring him to court. Show him what the play is like on the grand stage."

The Emperor toyed with his drink, slowly rotating the tumbler. His instincts told him that he was about to make a bigger decision than Mahoney realized.

He flipped the mental coin. Saw how it landed. Polished off his drink.

"Give him a shout, Ian," he said. "I have just the place for him."

CHAPTER THIRTY EIGHT

ENDGAME

In the darkened chamber the twelve fathers were gathered about the table, golden goblets before them.

Sitting in the command chair, Father Huber brought the meeting to order.

"Blessings upon us all, brothers," he said.

"Blessings," the others murmured, and they all drank deeply.

At the end of the table the deposed Father Raggio was pale and drawn.

Huber said, "With the failure of the *Demeter* mission, it is plain to you all that I was right to be concerned about Venatora. Unfortunately, this realization came too late. Anthofelia is dead and now we have no replacement at hand. We have to start from square one. Pick a new queen, then begin the long process of training and indoctrination. And it is all the fault of Father Raggio."

Raggio grew angry. He started to come to his feet, hand going to the dirk at his side. But Father Argon, who sat next to him, placed a hand on his arm.

"Restrain yourself, Brother," he whispered. "For the sake of all of us."

Raggio relented and sat back down. He said, "Was *Demeter* a disaster? Of course it was. But no one could have predicted the extent of the disaster.

"I've apologized to you all. I've freely relinquished the chair. And I'm more than willing to pay any reasonable fines for my errors. What more do you want of me?"

From the look on Huber's face there was no doubt that what he wanted was Raggio's head.

Before he could speak, Jesop broke in, "Fathers, this is no time to grind in blame. Fault has been admitted. Restitution promised.

"The important question before us now, is who will be our next Queen Of The Himmenops? Each of you has a candidates' list before them. We have all studied the list thoroughly and have discussed the various merits of each candidate.

"Now we must choose—and choose quickly before the Himmenops revolt."

"They may have already revolted," Argon said. "The fortress has been shut down and there hasn't been a whiff of activity, nor has anyone answered our attempts to communicate.

"In short, Fathers, no one has heard one peep from the Himmenops since the *Demeter* debacle."

Huber sighed, momentarily defeated. "Very well," he said. "I call for a vote. Who will we choose for our new queen?"

"In the spirit of unity, peace and reconciliation," Father Raggio said, "I second the motion."

But before the vote could begin a great door crashed open.

Light came exploding in, momentarily blinding the Fathers.

Then, through bleary eyes, they saw who had so rudely interrupted their proceedings.

It was Venatora.

She stood before them, battlerifle at ready. Marta and Nalene flanked her, their weapons locked and loaded.

"Hello, boys," Venatora said.

And opened fire.

COMING SOON: A NEW STEN ADVENTURE

A LETTER FROM THE AUTHOR

Dear Reader:

I hope you have enjoyed this edition of the Sten series. I know how busy you are, but the care and feeding of a Mantis team is clotting expensive. So please stop off at Amazon.com and say something nice about Sten and his pals. Honestly, it really does help. And while you're there you'll see there are nine more Sten novels, along with two companion books, and a short story. They're available in all three flavors: paperback, e-books and audiobooks. For quick and easy links to all the editions just hop on The Sten page at stenbooks.blogspot.com.

Meanwhile, here is the usual "About The Author" hype:

ALLAN COLE is an international best-selling author, screenwriter and former prize-winning newsman. The son of a CIA operative, Cole was raised in the Middle East, Europe and the Far East. He is probably best known for the Sten series, which he wrote with the late Chris Bunch. His other works include The Timura Trilogy, The Far Kingdoms series, The Shannon Trilogy, Lucky In Cyprus, and S.O.S. Allan has published more than two dozen books and sold more than 150 screenplays. For further details visit his website at http://www.acole.com. He's also listed at Wikipedia.com and the Internet Movie Data Base—IMDB.com. For more information about **Chris Bunch**, see his Wikipedia and IMDB entries.

Stregg Forever

Allan Cole
Boca Raton, Florida
Nov. 5, 2018